Praise for the Da[r]
DONNA

"Loaded with subtle emotions, sizzling chemistry, and some provocative thoughts on the real choices [Grant's] characters are forced to make as they choose their loves for eternity." —*RT Book Reviews* (4 stars)

"Vivid images, intense details, and enchanting characters grab the reader's attention and [don't] let go."
—*Night Owl Reviews* (Top Pick)

Praise for the Dark Warrior novels

MIDNIGHT'S KISS

5 Stars TOP PICK! "[Grant] blends ancient gods, love, desire, and evil-doers into a world you will want to revisit over and over again." —*Night Owl Reviews*

5 Blue Ribbons! "This story is one you will remember long after the last page is read. A definite keeper!"
—*Romance Junkies*

4 Stars! "The world of the Immortal Warriors is a thoroughly engaging one, blending powerful ancient gods, fiery desire, and touchingly human love, which readers will surely want to revisit."
—*RT Book Reviews*

4 Feathers! "*Midnight's Kiss* is a game changer—one that will set the rest of the series in motion."
—*Under the Covers*

MIDNIGHT'S CAPTIVE

5 Blue Ribbons! "Packed with originality, imagination, humor, Scotland, Highlanders, magic, surprising plot twists, intrigue, sizzling sensuality, suspense, tender romance, and true love, this story has something for everyone." —*Romance Junkies*

4 1/2 Stars! "Grant has crafted a chemistry between her wounded alpha and surprisingly capable heroine that will, no doubt, enthrall series fans and newcomers alike." —*RT Book Reviews*

MIDNIGHT'S WARRIOR

4 Stars! "Super storyteller Grant returns with…A rich variety of previous protagonists adds a wonderful familiarity to the books" —*RT Books Reviews*

5 Stars! "Ms. Grant brings together two people who are afraid to fall in love and then ignites sparks between them." —*Single Title Reviews*

MIDNIGHT'S SEDUCTION

"Sizzling love scenes and engaging characters fill the pages of this fast-paced and immersive novel."

—*Publishers Weekly*

4 Stars! "Grant again proves that she is a stellar writer and a force to be reckoned with." —*RT Book Reviews*

5 Blue Ribbons! "A deliciously sexy, adventuresome paranormal romance that will keep you glued to the pages…" —*Romance Junkies*

5 Stars! "Ms. Grant mixes adventure, magic and sweet love to create the perfect romance story."

—*Single Title Reviews*

MIDNIGHT'S LOVER

"Paranormal elements and scorching romance are cleverly intertwined in this tale of a damaged hero and resilient heroine." —*Publishers Weekly*

5 Blue Ribbons! "An exciting, adventure-packed tale, *Midnight's Lover* is a story that captivates you from the very first page." —*Romance Junkies*

5 Stars! "Ms. Grant weaves a sweet love story into a story filled with action, adventure and the exploration of personal pain." —*Single Title Reviews*

4 Stars! "It's good vs. evil Druid in the next installment of Grant's Dark Warrior series. The stakes get higher as discerning one's true loyalties becomes harder. Grant's compelling characters and the continued presence of previous protagonists are key reasons why these books are so gripping. Another exciting and thrilling chapter!"

—*RT Book Reviews*

4.5 Stars Top Pick! "This is one series you'll want to make sure to read from the start…they just keep getting better…mmmm! A must read for sure!"

—*Night Owl Reviews*

DON'T MISS THESE OTHER SPELLBINDING NOVELS BY DONNA GRANT

THE DARK KINGS SERIES

Dark Heat

Darkest Flame

Fire Rising

Burning Desire

Hot Blooded

Night's Blaze

THE DARK WARRIOR SERIES

Midnight's Master

Midnight's Lover

Midnight's Seduction

Midnight's Warrior

Midnight's Kiss

Midnight's Captive

Midnight's Temptation

Midnight's Promise

THE DARK SWORD SERIES

Dangerous Highlander

Forbidden Highlander

Wicked Highlander

Untamed Highlander

Shadow Highlander

Darkest Highlander

FROM ST. MARTIN'S PAPERBACKS

SOUL SCORCHED

DONNA GRANT

This is a work of fiction. All of the characters, organizations, and events portrayed in this novel are either products of the author's imagination or are used fictitiously.

SOUL SCORCHED

For information address St. Martin's Press, 175 Fifth Avenue, New York, NY 10010.

ISBN: 978-1-250-07193-4

Printed in the United States of America

St. Martin's Paperbacks edition / July 2015

St. Martin's Paperbacks are published by St. Martin's Press, 175 Fifth Avenue, New York, NY 10010.

10 9 8 7 6 5 4 3 2 1

To Casey Rogers –
Wonderful person and cherished friend,
I’m very thankful to have you in my life.

ACKNOWLEDGMENTS

Words can never express how much I love working with my extraordinary editor, Monique Patterson. I love our partnership!

To Alex, Erin, Amy, the truly amazing art department, marketing and everyone at SMP who was involved in getting this book ready. Y'all rock!

To my agent, Natanya Wheeler, thank you for falling so hard for my dragons!

A special thanks to my family for the never-ending support.

SOUL SCORCHED

CHAPTER ONE

Dreagan Industries
October

Warrick reclined in the overstuffed chair, his feet propped on the stool before him as he randomly looked through Facebook pages, Twitter posts, and Instagram pictures.

He was constantly amazed at the brilliant and idiotic things humans imparted about their lives. For some reason, the mortals truly believed everyone wanted to know every detail of their lives like when they got up and what food they chose to eat.

Warrick didn't understand this need humans felt to convey such mundane intricacies. Nor could he fathom why he looked at their posts almost every day.

He clicked on a link that took him to YouTube where he watched a video of a kitten attempting to jump from a table to the windowsill, only to miss by several inches and falling.

To his horror, he watched it three times—smiling each time.

There was a kind of lull at Dreagan, and had been for

a few weeks. It began once Rhys broke the spell preventing him from shifting into dragon form. It was their true form, and it had been the worst sort of hell for his friend.

Rhys also found love in the arms of Lily, a human. But he wasn't the only Dragon King to do so. Hal, Guy, Banan, Kellan, Tristan, and Laith had also fallen in love with mortals. Kiril was the only one among them to choose a Fae as his mate.

Thinking of the Fae turned Warrick's thoughts to Rhi, the Light Fae who had loved—and lost—a Dragon King. No matter what Rhi said, the Kings knew she still carried love in her heart for her King.

If only the bastard would realize what he was missing and take Rhi for his own once again. The Light Fae had helped the Kings more than any other ally they had. And since the Dragon Kings were the strongest beings on this realm, they had few allies.

Warrick went to Rhi's Facebook page—The Real Rhi. He chuckled when he saw yet another picture of her nails. She loved nail art, and she was constantly having her nails painted, changing the colors almost daily.

This photo was of her nails done in racing stripes using OPI's Ford Mustang colors. He laughed at the color names that Rhi always mentioned. The base of her nails was a hot pepper red named Race Red, and the two white stripes running down her nails was called Angel with a Lead Foot.

Rhi never posted a picture of her face. She, like most Fae, was fascinated by the humans. Both the Light and Dark Fae craved being around them. Where the Light would have sex with them once only, the Dark would kidnap mortals and use them until they drained them of their souls, making the humans dependent on sex with the Dark just to stay alive.

It was one of the many reasons the Dragon Kings had

gone to war with the Fae. That war lasted for countless decades with the Dragon Kings finally winning. For all of that, it looked as if they were about to go back to war with the Dark Fae.

At least this time the Light Fae were on the side of the Kings.

Warrick didn't want to go back to war, but there was no denying it now. Not after all the Dark had done to the Kings and humans. Then there was the matter of Ulrik.

He was a King, or he had been. Everything had changed in one day, shattering the peaceful world they had lived in with the mortals. All because Ulrik's human lover tried to betray him.

To this day Warrick didn't know how Constantine had discovered what the female had tried to do, but then again, the King of Kings had his ways of gaining information. It was lucky Con learned of her treachery before she could put her plan into action.

Warrick had never questioned any of Con's decisions. When the King of Kings sent Ulrik on a mission and called the rest of them to find the human, Warrick was one of the first to Con's side.

He was also one of the first to thrust his sword into the mortal. It's what she deserved for even thinking of betraying Ulrik. Ulrik hadn't just sheltered her, clothed her, fed her, and loved her. He was going to bind himself to her, which would have ensured she become immortal and live as long as he did.

The Kings were doing Ulrik a favor in taking the mortal's life. Or so Warrick thought until Ulrik returned. To this day, thousands of years later, Warrick still wasn't sure if Ulrik was angrier at them for killing his woman, or Con for going behind his back.

Either way, the kind, laughing King of Silvers changed.

Ulrik became hard, grim, and relentless in his destruction of humans.

He had killed without thought, without conscience. His Silvers, some of the largest dragons, were right by his side.

Since the Kings were supposed to protect the mortals, Con had no choice but to stop Ulrik. Except the humans began to kill dragons.

Warrick still dreamed of those days. The angry roars of the dragons, the bellows of fury from the humans. Then there were the dying cries of the dragons, and the screams of pain from the mortals.

But that wasn't the worst.

The worst was when the Kings had to open the dragon bridge and send their dragons to another realm. Warrick had never felt so empty as he watched his Jades flying away.

The Dragon Kings then disappeared, hiding in the mountains on Dreagan to sleep away a few centuries. The area pulsed with their dragon magic, preventing any human from settling on their land or accidentally finding them.

After that, the Dragon Kings hid in plain sight among mortals, only taking to the skies in their true form at night or during a thunderstorm when no one could see them.

Unlike the other Dragon Kings, Warrick had a different view of the beings that shared their realm. He didn't hate the humans for what happened. However, he wished he didn't sympathize with them or understand that they feared the power and magic of the Kings.

Warrick wanted to hate the mortals, but he found them interesting, fascinating. Their lives were so short that they lived each day to the fullest. Their bodies so frail, but still they did daring, dangerous things. Nothing held them back. Some were astonishingly intelligent, while others captivated him with their works of art—be it painting, music, dance, or singing.

Humans were inferior to Kings in their magic, mortality, and senses, and yet Warrick was enchanted by them.

Oh, there were a few mortals who had magic, like the Druids. But Druid magic couldn't come close to matching dragon magic.

Warrick went to another Web site that had entertainment news about Hollywood's actors. His addiction to the site was one he kept closely guarded. He loved learning who was dating who, which actor got what role, and anything else he could find. Especially anything about Usaeil, the queen of the Light Fae who had been masquerading as an actress for several years now.

He was deep into a write-up on a new couple alert when there was a quick knock. His door opened and Ryder poked his head inside. Warrick easily clicked on another tab to hide what he had been reading.

Ryder's blond hair was messy from his fingers running through it. That was an indication that he had been diligently monitoring the roomful of computers and found something interesting.

"Busy?" Ryder asked.

Warrick closed the laptop and motioned him inside. "You look wired."

"I am." Ryder's smile was large, his hazel eyes wide as he walked into the room and shut the door behind him. "I thought Darius would recruit you to wake up everyone with him."

Warrick still couldn't believe Con wanted every Dragon King woken, but then again, they needed all Kings to fight Ulrik and the Dark Fae. "I'm no' exactly the one sent when things need to be achieved with a gentle hand."

"You're mellow, Warrick. You just prefer to be on your own."

"Exactly." Not to mention he had a hard time talking

to others—even Kings. "I gather Darius is waking the others by himself then?"

Ryder shrugged. "I caught a glimpse of dark blue scales in the clouds. Banan may be helping out."

"You didna come in here for small talk," Warrick stated. He was now curious as to why Ryder would seek him out. "What is it?"

Ryder leaned back against the door. "You were on patrol duty when Con called the last meeting, so you doona know that Kellan, Rhys, Dimitri, and Laith are following Ulrik."

Warrick set aside the laptop on the floor and dropped his feet to the ground as he sat forward. The calm around Dreagan had been great for the females mated to the Kings, but it was anything but for the rest of them. The Kings were restless and edgy, waiting on the next attack as they tried to get ahead of Ulrik, the Dark Fae, and MI5.

"Con has had Ulrik watched for centuries," Warrick said. "He's no' going to kill Ulrik now, or he'd be the one following him."

"Aye, but Con is tired of waiting. We all know there's going to be a battle between Con and Ulrik. It's coming sooner rather than later."

Warrick cocked his head to the side. "You doona want them to fight."

"Nay." Ryder sighed and shook his head. "I may have reacted just as Ulrik did, had our positions been reversed. Who's to say that any of us wouldna have attacked the humans when we discovered the woman we loved was set to betray us?"

"Con gave Ulrik the chance to stop killing the humans."

Ryder's gaze lowered to the floor. "When we have that much anger, that much need for retribution flowing through our veins, could any of us have set it all aside and forgotten what was done? Nay, I doona believe even Con could have."

"Con likes to have everyone think he has a cool head at all times, but I've seen the anger in his black eyes before."

"My point is that I doona think the answer was to banish Ulrik. We killed his woman. It was his right to confront her. Then we went against him when he wanted to wipe the realm of humans. How did we repay him after that? We stripped him of his magic, prevented him from shifting into dragon form, and locked away four of his Silvers in our mountain. And we're surprised when he sets his sights on taking Con down?"

Warrick got to his feet. "At any time Ulrik could've stopped what he was doing. At any time he could've realized aligning with the Dark was the worst thing to do. But he didna just come after us, he targeted certain humans. The worst was when he mixed Dark magic with his and cursed Rhys. That's unforgiveable."

"Aye." Ryder ran a hand through his hair. "We're all to blame, Warrick. It's no' just Ulrik's fault he's like he is. Honestly, I'm surprised it's taken him so long to come after Con. I think I'd have done it much sooner."

Warrick frowned as Ryder opened the door to leave. "Did you need me for something?"

"I did actually," Ryder said as he halted and looked over his shoulder. "Con knows you like to work alone so he wants you to go to Edinburgh. We have reason to believe Ulrik is visiting someone."

"Why do we care who Ulrik sees if it's no' the Dark?"

Ryder blew out a breath. "There's a verra good chance it's the Druid who was able to unbind his magic."

That would be a huge achievement for the Kings if they could find the Druid and possibly prevent her from unbinding the rest of Ulrik's magic. "I'll be ready then."

Ryder left without another word, the door closing softly behind him. There was a growing divide among the Kings, one that hadn't been there since before Ulrik was banished.

When Ulrik was at war with the humans, there were many Kings who had sided with him. It was only through Con's constant working to unite all the Dragon Kings that he eventually won everyone over except Ulrik.

The battle between the two former best friends—Con and Ulrik—had been building for millennia. If Ulrik killed Con, then Ulrik would take over as King of Kings.

Ulrik had been the only one who could've challenged Con all those ages ago, but Ulrik hadn't been interested. Especially since it was a fight to the death, and neither relished the idea of killing the other.

Banishment, along with walking around only in human form for thousands of millennia, tended to change a person.

Through the years, Warrick saw Ulrik from afar on occasions, but last month was the first time he had an up close encounter with the King of Silvers since before Ulrik's banishment. Not only had Ulrik appeared cruel and hard, there was a darkness about him that hinted at a barely leashed beast within that he was waiting to let loose.

Worse was that Warrick saw firsthand that Ulrik had somehow managed to get his magic back. He wasn't at full strength yet. When that happened—all hell would break loose.

CHAPTER TWO

Edinburgh, Scotland

Darcy sat straight up in bed, her chest heaving from her gasping breaths. She clawed at the hair that clung to her face with her sweat and blinked several times to make sure the dragon who had been bearing down on her with its mouth open wasn't real.

She hunched over and buried her face in her hands, her entire body shaking. It was the same dream from two days earlier. For the past month, the dream kept recurring every few days. There was no rhyme or reason to when the dreams came or when they didn't. All Darcy knew was that the dragon was after her.

She lifted her face to peek out her window. Dawn had arrived. She took several deep breaths before she threw off the covers and rose to walk to the bathroom. After a quick shower, she pinned up her hair and pulled on a sweater, jeans, and boots before she walked to the kitchen of her flat. A quick inhale of the smell of coffee brought some semblance of a smile to her face.

Darcy poured the dark liquid into a tall thermal container

and screwed on the top. She put on her coat and pulled her purse over her head, settling it across her body. As she made her way to the door, she grabbed an apple from the basket.

She walked the few blocks to work slowly. She wasn't in a mad dash like others in the city heading to their corporate jobs.

By the time she reached the black door of her shop, she had finished the apple. Darcy opened the door and stepped inside. She shut and locked the door behind her. It was a few hours yet before she would officially open, but she always came in early.

She walked past the round table painted black set in the middle of the floor. All around the front of the small store were decorations that people expected to see, like a crystal ball and crystals of various sizes and colors hanging from the ceiling.

Simple was best, and it was what she liked. Darcy didn't put up any brightly lit signs announcing that she read palms. People always found her, and her clients returned again and again.

Although she could read palms anywhere, she preferred the place kept darkened. So the lights were dimmed and candles lit. The walls were painted a dark purple, and the hardwood floor was covered with black rugs of various sizes and shapes.

She walked through two sets of dark hanging curtains to the back of the store that held boxes of different tarot cards, runes stones, and books about reading the tarots and runes, as well as palm reading. She made the bulk of her money from her clients, but she made a nice chunk with her online sales.

This was the place she called her mini-warehouse because of all the boxes. She had a small desk that housed her computer and printer. All her shipping supplies were in cabinets hanging on the wall above her desk, which meant it was as neat as it was going to get.

Darcy hung her purse on the coatrack, and her coat soon followed. She tapped a key on the computer keyboard to wake it up as she walked to the back door.

She quickly threw open the door and sighed. This was the place she craved to be. This is what the money from her palm readings and online sales allowed her. She was finally able to find some semblance of comfort since the dream woke her.

The conservatory was long and narrow, going back as far as it could until it reached the building behind hers. Darcy took a deep breath, the air filled with the fragrance of dozens of flowers. This is what calmed her. It was the place she went to ease her mind and find peace that eluded her out in the world of crazies.

Darcy didn't bother with gloves. She pushed the sleeves of her sweater up her arms and put on the apron that held the tools she would need to tend to her flowers.

She looked over the tables of plants to the planters in the back that held the tallest flowers. Then she walked to the table to her left.

One by one Darcy lovingly touched their leaves and inhaled their fragrance while she checked the soil and pruned as needed. She went down the first row, moving to her right until she reached the end.

She was at the middle table working her way back to the front when she noticed the Scottish primrose she had planted from a seed. It had sprouted well enough, but yesterday it began to look as if it was struggling to live.

Darcy leaned close and cupped her hands around it. She let her magic fill her before she released a small portion of it through her fingers into the plant.

She didn't normally use her magic with her plants, but the primrose had been a gift from her sister. It had taken her six years to get up the courage to plant it, and now that she had, she didn't want it to die.

As she watched the leaves of the flower begin to brighten, she dropped her hands to her side and straightened. She didn't need to turn around to know who had come into the area. There was only one person who would dare to intrude upon her privacy.

"I honestly didn't expect to see you again."

"And I didna expect to see you cheating by using your magic," came the masculine reply in a deep, soft Scottish accent.

Darcy turned and faced the man who had first walked into her shop three years earlier. She looked over his long black hair that hung loose about his shoulders to his gold eyes. As usual, he was in a dark suit, the crisp white shirt beneath the jacket left open at the collar.

Ulrik.

Her first foray into a world she hadn't known existed—the Dragon Kings.

"It's not cheating. I'm merely helping it along."

He raised a black brow. "It must be special for you to use your magic. I've never known you to do so before."

Darcy looked down at the primrose. She couldn't wait until it flowered, showcasing the small, bright purple petals. The plant itself would only grow to be a few inches tall at most.

"It is special." But she didn't want to think about why it meant so much to her. Darcy slid her gaze back to Ulrik. "I'm not sure I can unlock any more of your magic. The last time nearly killed me."

"I know." He leaned back against the wall near the door and crossed one ankle over the other. "I'm no' here for that. I'm here to warn you that you may be targeted soon for helping me."

"Why not just call and tell me this?"

"So you would know how important it is that you keep your guard up."

The way Ulrik's gold eyes went cold told her all that she needed to know. Whoever was after her was dangerous. "How will I know who they are?"

"You'll know. They're too bloody curious as to how I got my magic returned. I've been evasive. But . . . they'll find out."

Darcy gawked at him. "Are you that stupid? They could've followed you."

Normally, she wasn't so idiotic as to call someone as powerful as Ulrik stupid, but she was more concerned with her life than his response.

"They'll find you one way or another," Ulrik said, though by his flat look, he wasn't happy with her choice of words.

Darcy put a hand to her forehead. She and Ulrik weren't exactly friends. He had needed something, and she was able to give it to him. In return, he'd paid her handsomely.

She dropped her hand to her side and studied the Dragon King. "You're not warning me out of the kindness of your heart. That's not you."

"No," he said, the barest hint of a smile upon his lips. "I'm warning you because I may need you in the future, and I doona want you harmed. I hope you'll be smart enough to remain safe."

"Who is coming for me?"

"An enemy."

She blinked. The only reason Darcy knew Ulrik's story was because she had seen his past while delving into his mind to undo what the other Dragon Kings had done to him.

Ulrik pushed away from the wall. "Close your mouth, Darcy. We all have enemies we'd rather no' talk about."

"I just . . . I just thought you were going to say the Dragon Kings," she said and shrugged.

He blew out a breath, his nostrils flaring. "Who says I'm no'?"

"You should let your true accent come out more," she said when he let it slip. "It suits you better than the fake British you use from time to time."

He continued on as if she hadn't spoken. "My enemies will kill you. They want to ensure I doona get any more of my magic returned."

"If your enemy is anything like you, there's nowhere I can go where I won't be found."

Ulrik stared at her for a moment. "You're a Druid from the Isle of Skye. You touched upon dragon magic and walked away without it taking your life. If there's anyone who can get through this, it's you." He pivoted to leave.

"I've been dreaming of dragons."

Ulrik hesitated. Without turning around he asked, "Any particular color dragon?"

"Yes," she said after a brief pause.

"What color?"

Darcy hadn't told Ulrik she had seen his past. She had never mentioned Constantine's name, nor would she knowing how much Ulrik hated the King of Kings. Ulrik wasn't a man she would cross. *Ever.* As long as he needed her, she was useful. So she would remain useful.

Ulrik turned to her, a frown upon his brow. "Darcy? What color?"

"It's not exactly clear."

"Is he gold?"

She gave a shake of her head. "No."

"If you see his color, call me immediately."

"Why?"

"So I can tell you who to expect a visit from."

With that, he turned on his heel and was gone. Darcy swallowed and leaned a hand on the table. Despite the danger that fairly radiated from Ulrik, she wasn't scared of him. She had a healthy dose of respect, sure, but perhaps she didn't fear him because he'd come to her before he had magic.

She saw the man struggling to deal with the life he had been forced into. When she saw his past the first time, she wanted to get as far from him as she could. Yet, she was intrigued by the world of the Dragon Kings.

Ulrik eventually told her a little about who and what he was, but he kept most of it to himself. It took her numerous tries before she was able to touch the thick and powerful dragon magic that bound his. At first, each time she came close, she was knocked unconscious.

She wasn't the only one affected. By messing with the dragon magic, Ulrik experienced a tremendous amount of pain that left him weak and exposed. He held back as much of the bellows as he could, but eventually, they were released.

Both of them had seen the other in their weakest times, but she never thought of him as a friend. The fact he visited her after almost three years let her know he was serious about the threat.

It had been seven long years since she left Skye. Maybe it was time to go back. She had left seeking . . . something. She hadn't known what, and she still didn't. Darcy had had this urging to go, and she'd followed it, fully expecting to find whatever it was that sent her from her home.

She wasn't exactly unhappy in Edinburgh. Her clients were many, and she enjoyed what she did. To return to Skye would mean returning to Corann's fold.

That she wasn't ready to do. Then again, she couldn't remain in Edinburgh. Ulrik was right. She was a Druid. There were few places she could go that his enemies would never find her.

Skye was one of them.

CHAPTER THREE

Darcy struggled all day to read palms and tarot as if she didn't know she was being targeted by someone. Normally, she would see a client's future laid out before her, but she never told them the truth. No one *really* wanted to know what awaited them.

She would give them hints and clues to try and steer a client away from something that could harm them, but ultimately it was up to each person to make their own destiny.

The code she had been taught on Skye was so deeply entrenched that she didn't even try to break free. Besides, she understood why that code was in place. To use magic to do harm, bring about death, or otherwise aid evil went against everything a *mie* was.

Each Skye Druid put a spell upon themselves to ensure they would never break the code. If she did, she would no longer be able to use her magic.

That's why, when she went the entire day only seeing bits and pieces of her clients' futures instead of a full picture, she began to freak out.

Magic was her life. Well, magic and her plants. She had

done nothing to go against the code. Of that she was sure. The only explanation was she was beyond stressed after Ulrik's appearance that morning combined with the dreams of dragons.

She closed up the shop at eleven in the evening and began the short walk home. The streets were abnormally empty. Every sound had her jumping. She had her magic at the ready, prepared to use it at any second.

Her hand shook when she reached her building and she tried to get the key in the lock. She finally gave up and unlocked it with magic.

Darcy hurried inside and then up to her flat to shut and lock the door behind her. With a wave of her hand she turned on all the lights in the flat. Only when she was sure that she was alone did she step away from the door.

Warrick let the Dark Fae fall to the ground, his gaze on the third floor windows of Darcy Allen's flat. The silly female hadn't even realized she was being followed—not just by him, but a Dark as well.

He was able to grab the Dark before the Fae could get to her. Thankfully, there was just the one, and Warrick had the element of surprise against the Dark.

But there would be more.

When Warrick found the palm reading store at noon, he kept an eye on who entered and who left. Nothing out of the ordinary occurred.

Even though Ryder had sent a picture of the Druid to his phone, Warrick hadn't expected to feel such a shock at the pretty mortal with curly auburn hair and long, lean legs.

Warrick dragged the Dark into an obscured alley. It would be so easy to dispose of the Fae with a burst of his dragon fire, but he couldn't chance shifting in the middle of the city. Besides, he wouldn't fit between the two buildings.

He stared down at the Dark and grimaced. His mobile phone vibrated in his pocket. Warrick took it out and saw it was Kiril calling. He answered curtly.

"I'll be damned," Kiril said. "I just lost a hundred quid because you answered."

In the background, Warrick heard Rhys laughing. Warrick sighed heavily. "If you didna want me to answer, then you shouldna have called."

"True." There was a smile in Kiril's voice. "How is it going? Have you seen the Druid?"

"Aye. And I've killed a Dark that was after her."

"Shite." The laughter was gone. Kiril was all business as he asked, "Do you need any help?"

Warrick looked at the body. "I doona want to leave the Druid in case more Dark show up, but I need to get rid of the one I've killed."

"I'll be there shortly."

The call ended. Warrick returned the mobile to his pocket and looked back to the windows of Darcy's house. Once the Kings following Ulrik had discovered who it was he visited, Ryder had all of the Druid's information pulled up on the screens at Dreagan.

Ryder had sent everything to Warrick's phone as he drove to Edinburgh. Warrick had glanced at her photo on his phone, but the image he'd formed from that and the woman who walked out of the shop tonight weren't one and the same.

He climbed a fire escape ladder to the top of the building across the street and set up watch. From his vantage point he would be able to see anyone coming for her. The only blind spot he had was the back of her building. This was supposed to be a one-man job, but it had just turned into a two-man watch, minimum.

Warrick worked better alone. Not because he didn't like

others. He just had a difficult time around anyone else. But he wouldn't put the life of the female in jeopardy simply because he didn't want others around. He pulled out his phone and dialed Con.

The King of Kings answered on the second ring. "How are things?"

There was no hello, no pleasantries. Just the way Warrick liked it. "No' good."

"Meaning?" Con asked, a note of worry deepening his voice.

"I'm no' the only one watching the Druid. There was a Dark who came after her. He was too intent on her to realize I was there."

There was a pause. "Was it a random Dark?"

"In Edinburgh? Nay. Perhaps Ulrik sent him."

"Perhaps." Con sighed through the phone. "I'm going to have to send someone to join you."

"It's why I called."

"Look for Thorn in a few hours. I doona want to bring more Kings there since it might alert Ulrik. It willna take him long to realize you're there."

Warrick watched as Darcy's lights went out. All except for one. He saw her silhouette walk across the window. "If he doesna already."

"If the Dark are after her, there will be more."

"I'm ready for them."

Con chuckled. "Of course."

The line went dead. Warrick returned his mobile to his pocket as he scanned the area for anyone who might be a threat to Darcy—Dark and human alike.

Ulrik hadn't just aligned with the Dark Fae. He also had MI5 on his side, or at least a small portion of them. The Kings also had an ally in MI5. Henry North. The spy, along with others in the organization, were trying to break the allegiance between the group and Ulrik. So far it hadn't gone so well. Henry had also been working at Dreagan tracking the movements of Dark around the world.

It was worrying the Kings that the Dark were being so blatant about showing themselves. As if they wanted the Kings to know what they were doing. Since the Dark Fae were never to venture onto UK soil once they signed the treaty after the Fae Wars. Something had certainly changed, and Warrick felt as if he were struggling to catch up. Which wasn't a good sign.

Warrick didn't remain on the rooftop. He jumped from structure to structure, working his way around Darcy's building several times. The night was quiet, too quiet.

By the time Warrick made his way back to the alley on his tenth trip, Kiril and Rhys were there. Rhys stood next to Kiril who kneeled beside the Dark.

Both wore only jeans, meaning they had gotten to one of the stashes around Edinburgh set up by the Kings after flying from Dreagan. Every city in the UK had such a supply.

"Do you recognize him?" Rhys asked Kiril.

Warrick watched Kiril. After Kiril spent months in Ireland spying on the Dark, no one would know them better than him—except of course his mate, Shara.

"Nay," Kiril said as he stood. He lifted his shamrock green eyes to Warrick. "Is he the only one you've seen?"

Warrick couldn't help but turn and look at Darcy's window again. She took down her hair, the length dropping down her back before she pulled off her shirt.

He looked back to Kiril and Rhys. "He's the only one. I've found no other sign of anyone else."

"Interesting," Rhys said, a knowing smile lifting half of his mouth.

Kiril held out his hand and a blast of magic shot from him, freezing the Dark into one big icicle. Rhys then knelt and slammed his fist into the ice, shattering it—along with the Dark—into thousands of tiny pieces that evaporated.

"Like he was never here," Kiril said while dusting off his hands.

Rhys got to his feet and nodded. "That was fun. I could kill Dark Fae all night."

"Ah, but you didna kill him," Kiril pointed out. "Warrick did."

Warrick rolled his eyes. Those two were always joking with each other, their banter that of close friends. He didn't understand it since he'd never had anything like it.

"Smile, War, you might like it," Rhys teased.

Warrick gave him a flat stare. He hated the nickname Rhys had given him centuries ago. "I do smile."

Kiril laughed, and then hastily cleared his throat. "It's just no' often. It's more of a rare event."

"Like Halley's Comet," Rhys quipped.

Warrick simply stared at Rhys who had a wide smile on his face. After all Rhys had recently endured, Warrick wasn't about to say anything. It was good to see Rhys smiling and laughing again, when a few weeks earlier, he was so troubled he disappeared, not even answering Kiril's calls.

Kiril slapped Rhys on the back. "I think we ought to leave before Warrick does you bodily harm."

"Wait," Warrick said. "Thorn will be here shortly. Until he does, I could use help keeping an eye on the Druid."

Rhys's smile vanished as he exchanged a look with Kiril.

Warrick inhaled deeply, waiting on their reply. Was it so odd for him to ask for help that it left them speechless? Well, now that he considered it, he had never asked for help.

He wouldn't now except that the Dark came out of nowhere. He didn't know why the Fae targeted Darcy, and until he did, he would feel better if there were more eyes on her.

"Of course," Kiril said. "Where would you like us to set up?"

Warrick faced the building, his gaze locking on the window again. "The back. I can no' see the back."

"I'll take the back," Kiril said and walked away.

Warrick felt Rhys's aqua eyes on him. He faced the King of the Yellows. "Have I actually made you mute?"

Rhys snorted. "I'm trying to figure out if it's the fact the Druid was able to release some of Ulrik's magic or the woman herself that has you acting so . . . strangely."

"Con may have only asked me to watch the Druid, but she's done what no others have. She has enough magic to undo our magic. Dragon magic is the most powerful on this realm. How was she able to do it?"

"I've a feeling you're going to get to find out."

"No' me. I'm the one sent in to keep watch and protect. I'm no' the one Con sends to befriend someone. That's for those like you and Kiril."

Rhys glanced at the sky and the few clouds that drifted past. "You may be just the right person this time, War."

"She knows of us because of her association with Ulrik. It doesna matter how much or how little he told her. He'll color his words to reflect himself in a positive light. She willna want anything to do with any of us."

"She doesna have to know we're Dragon Kings."

He cut Rhys a look. "She's a Druid. She'll know."

"We'll see," Rhys said as he walked away.

Warrick climbed the ladder to stand on the roof once more. He checked the streets again, but his gaze was drawn back to the window time and again.

The light shone like a beacon in the darkness. To his delight, her silhouette appeared once more. A long shirt stopping mid-thigh skimmed her lithe body. She pulled back the covers of the bed and climbed in before reaching over and cutting off the light.

Warrick still didn't move. "Who are you, Druid?" he whispered. "How were you able to touch our magic?"

He didn't want to be intrigued, or care about her as he did. His duty to Dreagan and the Dragon Kings was tested again in his compassion for the humans.

All he could hope for now was that no one realized just how much he cared about the mortals.

CHAPTER FOUR

Darcy stumbled to the kitchen in her robe for a coffee. She'd slept very little as her conversation with Ulrik had been mixed with images of the dragon from her dream.

Not even a shower could help wake her. Afterward, she leaned against the counter sipping the hot liquid while her hair dried. She didn't move until the mug was empty. Only then did she make her way to the wardrobe with a yawn. She opened the doors and looked over her clothes and groaned.

She wanted to be comfortable, but there wasn't a single thing she had that she felt the urge to wear. With a loud sigh, she turned away and got the blow dryer. Not that she could do anything with her curls. They had a mind of their own, and no matter what hair product she used, her hair did its own thing.

After it was dry, Darcy looked in the mirror and winced. There were dark circles under her eyes. She didn't normally wear makeup on a daily basis, but today certainly called for some. She concentrated on her makeup as she applied it. A quick glance to be sure she didn't have mascara anywhere but her eyelashes and she returned to the wardrobe.

It was one of those days where she would stand in front

of her clothes for hours and still not find anything to wear. So she grabbed the first thing she saw—a pair of black leggings. Darcy paired it with her favorite faded purple and black plaid flannel shirt.

Darcy added a cream long-sleeved tee beneath the shirt, letting both hang down to her hips. She then tugged on the pair of black leather Ugg boots with the lamb's wool within that would keep her feet warm.

She was running late, so she threw on her jacket and purse, and grabbed an apple on the way out the door. It was halfway between her flat and the shop that she realized she'd left her jewelry. Darcy ate the apple and tugged her coat closed. The wind was fierce coming off the sea that morning. She was happy to be inside the shop after such a frigid blast first thing.

She tended to her plants, expecting to see Ulrik again, but she should've known better. He'd told her all he would. She would have to take it from there. After she finished with her plants, Darcy returned to the front of the store and flipped the OPEN sign over before unlocking the door.

She had a client coming that morning who hadn't missed a week in five years. Dorothy MacAvoy was an elderly lady deeply rooted in the occult. She claimed to have ancestors who were Druids.

Mrs. MacAvoy wasn't the first client to say such things, and Darcy never let anyone know she truly was a Druid. Mostly because the perception of a modern-day Druid was so far removed from what she really was.

Instead, she let Mrs. MacAvoy talk of the magic she felt was within her and how she wished she were born in a different century. Mrs. MacAvoy was sweet and always had a kind smile.

The door opened, and Mrs. MacAvoy stepped inside. She rubbed her hands together as she spied Darcy. "It's a cold one, dear. I suspect we'll get snow soon."

Darcy rose and helped her remove her purse and coat. She hung both on the hook for Mrs. MacAvoy. Then, together they walked to the table.

It took a little while for the woman to settle her old bones in the chair. When she was comfortable, Darcy walked around the table to her chair and sat. She looked at Mrs. MacAvoy and noticed something decidedly different about her today, though she couldn't pinpoint what it was.

"Shall I read the cards now?" Darcy asked.

Mrs. MacAvoy always booked two hours. During that time Darcy would read the cards, but most of it was spent talking about whatever Mrs. MacAvoy wished.

"Not yet," she replied and held out her hands.

Darcy took the woman's hands as they had done from the first time Dorothy entered the shop. "All right. Have you had any more dreams of Mr. MacAvoy?"

"I'll be joining him soon," she said, her smile slipping.

Darcy was taken aback. She knew Mrs. MacAvoy's life was counting down, but she'd never let her client know that. "What makes you think that?"

"I have one more task to complete, and then I can join my Rupert." Mrs. MacAvoy squeezed Darcy's hands. "Will you help me with my task?"

"Of course," she replied without thinking about it. What could the old woman possibly need her to do that she wouldn't accept?

Mrs. MacAvoy took a deep breath. "There was a wrong that happened thousands of years ago. It needs to be set right, Darcy. It's important that it's set right."

Darcy blinked, suddenly wary. "There's a lot of history that happens in thousands of years. What are you talking about?"

"You'll know when the time comes."

"I could use a little more information."

Mrs. MacAvoy's smile was a little sad. "We all have our destinies. I've known mine since I was a little girl. I think you know yours is important."

"Why do you say that?" Darcy asked, becoming uncomfortable with the way the conversation had turned. Normally, Dorothy would talk of her husband and their children before Darcy read the cards.

"You came to Edinburgh, didn't you?"

"How do you know I wasn't born here?"

Mrs. MacAvoy chuckled. "You've the look of the isle about you, girl. There's no mistaking that."

Darcy swallowed, trying to figure out where Dorothy's conversation was taking them. "You think I was brought to Edinburgh? I chose this city."

"Fate likes to let us think we make our own decisions, but the big ones are already laid out before us."

"I don't believe that. We make our own fate."

Mrs. MacAvoy tightened her fingers on Darcy's. "You'll discover the truth soon enough, my dear. We all do."

The room spun around Darcy for a moment, causing her to squeeze her eyes closed. The lack of sleep was playing havoc with her. "I thought I was the one who read the future," she said with a forced smile.

"Good luck with what's coming, Darcy. You're going to need it."

Darcy could only sit there as Mrs. MacAvoy rose and put on her coat before she walked out of the shop without the cards being read.

It had been an incredibly strange morning, and much to her dismay, the day didn't get any better. Not only did she feel drained, but she couldn't focus. The day seemed to last forever. It was a rare thing indeed for Darcy to be glad to leave the shop.

She locked the shop and turned around. The city pulsed around her, and yet she felt utterly alone somehow. She blamed Ulrik and his mysterious words, but it went deeper than that.

It was almost as if the fates that Mrs. MacAvoy mentioned were involved, positioning things their way.

At the thought of the fates, Corann's voice filled her head with one of his old sayings. *"You always think such polite and good thoughts, Darcy. That's no' always a bad thing, lass, but you need to remember there is evil out there. You think it may be the fates, when in fact it is evil."*

She shoved her hands in her coat pockets. Evil. There was certainly enough out in the world. Every day the news held nothing but horrible stories of war, murder, rape, and other such crimes.

How could she forget there was evil when it fairly surrounded her? How naïve she had been on Skye. There she and the other Druids were sheltered from the realities of the world.

There were times she truly missed those days of innocence.

But she chose to trade her innocence for freedom. Away from Corann and the rest of the elders of Skye, she was allowed to make her own way.

She hadn't always done a good job. There were times she didn't just stumble, but fell flat on her face. Yet, she picked herself up and tried again.

Darcy was proud of what she'd accomplished. Through all her decisions and failures, she hadn't broken the code of a Skye Druid. She still had her magic. Corann could be pleased about that, if nothing else.

As she walked home, she found herself lured by the sound of music coming from a pub. She occasionally stopped there for dinner and a drink. After the day she'd had, she needed a drink.

Or two.

* * *

Warrick shifted in the shadows so he could see Darcy enter the pub. The bright lights and loud music along with the crowd made it difficult for him to keep track of her.

"You're going to have to go in after her," Thorn said as he walked up.

Warrick looked over at his fellow Dragon King. Thorn's dark hair hung past his shoulder. Having only recently been woken, he hadn't cut his hair. Not that Warrick thought he would.

Thorn did his own thing. He had an air about him that always brought danger close. Women were attracted to that dangerous thread.

When Thorn had arrived the night before, there had been few words exchanged between them as Thorn set up his watch and Kiril and Rhys returned to Dreagan.

"You do better in crowds," Warrick said.

Thorn crossed his arms over his chest. "I've no' been awake long. You really want me in a crowd like that?"

"Shite," Warrick mumbled.

Which meant Warrick had no choice but to go into the pub if he wanted to ensure Darcy didn't end up with a Dark Fae. He walked from the shadows, hating the idea of being around so many people.

"You might want to mask that glower," Thorn called.

Warrick stopped and took a deep breath. Thorn was right. He had to pretend to at least like going into such a place.

It was a conundrum. Warrick was completely fascinated by humans, but he couldn't stand being around so many beings whether it was humans, Fae, or Kings. Crowds made him immensely uncomfortable. He felt closed in and became agitated, which made people wary and anxious.

It wasn't much better with those he knew well. The Kings were his brethren. He would do anything for them—and had on many occasions. Yet, he found it nearly impossible to sit in Con's meetings around so many of them.

It took a bit of effort to erase his anger, but Warrick managed it. He glanced back at Thorn to see the prick give him a thumbs-up with a wide grin. Warrick rolled his eyes and continued to the pub.

As soon as he pulled the door open, the music and conversation deafened him. He was tall enough to see over most everyone, which made it easy for him to pick out Darcy.

She stood at the bar and had her head bent, her auburn curls falling forward as she looked over the menu. It didn't take her long to place her order and grab the glass of ale. As she turned around, someone bumped into her, spilling some of the ale. She easily deflected the drunken man with just a small blast of magic.

Warrick was surprised to find himself grinning. He let it drop and slowly made his way through the pub to get closer to Darcy after she found a table.

He walked past her table as she tilted her head. One auburn curl slid down, brushing the back of his hand. He didn't stop until he reached the back and found an empty table. Warrick moved the chair so that it backed against the corner. He sat and motioned to a waitress.

His gaze quickly scanned the liquor lining the back of the bar to see if they stocked Dreagan whisky. Unfortunately, they didn't. He ordered an ale instead. Then sat back and observed the humans.

Few knew—or recognized—the limits of their bodies. They drank too much, smoked too much, and indulged in everything too much. But it was appealing to watch them. They didn't care that smoking could give them lung cancer or that it made their breath smell bad.

They would get drunk every night, heaving the contents left in their stomachs the next morning, and that evening return to the pub to do it all over again.

It didn't make sense to him, no matter how many times

Warrick tried to understand what caused the mortals to do the things they did.

Warrick's gaze landed on Darcy. Her head nodded slightly to the music playing. He noticed her toe tapping with the beat while she was typing something on her phone. Her ale was sipped slowly, and that didn't change when her food was brought.

He finished two ales in the time it took for her food to arrive and for her to eat. When she paid and stood to leave, over half of her ale was left.

Warrick rose and tossed money down on the table. He did a double take when the doors opened and two men walked into the pub. Except they weren't men. They were Dark Fae. They each used glamour to hide their red eyes, but neither did anything about their black hair streaked with silver—a trademark of the Dark.

There was a push against Warrick's mind from Thorn. He opened the link shared by all Dragon Kings. *"I see them."*

"There are three more of the assholes outside," Thorn said contemptuously.

"They're no' here by accident."

Thorn grunted. *"Nay. I'll take care of the ones out here."*

"No' yet. I doona want them to know we're here."

"I doona like it, but all right."

Warrick watched Darcy walk past one of the Fae. The Dark reached out and grasped her arm. She frowned and turned to him.

Warrick hoped she would be immune to the Dark like some of the humans were, but Darcy fell under their spell immediately. Warrick cursed beneath his breath. So much for keeping Darcy away from the Dark.

CHAPTER FIVE

Darcy was disoriented and baffled. She was on her way out the door when the man grabbed her. Not one for being manhandled, she turned to give him a piece of her mind. Then she looked into his eyes.

She couldn't name the color. They kept changing, showing flashes of red. It should scare her, but it didn't. No longer did she care about going home., the dragons, her magic, or . . . anything other than the extremely handsome man looking at her.

"Stay," he urged softly, a smile upon his lips.

She recognized the Irish accent. He was gorgeous. The kind of man who was too beautiful to be real, like Chris Hemsworth. And the man was talking to her.

Somewhere in the back of her mind, Darcy knew something was off. But she couldn't put her finger on it. She wanted to stay, which she knew was wrong. Yet she couldn't make herself leave.

The man gently touched one of her curls. "I've been looking for you."

"We both have," said a second man, his voice just as seductive as the first.

He came up behind her so she was sandwiched between the two of them. She couldn't catch her breath, and the urge to give herself to them was irresistible, engulfing.

Uncontrollable.

The first leaned close, pushing her back against the second man. He bent and put his lips by her ear. "Leave with us."

"We'll show you untold ecstasy," whispered the second.

Darcy was nodding before their words registered. With one on each side of her, they guided her out of the pub. She willingly went with them, her body eager to feel their hands on her. Her legs were jelly, her chest heaving as if she were winded. Her body was a riot of need and hunger clawing at her, demanding release that instant.

As soon as the cool wind hit her, she expected to shake off whatever assaulted her, but she couldn't. In fact, the desire only intensified. She was nearly crying with the longing to ease her body that was on fire for them.

With their hands on her lower back, they applied just enough pressure to keep her moving at a steady pace. When they turned the corner of the block, the first pushed her against the building and took her face in his hands.

"I'll not go farther until I have a kiss," he said in a husky whisper. He claimed her mouth in a kiss that seemed to sap her very soul.

"We share everything," came the second voice.

He began to kiss down her neck, his hands everywhere, touching every part of her. Her flannel shirt was suddenly unbuttoned, and her tee was shoved up and over her breasts.

Her body throbbed for more while she begged them between kisses never to stop. She grasped the brick of the building to keep on her feet. For the life of her Darcy couldn't understand how she loved every moment of their touch while at the same time her mind screamed for her to run.

"Leave some for us," came a third male voice.

Her lids were heavy, her limbs weighted down. She was only on her feet because they kept her upright. Three men? Yes!

No!

Something was wrong. She never gave herself so easily to a man—any man, much less two. Or three.

But it feels so good. Their hands, their mouths.

Darcy closed her eyes as her sex ached to be touched. She found herself grinding against one of the men. And somehow through the haze of passion, she realized the feelings within her weren't her own. They were being forced.

She pushed the two men kissing her away. They were so unprepared that she managed a little distance. That's when she spotted three more standing behind them for a total of five. By the way they were eyeing her—like she was a meal—she finally registered the warning her mind kept telling her.

Darcy tried to halt the need pounding through her, but it was too much. She struggled to stay on her feet even as she yanked her bra back into place and pulled her shirt down.

"No," she said.

The man closest to her, the one who had kissed her senseless merely laughed. "No?" he repeated in his Irish brogue. "You really don't mean that. You want us. I felt it in your kiss, in the way your nipples hardened beneath my hand. All you have to do is lie there and let us give you pleasure."

Darcy clamped her lips tight when she began to admit that she did want them. What the hell was wrong with her? She knew they were dangerous. Why did her body continue to ache for them?

Magic. The realization hit her suddenly. They were using magic. That was the only explanation.

She looked closer at them and sucked in a breath when she saw their red eyes. Red eyes? That wasn't possible. Was it?

"Leave me alone," she said in a breathless voice.

In her mind she screamed it. Why hadn't it come out more forcefully? Why wasn't she able to have more strength to shove their hands off her as they continued to touch her? Why did she crave their touch as if it were life itself?

"We can't do that," one of them said, the Irish brogue deep. "You're ours now."

Darcy sank into her mind. It was a trick she'd learned as a child when she needed her magic, but whatever the beings were doing to her, it was making it difficult for her to think of anything other than removing her clothes to make it easier for them to touch her.

She managed to drag up some of her magic. She held out her hands and directed it at all five of them. The men stumbled backward, their arms up to block the assault. It gave her the time she needed to run.

She pumped her arms, running as fast as she could along the hilly, winding streets. But she didn't get far before she was tackled to the ground.

"We could've played nice," said an angry voice in her ear.

He flipped her onto her back and straddled her. Darcy didn't scream or panic. Anger flooded her, helping to push away whatever stifled her magic and made her wanton. She called to every ounce of magic within her and let it build and build. The men were physically too strong for her. She would have to fight them with magic.

They laughed when she threw magic at the man atop her, which took her aback. The fact they weren't shocked at her use of it told her they knew all about her.

Suddenly, the man was thrown off her. Darcy looked around, but saw nothing. She rose up on her elbows to see the man climbing to his feet, shaking his head to clear it. His four comrades were looking up to the sky nervously.

A huge, dark shape descended from the sky, vanishing quickly. Along with one of her attackers. Darcy was afraid to move and be taken as well. She remained still, her chest heaving.

Another shape formed out of the dark sky. She could only stare openmouthed at the dragon coming right for her.

Just before he touched down, the dragon shifted, taking the form of a man—a man that left her breathless and awestruck.

There was no denying she was looking at a Dragon King.

He stood naked, his hands at his sides while his gaze was riveted on the men who accosted her. The shadows kept much of him out of sight, but the streetlamps shed enough light on the hard sinew of his body that she wanted to see more.

His lips peeled back in a snarl as he fought the four remaining men. He moved quickly, as if it were as effortless as breathing.

The men began to throw huge bubbles of magic at the Dragon King. He dodged many of them. The few that hit him barely made an impact other than to infuriate him, if his bared teeth were any indication.

The man—or whatever he was—who had stopped her in the pub was struck down with lethal force by the Dragon King. Darcy almost cheered, but it got lodged in her throat when she saw something out of the corner of her eye.

Had she not turned right then, Darcy would never have seen the second dragon swoop from the sky and wrap its talons around another of the men before flying away, crushing him.

That left just two of her attackers. They and the Dragon King circled each other on the street.

"She's ours," one of the red-eyed men said.

The Dragon King merely raised a brow. "Think again, Dark."

More globes of magic flew from the two Dark, but the Dragon King was too fast. He came up behind one of the Dark and ripped out his spinal column. The same instant the dragon grabbed the other. Both Dark fell lifeless to the ground a moment later.

Darcy hadn't moved a muscle in the few minutes that had passed. The need that had assaulted her earlier with the Dark was now gone. But she wasn't alone.

The Dragon King's gaze turned to her. Darcy watched him standing in the glow of the streetlight, completely mesmerized by the dragon tat that ran from the King's right shoulder, under his armpit, and down his side to the top of his right thigh.

The dragon's head was at the front of the man's shoulder and had his mouth open as if on a roar. He was rearing with his wings up and out. It was his long tail that stopped at the King's thigh.

The King glistened with sweat that made his muscles gleam in the light. Darcy had the absurd notion to run her hands all over his body, learning the feel of his hard muscles and warm skin.

Her gaze traveled down his wide chest to his washboard stomach and narrow waist. She bit her lip when she saw his cock. His rod twitched, and her eyes jerked to his face.

Out of nowhere, a pair of jeans came sailing through the air. The King caught them without looking and tugged them on. Once the pants were fastened, he walked barefoot to her and held out his hand.

"You've no idea how close you came to death. Again."

She frowned. "Again? You make it sound like this wasn't the first time those creeps came after me."

"It isna," he said.

Darcy stared at his large hand. He held it palm up, and despite herself, she wanted to read his palm. Instead, she slid her hand in his.

His long fingers curled gently, firmly around hers before he tugged her up. She stood staring up at a face she knew she had never seen before, but the rugged planes looked familiar. As did his square chin and hard jaw, his intense cobalt eyes, and the thick lashes. She knew his sinfully full lips and his warmth.

Just as she did his short blond hair that was disheveled from the fight. The full waves made her itch to sink her hands into the strands.

She knew she hadn't released his hand, but for the life of her, she couldn't. She enjoyed the feel of his strength, his comfort.

He was watching her as intently as she watched him. Darcy wondered what he thought of her frizzy hair and pale complexion. And she couldn't forget the freckles across her nose.

"You called those men Dark," she said, hating her hoarse voice.

He glanced at the dead men. "They're Dark Fae."

Thankfully, her knees held her. "Fae," she repeated since she couldn't think of anything else to say.

"She took that rather well, I think," said a deep voice from the shadows to her right.

The King's forehead furrowed before he glared into the shadows. He didn't utter a word, but there was no need. He was perturbed that they had been interrupted. As was she.

Darcy looked back at him to see his gaze lowered to

their clasped hands. Hers looked so small within his. He loosened his fingers, and she reluctantly withdrew her hand. She let it fall to her side and took a step back. The night had given her a swift kick in the butt.

She needed her mental armor back in place, and thankfully it didn't take her long to find it. "Of course I took it well."

What better way to face a situation like this than to lie? She would laugh at her pluck, if the circumstances weren't so dire.

"I know you're Dragon Kings," she said to the one before her.

His cobalt gaze bore into hers. Silence stretched as he studied her. "You know that because you helped Ulrik."

"Why do I have the feeling you didn't just happen to be here?"

"Because we were no'," came the voice from the shadows.

"Thorn," the King said, though no heat was in his voice. "Enough."

Darcy lifted her chin. "Is that a nickname because he's apparently a thorn in your side?"

"It's my bloody real name," came the terse reply.

The King's lips softened just a fraction, but not nearly enough to call it a smile.

"And your name?" she asked him.

There was a long pause before he said, "Warrick."

"Warrick," she repeated, letting it roll off her tongue. After watching him in battle with the Dark Fae, the name suited him to perfection. "Thank you both for helping me with the Dark."

Thorn made a sound at the back of his throat. "Doona go thinking that's the last you've seen of them."

"Please come out so I can see your face," Darcy said.

There was a smile in Thorn's voice when he said, "I gave my jeans to Warrick. I'm no' shy, lass, but I doona want to embarrass Warrick."

A growl rose up from Warrick as he faced the shadows, his nostrils flaring. Darcy ducked her head to hide her own laughter when she heard Thorn chuckling.

She couldn't quite manage to hide her smile when Warrick turned back to her. "I'm Darcy."

"It's late, and there may be more Dark. It might be best if we get you home," Warrick said.

She looked around at the dead Fae. If the Kings weren't here by accident, that meant they were watching her. She was sure they knew her name as well.

As much as she didn't like being followed, she was immensely grateful that the Kings had been there to stop the Dark. "What happens with them?" she asked, pointing to the Dark that littered the street.

"I'll take care of them once you're gone," Thorn said.

Warrick bowed his head. "And I'll walk you home."

Darcy turned toward the direction of her flat, a bubble of something causing her stomach to flutter. It couldn't be because of the quiet, brooding giant of a man with blond hair and blue eyes beside her.

They walked a little while before she asked, "Why were you here?"

"You."

One word. She rolled her eyes. "I figured that one out. Is it because I helped Ulrik get some of his magic back?"

"Did you ever stop to wonder why we bound his magic?"

"Yes."

He shot her a glance as they walked. "And you helped him anyway?"

"Yes. Are the Dark after me because I aided Ulrik?"

There was a long pause before Warrick lifted a thick

shoulder in a shrug. "The Dark have your scent now, Druid. They'll keep coming for you."

"Until I'm dead?"

"They'll take you to their realm and use your body, draining you of your soul."

Well, hell. That sounded pretty damn awful. "I can't let that happen."

Warrick stopped and turned to her. "Nay. We can no'."

CHAPTER SIX

Rhi thought by going with Balladyn that it would calm some of the turmoil within her. Instead, everything ratcheted up to the nth degree.

Balladyn's hold on her hand was firm. If she wanted her hand back, she was going to have to pull it loose—and probably use a bit of magic in the process.

Neither spoke as they walked to a Fae doorway a few hundred yards from the streets of Pompeii where he'd found her. Rhi had no idea where he was taking her, and it didn't matter. She knew that she could take care of herself against anyone—and anything.

That realization made her look at things differently. It wasn't that she wanted anyone to know how much power she had. In fact, she would rather keep it to herself. Rhys knew, but that was different. Rhys would never tell anyone. Well, except perhaps Lily, but Lily wouldn't repeat anything.

Rhi kept pace with Balladyn as they stepped through the doorway and arrived in Ireland. She almost rolled her eyes. Of course he would want her back in Ireland. It was a stronghold of the Fae, a mistake the Dragon Kings allowed to happen.

Stupid, Constantine. So stupid.

Rhi stopped her inner dialogue. There was no way she was going to think about that arrogant douche canoe. Let him figure a way out for the perfect Dragon Kings in this crater of a mess they were in.

To her surprise, Balladyn didn't remain in Ireland. He turned her to the left and immediately took her through another doorway. This time when she stepped through, her feet sank into sand.

Rhi blinked against the blinding sun. With just a thought, she had her favorite pair of Maui Jim sunglasses in place and looked at the mountains of sand around her. She then turned her head to Balladyn.

He looked out over the sand, a small, confident smile in place.

Another douche.

What was it with men? She didn't bother even trying to come up with an answer—because there wasn't one. Males were males, no matter what race they were.

"I knew you'd come to me," Balladyn said. He swiveled his head to her, his smile growing. "I knew it was just a matter of time."

For a moment, Rhi thought she was looking at the Balladyn who had been by her side for centuries. Then she stared into his red eyes and remembered. He was Dark.

He'd tortured her, tormented her. She'd suffered through unimaginable, unspeakable pain by his hand while he gloated during all of it.

He blamed her for his turning Dark.

And lest she forget, he wanted revenge.

Rhi glanced at their hands. His fingers tightened, as if he knew she wanted to yank away from him. She tucked her hair behind her ear with her free hand and faced the desert.

Balladyn had gotten some of his revenge, but he didn't yet comprehend that she wasn't Dark. Rhi had doubts about her being Dark up until that moment. She was Light, and not even the tide of darkness within her was going to change that.

"Do you have nothing to say?" he asked.

Rhi shrugged, her gaze following the rolling hills of sand against the stark blue sky. "What do you want me to say? I didn't come to you. You found me."

"You took my hand."

His voice had a hard edge now. Rhi often let her emotions rule her decisions, but for once, there was no anger or fear or confusion. She knew exactly what she had to do.

Rhi shifted so that she faced him. "I did."

"You're mine now."

A flash of anger began, but she hastily stamped it out. "I belong only to myself."

Balladyn's red eyes narrowed. He released her and ran his hand down his face, over his hollowed cheeks to the hard line of his jaw. At his temple, a muscle ticked, indicating that he was growing upset.

Rhi didn't bother to say more. She let her statement sink into Balladyn's head while she waited for whatever he would say next.

His look was hard as he stared at her. "There is darkness within you. I feel it."

"There is darkness within every creature, just as there is light. You brought more darkness out in me, but I didn't give in to it."

"You just need more time with me."

Rhi held up a hand when he took a step closer, halting him. She cut him a look as she hooked her thumbs in the belt loops of her jeans. "Hold up with the crazy. You wanted revenge for what happened to you. Guess what, wanker? You got what you wanted."

"No." He shook his head from side to side. "If I had what I wanted, your eyes would be red and there would be silver in your hair. And . . . you would be in my bed."

Usaeil had warned her, but Rhi hadn't believed the queen. Balladyn had taken the place of her brother when hers had died. Sure Balladyn was gorgeous, but she'd never thought of him that way.

"You changed me," she argued. "Regardless of what you think, your revenge was thorough."

"Not nearly thorough enough."

"What do you want? To hurt me? You've already done that."

"I did want to hurt you. Now . . ." He shrugged, a frown marring his brow. "Now, I just want you."

Rhi didn't move when he closed the distance between them and brought a hand up to her face. His touch was light, his caress gentle as his thumb stroked her cheek.

"All I've thought about for years was you, pet," he whispered. "I loved you before I went off to war with your brother. I was going to tell you when I returned, but you took his death too hard. Then you met—"

"Don't you dare say his name," she ordered.

Balladyn's gaze lowered to her mouth for a moment. "It killed me to see you with that dragon. The Dragon King never deserved your love. Not then. Especially not now."

"He never tortured me."

"Really?" Balladyn asked. "Isn't seeing him every time you go to Dreagan torture? Isn't knowing he's there, but he chose to let you go torture?"

How she hated when Balladyn was right. Rhi swallowed as his head dipped a fraction. She'd gone millennia without a kiss, and then, in less than two days, she'd kissed two men with a third about to be added.

"Choose me, Rhi," Balladyn urged in a soft voice. "I can give you everything you need. I'll never stop loving you. I'll always be here for you, and I'll never hurt you again."

His thumb was at her bottom lip, slowly tracing it. She blinked, just noticing that sometime while he had been talking that he had removed her sunglasses. They were perched atop her head.

Rhi looked into his red eyes. The love was visible there, though it seemed odd that a Dark could love. That emotion was part of the light, not the darkness within a person.

"Choose me," he said again as his other hand came up to cup her face.

Then his lips were on hers, tenderly nipping at her mouth until she opened for him. Then the gentleness vanished. He held her tight, pressing her body against his from shoulder to hip.

He kissed her as if there were no tomorrow, as if he were releasing thousands of years of desire.

And to her shock, she wasn't unmoved.

There was a spark of . . . something . . . that flared to life within her. It scared her so badly, that she abruptly ended the kiss.

"I love you," Balladyn said.

He took a step back and dropped his arms to his sides. There was a sad smile as he took another step away. "I'll not force you to come with me, pet. That choice has to be yours. You broke the only chains that I knew would hold you."

Rhi drew in an unsteady breath, unsure of what to do.

"You've no idea of the power flowing within you, do you?" Balladyn chuckled. "I didn't either until you leveled my compound. We can rule the Dark. You've had my heart for years without knowing it, but I'm freely handing it to you now."

They stared at each other. The expectant look on his face only confused her more. She didn't know what to say. So she chose not to speak at all.

"You know how to find me," he said before he stepped back through the doorway and disappeared.

For long moments, Rhi stood staring at the doorway, Balladyn's words running through her head over and over again.

She compared Balladyn's kiss with Henry's, which had been pleasant. She knew it had been wrong to kiss the mortal, but the way Henry looked at her had been too much. She missed being a part of something special with someone else. Henry was sweet, and he kissed well. Still, she wasn't one to dally with mortals.

As for Ulrik—his kiss had been swift. She'd barely realized what he was doing before he pulled back. Which was too bad really. She would've liked to know more of his kiss.

Which brought her back to Balladyn. There was only one other man who stirred such a reaction in her. But her King didn't want her anymore, and hadn't for some time. Perhaps it was time to move on.

Unrequited love was the worst. It killed souls, slowly destroying all hope until all that was left was a hollow shell. A soul that was withered and dry. Like hers. It was also the reason the darkness was able to enter her as it had.

Just another reason to resent her Dragon King. If there weren't hundreds already.

She dropped her face in her hands and let out a shaky breath. There was no way to force love any more than there was a way to stop loving someone.

But when did the time come to let go of the past? When

did she stop longing for what could never be and look to the future?

Now. Do it now or you'll never let go.

Rhi lifted her head and squared her shoulders. Yes. She had to let go now. It was the right thing to do.

Why then did her heart feel as if it were shattering all over again?

CHAPTER SEVEN

Warrick looked into the fern green eyes of Darcy Allen. She stared calmly back at him, even though he could see the tension in the way she stood. She was frightened, but she was holding it in check.

Her auburn curls fell around her. Her bearing was that of someone with an old soul, someone who was rarely ruffled. She dragged in a breath and adjusted her purse on her shoulder. Her wide eyes glanced down at his tat, making his skin warm at the thought of her interest.

Her gaze returned to his face as he took in her beauty. With her oval face, her eyes were what kept his focus, but there was no denying the appeal of her smooth skin, high cheekbones, and plump lips. There was a spattering of freckles across the bridge of her nose that he found appealing in ways he couldn't describe.

"So, these Dark Fae are dangerous. Got it," Darcy said nervously.

Warrick realized that once more he'd done something wrong. It's another reason he preferred to be by himself. Even when he didn't talk, he made others uncomfortable.

"Aye. I was going to have a look in your flat, but perhaps that isna a good idea."

"Why?" she asked with eyes wide with surprise. "Do you think they won't venture there?"

Warrick glanced up at her windows. "They most certainly will. I just assumed you would rather I get Thorn."

She rolled her eyes and unlocked her door. "You're already here. Why make me wait for someone else?"

Warrick had no choice but to follow her inside. He glanced around to make sure there were no Dark near, even though he knew Thorn was watching the building as well.

Following Darcy, Warrick tried—and failed—not to notice how her hips swayed as they walked up the stairs. Her legs went on forever, and the leggings that clung to her slender limbs brought his attention to them again and again.

The woman had no idea of her allure, of how she tempted him. And he was exceedingly thankful.

"I expected anger," she shot over her shoulder.

Warrick jerked his gaze from her shapely behind to her face. "What?"

A frown formed between her brows as she reached the landing to her door. "For my helping Ulrik. I thought if a Dragon King did come, I would be met with resentment and fury."

"What you did is done. There's no reason to be upset."

She made a sound at the back of her throat as she unlocked the door. "I doubt the rest of the Kings feel that way."

Warrick stopped her with a hand on her arm before she could enter. He motioned for her to stay put as he pushed open her door and stepped inside.

It didn't take him long to look in her studio since the

only other room was the bathroom. When he knew everything was clear, he walked back to the door. That's when he saw the carvings in the doorway. His gaze slid to Darcy.

"I'm a Druid," she said with a shrug. "You think I'm going to move into a place and not protect it?"

"These willna keep the Dark out."

Her lips flattened for a moment. "No, I'm going to need something much stronger."

Warrick moved aside and let her enter. He glanced at the Celtic carvings. It was rare for Druids to use spells in carvings. However, since she was from the Isle of Skye, it made sense. Those Druids clung to the old ways more so than in any other place in the world.

He shut the door behind him and took in the flat. Before he had been looking for Dark Fae. Now, he could look his fill at Darcy's home.

She liked things simple and eclectic, though she had a taste for a few floral items like an old round yellow pillow with a small floral print atop the frayed cream sofa. There was also a fringed scarf in a soft pink floral hanging on the corner of the armoire.

Aside from the florals, Warrick found himself liking the gray walls and white trim. There were just three pictures hanging on the walls, but it was the two long sections of dried orange slices hanging from the ceiling near the kitchen window by the sink that caught his eye.

"I like the smell," Darcy said as she walked up beside him. "And I like the way the sunlight hits them."

Never in all his years had Warrick ever thought to cut an orange into slices, dry them, and then hang them from the ceiling. Just another way the mortals intrigued him.

"They do smell nice."

Darcy smiled and took off her purse and coat. "I suppose it's a girl thing."

It was a mortal thing, but he didn't bother pointing that out.

She walked to the small stretch of kitchen countertops. Then she took a deep breath and asked, "Tell me all about the Dark. I need to know how to defend myself."

"You saw firsthand tonight what they are. As for defending yourself, if they get near you, it's over."

"They used some magic on me, didn't they?" she asked angrily.

Warrick leaned back against the door and shook his head. "It's no' magic, exactly. It's a part of a Fae—Light and Dark alike. Humans are attracted to them. That pull you felt? It'll happen again."

"Surely there are those of us who aren't affected," she said, worry tingeing her voice.

"Those humans are few and far between."

Darcy's fern green eyes narrowed. "You know something else. I can see it in your eyes. What aren't you telling me?"

"The only other ones I know who are no' affected by the Fae are the females mated to a King."

"Mated as in . . ." She trailed off, her eyebrows raised expectantly.

"Married."

She nodded. "Ah. Well, then. Looks like I need to come up with something myself."

"You're against marriage?" Warrick had no idea why the question came out. He waited for her to tell him to mind his own business.

Instead, Darcy reached up and touched one of the dried orange slices, before her eyes skated to him. "Not at all. I just can't see myself married. It's not like I could tell just any man what I am. Many would think I'm daft."

"And the Druids on Skye?"

"So you do know all about me," she said with a flat look.

She sighed loudly. "It's a rather long story, but to condense it—there's nothing for me on Skye."

"It could be the safest place for you."

Darcy turned so that her back was to the countertop, a hand braced on either side of her. "I left because I didn't want to be confined. I'm certainly not going to go back knowing that I could never leave that place."

"Is it no' better than death?" He might know the basic facts about her, but he was innately curious as to what made her leave Skye—and why she wouldn't go back.

"Don't get me wrong. I don't want to die, which is why I want to know all there is about the Dark Fae. So, back to the topic."

Warrick crossed his arms over his chest. "All they want from humans is sex. They kidnap or lure mortals with the promise of untold pleasures. Once a mortal has sex with a Fae, another mortal could never measure up."

"So they ruin us for anyone else," she stated with a twist of her lips. "That sucks."

"Aye. The Light Fae have banned having sex with humans, but it still happens. When it does, they're careful to only have sex once."

"That one time is all it takes, isn't it?"

"Aye."

Darcy slumped back against the counter. "That's good to know, I guess. How can I tell who a Light Fae is?"

"Their beauty. And you'll recognize the same pull you felt tonight."

She nodded slowly, as if filing it all in her mind. "And the Dark? I gather they don't have sex with us just once?"

"They live for evil. Remember that. They can use glamour to disguise their eyes and hair, but there's no denying the appeal they have. If nothing else, you'll be able to recognize that."

"Glamour. Got it."

The more he spoke, the whiter she became. Her voice and words said she was doing fine, but her demeanor and pallor said otherwise. Warrick almost stopped. Then he remembered why he was there. "Perhaps I should give you time to digest what I've told you so far."

"No, please," she urged, her gaze beseeching him. "Finish."

He hesitated for a moment. Then he said, "The Dark take a person and never release them. The females are known to be gentler with the men, prolonging their lives for years. The males have no compunction. For each time a Dark has sex with a mortal, they drain that mortal of their soul."

"How didn't I know about them?" Darcy said as she hurriedly walked to the sofa and sank onto it, her head buried in her hands.

Warrick dropped his arms and moved closer to her, though he didn't get too near—even when his fingers itched to wind a curl around a digit.

She lifted her face and speared him with a look. "Do the Druids know of the Fae?"

"No' many do. Corann does."

"Of course he does," she said tightly.

"I'm sure there are reasons your elder didna tell you about the Fae. We know of them because they tried to take over the realm and we fought them for centuries."

"Did you lose? Is that why they're still here?" she asked, her voice pitched higher.

Warrick ran a hand through his hair. "We won, but we allowed the Fae to remain on this realm with the understanding that we protected humans and that they didna try to live here. The Dark were quiet and smart in how they began to take over Ireland."

"They actually suck out the soul?"

Her face was pinched in fear and worry, sending a peculiar feeling though him that he couldn't quite name. "The Dark females only take a wee bit at a time. They like the idea of the humans, and want their men to remain that way as long as possible. The Dark males can go through a woman a night."

"I won't let them get their hands on me." She rubbed her palms on her thighs and sat up straight. "Now that I know they're out there, I can prepare. Right?" she asked.

Warrick studied the Druid for long moments. "You've ancient magic from Skye. I doona know if it can deter a Dark forever, but you might be able to find a spell that will give you enough time to get somewhere safe."

"I'm not leaving Edinburgh. I briefly considered it when Ulrik told me . . ."

She trailed off, which set off warning bells. Not to mention she'd said Ulrik's name. "What did Ulrik tell you?"

"Well, he didn't outright say it, but he implied that I might get a visit from the Dragon Kings."

He knew she wasn't telling him the entire truth, but Warrick recognized that he couldn't force it out of her. It would have to be something Darcy told him on her own.

"If you're no' leaving town, then you better ward this place and the shop as much as you can."

"And you? Where will you be?"

Why did his heart jump at her question and the hope in her gaze? Then he reminded himself that she wanted to live, and if that meant having Kings around, she would accept it. "I'll be near, as will Thorn."

"I know you didn't help me because you wanted to, and that's all right. I'm very grateful that you did, however." She got to her feet then.

Warrick took a deep breath and gave the flat one more

look before he headed to the door. "Doona venture out again tonight, and be vigilant from now on."

"I will. I promise."

With nothing else to say, Warrick reached for the door. He opened it and walked out, amazed that for the first time that he could ever remember, he wasn't ready to leave someone's company.

CHAPTER EIGHT

No matter how hard Darcy looked through her books at the shop, she couldn't find any known spells that would protect her from the Dark Fae. It didn't help that she couldn't stop thinking about Warrick and how he'd saved her.

The words in the book blurred as her mind went back to the night before and how he stood dripping with cold danger. His wrath was palpable, his loathing obvious. He moved quick as the wind, his motions lethal.

The Dark Fae hadn't stood a chance. No one did if the Dragon Kings were angered.

Darcy closed the book and shoved it aside. She rose and poured herself another cup of coffee and held it between her hands as she leaned back against the desk.

Sleep had come in snatches during the night. Every sound woke her, because she knew that no matter how many protection spells she put on her flat, the Dark could get through. Not even putting the spell up to alert her if someone came into her flat helped.

On the walk into work, Darcy had expected—and hoped—to see Warrick. To her disappointment, she didn't spot him anywhere.

She took his words to heart, however, and was vigilant. Any man who she suspected might be Fae she steered clear of. Once she reached the shop, she quickly added dozens more protection spells. They would at least give her a bit of time if a Dark did show up.

Darcy rubbed a hangnail on her finger with her thumb. She couldn't stand long nails, so kept hers cut short at all times. She might not like her nails to grow, but she was meticulous about keeping them neat. Now that she realized the hangnail was there, it was all she could mess with.

It didn't help that her mind was occupied between fear of the Dark and Warrick. The King had no idea how handsome he was. He'd met her gaze evenly, but there was no conceit or arrogance in his cobalt eyes.

She sighed as she thought of the deep blue color. She didn't know blue could get so dark, or make her so weak in the knees. There was something about his eyes that trapped her, ensnared her. She could hardly look away, and when she had, it had been down to the hard line of his jaw, his wide lips, and his magnificent body.

Nudity obviously didn't bother him as he'd stood in the middle of the Edinburgh streets uncaring if anyone saw him. She doubted there was an ounce of fat on his body. Every muscle was toned as hard as granite.

At first glance, Warrick had a reserved look. Yet the more she watched him, the more she discovered how interested he was in everything. He wasn't obvious about it, but the curiosity was there if someone looked for it.

Darcy covered her mouth as she yawned. Then she walked to the bookcase that housed the majority of her books. There were a few she'd looked through at her flat, but none had given her information on the Fae or the Kings.

After another two hours of searching—and three cups of coffee—she slammed the book shut and shoved it back into its spot on the shelf. There was no point in looking online for spells, because they wouldn't be there.

There were some Druids who posted spells online, but they were the simple spells for love, money, or the like. What she needed was a grimoire. Too bad she couldn't get her hands on one, not that the Druids would ever put one together.

All the Druids she knew committed spells to memory, which left her with nothing. She didn't want to die, but she couldn't go back to Skye. The pull that initially made her leave the isle was still there, refusing to release her. If only she knew what she was supposed to do, then she could do it and be free.

But it wasn't just that. She had no desire to be back under Corann's rule. He was a good man, and a powerful Druid elder, but she felt confined on Skye. It wasn't just the rules she had to follow as a Druid, but the way the elders protected the isle and the Druids limited everyone.

Most didn't mind it, but Darcy chafed at it from the moment she realized what was going on. No one in her family understood how the restrictions made her feel. They all tried to talk her out of leaving. The only one who understood was her sister who urged her to go.

The funny thing was that Darcy still followed the same rules from Skye. That's when she knew it wasn't the rules—it was the elders, namely Corann. Now that she knew he consciously didn't tell her about the Fae, it infuriated her even more. That information could have prevented last night from happening.

Darcy sat down on the floor and crisscrossed her legs. She placed her hands on her legs and closed her eyes. Meditation had helped her work out problems or spells in the past. There was no reason why it couldn't work now.

She emptied her mind of everything, though it took a

few tries because Warrick's handsome face kept popping up. Next, she searched her memories of all that she knew of the Dragon Kings. The problem was, what was stored in her mind wasn't her memories. They were Ulrik's. But something was better than nothing.

Constantine's face came into her mind's eye. It was before he was King of Kings, when he and Ulrik were still as close as brothers. Con's blond hair was long and wavy, flowing freely past his shoulders. His black eyes were crinkled in the corners as he laughed at something Ulrik said.

That image faded, replaced with another of Con. His hair was pulled back in a queue, and he no longer smiled so freely.

"I'll no' fight you," Ulrik said.

Con's gaze hardened. *"You're the only one who can challenge me. If you doona, it makes you look weak. The strongest of us needs to be King of Kings."*

"Then let me appear weak. I'll no' fight my best friend. Take the crown, Con. It's yours. You went through enough to ensure that it was."

"You think I want to fight you?" Con asked, an offended look coming over his face.

"Nay."

Though Ulrik began to suspect otherwise. He alone knew Con had killed the previous King of Kings. It's wasn't murder, but a challenge. The strongest of the Kings was King of Kings, and Con wanted to be uncontested.

Thankfully, that memory faded to one with Ulrik holding a woman in his arms. She was amazingly beautiful with her flame red hair and green eyes. Ulrik's love was there in his memories. He would've done anything for the woman.

Darcy prepared herself for what was next. The first time she'd experienced the memory of his lover's betrayal she had vomited.

She tensed as the memory flooded her mind. One moment Ulrik was flying back to Dreagan, and the next he was confronted by Con and the rest of the Kings.

At first Ulrik refused to believe them, holding onto denial. Then the fury he felt at that moment assaulted her.

Her eyes snapped opened as she gasped for air. She didn't have to run to the bathroom, but her stomach rolled for several minutes.

There wasn't a King out there who understood what Ulrik went through. He'd needed them the most during that time, and they'd turned their backs on him.

Darcy didn't fool herself though. She'd seen enough of his memories to know he hadn't exactly been a good person during the time he walked the earth in human form.

Still, she couldn't help but feel for Ulrik. Not that she would ever tell him that. You didn't pity a man like Ulrik.

She hoped, delving back into his memories, that she might uncover something important about the Kings. All she found out was that Con might or might not have wanted to kill Ulrik. By taking Ulrik's magic, banishing him, and condemning him to eternity in human form, Con guaranteed he was unchallenged.

As interesting as that was, it didn't tell her any more about the Kings.

Darcy got to her feet. She paced her small office for a moment before she went to the back with her flowers and walked among them.

She didn't know how long she paced before she looked up, halting when she saw a tall, broad shouldered man with long dark hair leaning against a post.

"It took you long enough, Druid," he said. "Would've sucked had I been a Dark."

As soon as he spoke, she recognized Thorn's voice from the night before. Darcy glanced around for Warrick, and when she didn't find him, she met Thorn's brown gaze.

"I see you found clothes."

He glanced down at his boots, jeans, and chocolate brown shirt. "So it seems. What has you so agitated?"

Darcy cut him a sharp look. "Really? That's the question you ask me after last night?"

"The Dark are verra dangerous to be sure. Is that all that has your dander up?"

"Where is Warrick?"

"Around. Would you rather talk to him? That would be a first," Thorn said with a slight grin.

What was that supposed to mean? Darcy ignored the last comment. "Are the Dark after me because I helped Ulrik?"

Thorn's grin vanished. He pushed away from the post and ran a hand over his chin that was shadowed with a beard. "If they are, it doesna make sense. Ulrik is aligned with the Dark."

"All of them?" she asked. "Couldn't there be some unhappy Dark Fae?"

"That would mean they would go against their king's orders. Taraeth would never abide such actions. If he doesna know, however, that's a different story. Unless Ulrik sent them after you."

She shook her head. "He didn't."

"How do you know that?"

Darcy whirled around at the sound of Warrick's voice behind her. His blond hair was windblown, and his eyes regarded her with a mixture of curiosity and wariness.

She licked her lips before she said, "I know because Ulrik told me he still needed me."

"Did you bed him?" Thorn asked from behind her.

Darcy threw him a withering look over her shoulder. "No. Besides, why would he kill the only Druid who can touch dragon magic and not die?"

Warrick's cobalt gaze narrowed. "Something I've been asking myself all night."

"It's not Ulrik," Darcy said.

Thorn walked to stand beside Warrick. "Then why are the Dark after you?"

"Balladyn," Warrick suddenly said to Thorn. "Henry said how much Balladyn hates Ulrik."

Balladyn. That name meant nothing to Darcy, but it obviously meant quite a bit to the Kings. It was time she learned all the players in this game to determine just where she stood.

Darcy waited until Warrick looked back to her. Then she said, "If you want any more information about Ulrik, I need details of what's going on."

Warrick and Thorn exchanged a look before Warrick nodded. "Deal."

CHAPTER NINE

Warrick considered doing serious bodily harm to Thorn when he entered Darcy's shop. All Warrick wished was to keep an eye out while he considered Con's plan, but Thorn thought they should take the time to get to know her better.

At first, Warrick hadn't followed him in. He waited outside, and intended to remain there. Then he began wondering what Thorn and Darcy were talking about and if Thorn was flirting.

Thorn wasn't a charmer like Kiril or Rhys. He lived life as wild and free as he wanted, which is why he spent the majority of his time sleeping. He and Con constantly clashed because Thorn couldn't care less if the mortals saw him in dragon form or not.

It wasn't that Thorn went looking for trouble, but it always seemed to find him. His willfulness and the unconventional way he did things set him apart from most of the Kings. Even Rhys, who was the most daring of them all, didn't always understand Thorn.

Perhaps that's why Con paired Thorn with him. Warrick

tended to think things through thoroughly. Just like barging in and interrupting Darcy's day.

The longer Warrick sat out there and thought of Darcy flirting with Thorn, the more irritated he became. He went in through the front door of the shop, unlocking it with magic, and followed the sounds of their voices to the back.

Like any male, Warrick had desires. He recognized the need that flooded him the first time he laid eyes on Darcy. It only intensified when he caught her gaze slowly running down his body after he'd fought the Dark the night before.

If he was to do his job correctly, he was going to have to do something about the desire that ruled him. A visit to his favorite bordello in Glasgow was in order. Quickly.

Then he forgot all about other women when Darcy turned to him. Her auburn locks were gathered loosely at the back of her neck, and the curve-hugging black sweater drew his eyes to her breasts again and again.

"That easy, huh?" she said with a slight grin. "Why do I get the feeling I'm not going to get much in the way of information?"

The more they learned what Ulrik was doing the better, which is why Warrick didn't think twice about striking that deal with her. It's what Con wanted anyway. Darcy already knew about the Dragon Kings. Whatever questions she had couldn't be much.

"Ask me anything," Warrick stated.

Darcy silently regarded him for long moments. Then she asked, "Who is Balladyn?"

"First lieutenant to the Dark Fae king, Taraeth," Warrick explained. "All Dark were once Light Fae who chose evil. Balladyn was one of the best warriors the Light had. He was injured in one of the many civil wars the Fae have, and Taraeth captured him, turning him Dark."

"Why does Balladyn hate Ulrik?"

Warrick hoped Thorn might answer, but the King of the Clarets simply returned his look. Warrick turned his head back to Darcy. "That's unclear. We suspect it has something to do with Ulrik being a King."

Darcy's brow furrowed. "You lost me."

This was why Warrick liked others to explain things. He never did an adequate job, and to make matters worse he was trying harder with Darcy than he had with anyone else.

"There's history between Balladyn and the Kings," Warrick said. "One of us had a relationship with a Light Fae named Rhi. Balladyn was in love with Rhi."

"One doesna simply fall out of love," Thorn interjected. "If he hates Ulrik, then Balladyn is still in love with Rhi. It's one of the reasons he kidnapped her."

"What?" Darcy asked. "Balladyn kidnapped Rhi? Why?"

Warrick touched the bright green leaves of a lavender rose. "He blamed her for his turning Dark. He wanted to turn her as well. He didna succeed."

"And Ulrik carried her out of the place," Thorn said.

Darcy's eyes grew large. "Is Ulrik her lover?"

"Nay. That King chose to end the relationship. Rhi, however, still loves him," Warrick answered.

"Did the King stop loving her?"

Warrick shrugged. "He refuses to speak of her."

"He's no' told anyone anything," Thorn said. "No' even Rhi."

Darcy's face scrunched. "I don't think I like this King. What kind of guy does something like that? It's just rude." She gave a sad shake of her head. "All right. So that explains why Balladyn might have sent Dark to kill me. He doesn't want Ulrik to have any more help. If it was that simple, why hasn't Balladyn come and killed me himself?"

"Taraeth," Warrick said. "Taraeth is the only one holding Balladyn back. For now. I suspect Balladyn will make a run to become king of the Dark soon enough."

"I won't be forgetting those two names anytime soon." Darcy reached for some clippers and cut off a dead bloom. "Are you here to try and convince me to return to Skye?"

Thorn made a sound at the back of his throat and walked to the back of the conservatory. "I'll leave you to it, Warrick."

Darcy's head swung from Thorn's retreating back to him. "What did he mean?"

If there was time, Warrick could gleefully punch Thorn in the face. Thorn knew Warrick wasn't thrilled with Con's idea. Now he realized why Thorn really came to see Darcy.

"Warrick?" Darcy called.

"Tell her, War," Thorn said as he exited the back.

Darcy set down the clippers and gave Warrick a hard look. "Spill."

Warrick sighed. He wasn't the one to talk to Darcy about this. He would muck this up, he just knew it. "I'm no' here to convince you to return to Skye."

"Really?" She lifted one auburn brow, her look unconvinced.

"Really. You wanted to know about the Kings. Ask away."

"How about you start from the beginning."

"It might be easier if you tell me what Ulrik has told you."

She was shaking her head before he finished. "There are two sides to every story. I'm asking to hear your side of things."

Now that intrigued him. He thought for sure she would take Ulrik's side after helping him. Perhaps he wouldn't have to work so hard to get Darcy to help them.

"You look surprised," she said and walked past him. She waved for him to follow her. "Let's get comfortable."

Why was it when those words left her mouth, he didn't picture them sitting in the cushy chairs in the front of the shop at the round table but falling naked on a bed, their limbs intertwined as he kissed her?

He shook his head to try and dislodge the image, but the image was firmly implanted now. His balls tightened when he looked down to see the way her faded jeans clung to her well-formed ass.

There was no denying it—he was in over his head where Darcy was concerned.

She pulled the chairs used for her clients out from the table and around so that they sat facing each other. Darcy sank into one, tucking a leg beneath her as she did.

Warrick took the empty chair, surprised at how comfortable it was. He ran his hands along the arms of the chair, liking the feel of the black velvet beneath his palm.

"So," she said.

Warrick admired that she got right down to business. "From the beginning, aye?"

"Aye."

He liked the way her Scots accent thickened when she repeated his words. Warrick took a deep breath and thought back to the days before humans. "For countless centuries, this realm was ours. You can no' imagine what it was like to see dragons everywhere. There were those who preferred the water and spent much of their time in the oceans, seas, and lochs. There were those who craved the ice and snow, while others were more at home in the deserts, and still others who made their homes in the jungles."

"Much like we do," Darcy said.

Warrick nodded slightly. "We were no' just different in our choice of environment, but in color and size. Each group of dragons had a leader."

"Were the leaders voted on?"

"Nay. We became Kings of our dragons because we had the most magic and were the fiercest."

Darcy frowned. "You're immortal. So once you become King, no one else can take your place?"

"No' necessarily. A Dragon King can only be killed by another Dragon King. There were a few skirmishes between packs, but sometimes it was a matter of another with more magic and power wanting to take over."

"Is that what you did?"

Warrick still remembered the day he became King of the Jades. "A dragon knows when he can be King. He feels the force of the magic and instinctively knows he has more than another. So do the other dragons. The previous King of the Jades wasna ready to relinquish his title. He attacked me, intending to kill me."

"My God," Darcy said with her eyes wide.

"It sounds violent, but it isna any more than what humans do to each other. It was our way, Darcy. It's how we lived."

"And you obviously won."

"Aye. I wouldna have challenged him for a few years yet, but he wasna content with that. It was kill or be killed."

She swallowed. "So you became King of the Jades."

"Aye. Several millennia passed before the first humans arrived."

"Arrived? Like on a spaceship or something?" she asked with a twist of her lips.

Warrick scratched his chin. "One day they were no' here, and the next they were. Once they arrived, each King shifted into human form. That allowed us to communicate with the mortals. They possessed no magic, so we vowed to protect them."

"You had to know that whatever accord was between you and the humans wouldn't last."

"Why no'? Why did it have to end?" Warrick asked, feeling anger begin to rise. "We protected them. The dragons even moved out of areas that had been their homes for eons to give the humans a place to live."

"Did you ever consider that they were scared of you?"

Warrick scoffed. "No' a single dragon harmed them. No' one of the smallest nor the largest of us."

"So you were happy to have humans share your realm?" she asked with a knowing look.

"I didna say that. Would you be happy if another race of beings suddenly arrived and you had to move entire populations from their homes for these new people?"

Her shoulders slumped, a sad expression coming over her face. "No. I doubt we would be so accommodating."

"There were angry dragons. We Kings kept them in check. It wasna easy, and we had resentment of our own. But a vow is a vow."

"And we ruined it."

Warrick sighed. "We should've seen it coming. With every mortal born, the humans became more and more aggressive. They wanted more of our lands. They didna just take our homes, they began to kill our food sources. Hungry dragons can become . . . violent."

"You mean the dragons didn't eat us?"

"We did our best to enforce it, but I know there was a human who went missing every now and then."

"And you wonder why the humans turned on you?"

"Did I mention that the humans hunted the smallest of us when they couldn't find food? We each did harm to the other. It's never one-sided, Darcy. Never."

CHAPTER TEN

Darcy shifted in the chair. She was sorry to say that it never occurred to her that humans had harmed the dragons. They were *dragons*! They had magic and powers. Why would a human ever think to hurt a creature who was protecting it?

She knew what came next in the story, at least from Ulrik's point of view, but she was eager to hear it from Warrick's.

He had a way of talking that sucked her into the story instantly. His brogue was deep and thick as he weaved his words around her. And she wanted to hear more. A person would have to be deaf not to have their stomach tremble with excitement every time his rich voice filled the room.

"Despite everything, there were Kings who took mortal females for themselves."

"Was it the power of a King that drew the humans?" she asked.

Warrick shrugged one wide shoulder. "It's a possibility. A dragon mates for life."

"Which wouldn't be too long since you're immortal and we humans aren't," she pointed out.

Warrick's cobalt gaze pinned her with a hard look. "It does when a human becomes immortal, irrevocably tied to her King until he dies."

Darcy knew her mouth opened in shock. This was something she hadn't gleaned from Ulrik's memories, and it surprised the hell out of her.

"Exactly," Warrick said at her lack of a response. "The mortals gained much by a King's love."

She closed her mouth, her mind racing as she tried to put herself in a King's shoes. No wonder they killed Ulrik's woman. "Will you tell me what happened with Ulrik?"

Warrick got to his feet and ambled around the shop, inspecting the crystals hanging from the ceiling. "Ulrik could've been King of Kings. Everyone knew it, including Con."

"He didn't want to fight Con."

"Nay, he didna." Warrick turned his head to her. "Ulrik was liked by all. He had that kind of personality. I think that's why we all reacted the way we did when we discovered the betrayal."

"How did you find out about his lover's betrayal?"

"Con. He didna exactly trust mortals, and he worried that there might be war one day. He kept a close eye on any human who got close to a King. I'm glad he did, because he was able to stop her."

Darcy switched legs beneath her as she tracked Warrick with her eyes. "What was the woman's name?"

"Ulrik didna tell you?"

He hadn't. In fact, even her name was removed from his memories. Her face was still there, but that was all. "No."

A small frown wrinkled Warrick's brow. Most of his face was hidden in the shadows, and Darcy wished now that she had turned up the lights.

"He's erased her," Warrick said, more to himself than

to Darcy. "She was beautiful, and Ulrik was completely in love with her."

Darcy tried to imagine the Ulrik she knew in love, and she just couldn't do it. He was hardened now, a wall erected around himself so that no one could get close—friends or lovers.

Ulrik had been hit not just with his woman's betrayal, but by his friends' as well. She felt the rage that was still within him. That kind of hate turned a person dark in ways she couldn't begin to fathom.

"Did Ulrik tell you how close he and Con were?"

Darcy jumped, not realizing Warrick stood behind her. She knew from Ulrik's memories how close he and Con had been. "In a way."

"I think Con expected Ulrik to challenge him for the role of King of Kings. It's no' something either of them have ever spoken about. But that's my guess. Whether a King agrees with Con or no', none of us can argue that he has our best interests at heart. He keeps watch over us at all times."

"Is that why he sent Ulrik away?" She craned her neck back to get a glimpse of Warrick.

He had a faraway look on his face. Then he blinked and looked down at her. "He wanted to save Ulrik from having to kill her."

Darcy turned so she could see Warrick better. "Did it never occur to Con that Ulrik needed to be there? That he needed to talk to her, to know why she did what she did?"

"You'd have to ask Con that." Warrick walked around her chair and made his way to the glass door. He looked out, his back expanding as he took a breath. "We all thought we were doing him a favor by killing her."

"Then he returned."

"Then he returned." Warrick paused, the seconds turning into minutes.

Darcy didn't want to push him since he seemed lost in his thoughts. She had the insane urge to walk up behind him and wrap her arms around him. Not that Warrick would ever want or need her touch.

It must be the melancholy mood that took her, talking about such awful happenings.

"Ulrik was always slow to anger. Until that moment. I've never seen such fury before." Warrick's words were spoken softly, the timbre of his voice pitched low. "He was outraged at her death and stunned at her attempted betrayal. But he was devastated by what we had done."

"You don't realize just how much that moment changed him."

Warrick turned to face her. "He told you?"

She shook her head. "I saw it in his memories. I felt all of his emotions. That moment tore him in two."

"You saw his memories?" he asked in shock.

Darcy realized her mistake too late. She saw the tightening of Warrick's jaw, the flattening of his lips. "I didn't mean to. I've never had that happen before."

"Does Ulrik know?"

"No, and I don't want him to."

Warrick walked to the chair he had vacated and leaned his hands on the back. "Did he tell you anything of his past?"

"Some. He condensed what happened to what made him attack humans. Ulrik didn't share anything without a reason. He wanted me to know why he had his magic bound."

"So you know that he began to attack the humans after that night?"

Darcy nodded woodenly. "He told me he thought them responsible."

"But you saw more in his memories," Warrick guessed.

Was she that easy to read? Darcy rose and put some distance between her and Warrick. Only then did she face him. "Yes, I saw more. I wished I hadn't. I wished all I knew was the story he shared, but I don't. I know that he recognized his friends were trying to help him, even though he hated each of you for it. It's why he didn't attack any of you."

"He and his Silvers slaughtered thousands."

"Yes."

"We tried to stop him," Warrick said as his head dropped to his chest. "There were some Kings who sided with him for a while, but Con talked them back to his side. That didna deter Ulrik."

Darcy shuddered, recalling the few seconds of a battle she'd seen through Ulrik's dragon eyes. "I know."

"By that time the humans rose up and began killing dragons. The war Con wanted to avoid was upon us. I still feel the pain of watching dragons being killed. They had to be saved." He lifted his head and caught her in his gaze. "We had but one choice—to send our dragons away."

Darcy rubbed her hands on her arms. "Did that stop Ulrik?"

"You didna see this in his memories?"

"No. What I did see was terrifying. I've no wish to ever see more."

Warrick straightened. "It didna stop Ulrik. We managed to send some of his Silvers with the others, but four of the largest remained with him. It took all the Kings to trap them."

"And send them with the others?" she asked. When he merely looked at her, she gasped. "They're here? On Earth?"

"The dragon bridge was already closed. We couldna send them. They're sleeping, Darcy. You doona need to fear them."

She put a hand over her stomach, feeling ill. "What happens if they wake?"

"They'll begin killing again."

She looked at Warrick askance. "Right. There's nothing for me to worry about."

"There isna. We willna allow them to wake."

Darcy couldn't think any more about the Silvers. "What happened to Ulrik?"

"We surrounded him. It took every one of us using our magic to bind his. In order to stop the killing, we stripped him of his ability to shift and talk to his dragons. We condemned him to walk this realm for eternity in human form. And we banished him from Dreagan."

"You don't think all of that was a bit extreme?"

"At the time, nay." He blew out a breath. "Now? Aye."

"Now you have him as a powerful enemy. No wonder you're pissed I was able to return some of his magic."

Warrick cocked his head. "Do you realize what will happen if he gets all of his magic returned? He'll challenge Con for the right to rule as King of Kings. If Ulrik wins, he'll wake his dragons and wipe the realm of humans."

Darcy tried to swallow, but all the moisture left her mouth. "No."

"Oh, aye. Did he no' tell you why he wanted his magic returned?"

She began to shake. This couldn't be right. She turned and hurried through the two sets of curtains to the back with her plants. There she took several deep breaths, her fingers running through the leaves as she slowed, letting the plants calm her.

"How did he convince you?" Warrick asked from behind her.

Of course Warrick would follow her. He wanted his answers, and she had made a deal with him to share information. Darcy waited until she was at the end of the table before she faced Warrick. He hadn't come any farther into the conservatory than the entrance, just as he had earlier.

"Ulrik came to me nearly three years ago," she began.

"He told me he had magic, and that it was bound. It's not uncommon for Druids to bind the magic of others for various reasons."

"Is that what you thought he was? A Druid?"

She couldn't hold Warrick's cobalt gaze. It was as if he could see right through her. "I've been in Edinburgh for seven years. His visit was the first I ever received where someone came in and knew I was a Druid. I realized he had to come from a world of magic, but he didn't act like any Druid I knew."

Warrick leaned a shoulder against the door. "And?"

"He told me he was a Dragon King." She had laughed at first, thinking it was a joke. That hadn't lasted long.

"That's all it took to convince you?"

"Of course not," she snipped. She took a deep breath to calm down. "I read palms. I see people's futures, and sometimes their pasts. It's my gift. Whether through tarot cards or palms, the truth is there."

Warrick had a shocked look on his face when he asked, "He let you read his palm?"

"Yes. That's when I saw truth—that he was a Dragon King."

CHAPTER ELEVEN

Rhi was edgy. She had been since Balladyn left her in the desert. Not even the new OPI Nordic shades could help, although the deep purple—Viking in a Vinter Vonderland—certainly didn't hurt. The added glimmer of My Voice Is a Little Norse on her tips usually made her smile.

Not today. Not since her talk with Balladyn.

Rhi held out her hand and curled her fingers inward to her palm and snapped a picture on her phone. She quickly uploaded it to Facebook before noting she had a thousand new likes on her page.

Even that didn't cheer her.

There was only one thing that could possibly make her forget about her troubles for a bit—irritating Con. It never took much. Usually, all she had to do was make an appearance. That was enough to make the vein in his temple pulse. Few knew that was a clue that he was furious. He hid his emotions so well, but Rhi had known him long enough that she knew many of his secrets.

She veiled herself and teleported to Dreagan, right into Con's office. When she wasn't immediately thrown out, she knew he had yet to carve the symbols found on the cottage doorway as he'd threatened.

The angrier he got when she popped into his office unannounced made her do it even more. She lived to irk him. It became an addiction, something she practiced and perfected just for the wanker.

Because she could.

Except, he wasn't in his office. Rhi remained veiled as she walked around his desk and peered down at the reports neatly stacked and the pen beside them.

The only thing that would tear Con away from finishing his work was an emergency, and since Rhi could hear Ryder's laughter from the floor above, there was nothing going on.

Curious, Rhi walked out of Con's office. The last time she freely walked Dreagan Manor, she had been with her lover. Sure she appeared all over Dreagan, and even in the manor at times, but she hadn't walked it in . . . ages.

She wandered the second floor, stopping at closed doors and putting her ear to them. Some were empty, but she found Cassie and Hal in one as well as Sammi and Tristan in another, though she didn't bother either couple. The rooms that were left open, she couldn't resist going into. She examined each before going up to the third floor.

Repeating the same process, Rhi made her way around the third floor until she came to the computer room. The door was slightly ajar, enough that she could easily squeeze into the room.

All the monitors were on, and each had something different on the screens. She watched Ryder open a new box of donuts, reaching for his favorite—jelly-filled. But her gaze was caught by the screen that had Ryder's attention.

It held the picture of a pretty auburn-haired woman with green eyes. Darcy Allen was the name at the top of the screen.

"You left him in there with Darcy?" Ryder asked.

Rhi jerked until she realized Ryder was talking to someone through his headset. She leaned close to hear the response.

"Aye. You should've seen his face. I'll catch hell later."

Rhi knew that voice, but she couldn't place who it belonged to. Which meant another of the Kings must have woken.

"You know, you could've used our link," Ryder said.

The King chuckled. "Aye, but I like this little device. A mobile phone. Ingenious."

"I didna get a chance to show you the computers. And your mobile is called a smart phone."

"A smart phone, aye? We'll see."

Thorn. There was something in his speech, the confidence and cockiness that was all Thorn. He was another that got under Con's skin almost as easily as she did.

Ryder chuckled. "Any more Dark show up?"

Dark? There were Dark Fae near? Rhi scanned the screen with Darcy's picture that had all her information off to the side until she saw Edinburgh listed.

"Nay," Thorn stated in a hard tone. "I suspect there will be more tonight."

"Con really thinks we can convince her to help us against Ulrik?"

"Apparently. Warrick has his doubts."

Rhi grimaced. Con had sent Warrick and Thorn to Edinburgh? That was like sending water and dynamite. More surprising was that Warrick agreed to a partner. Yet, it was the knowledge that the Dark were after Darcy that kept her attention.

She couldn't figure it out, until she read the bottom of the screen—Druid. Then it all made sense. Ulrik had used a Druid to have some of his magic unbound, and Rhi would wager her best Jimmy Choos that Darcy was that Druid.

Rhi was about to teleport to Edinburgh to get a look at Darcy for herself when something on the screen caught her eye. Darcy was raised on Skye.

A Skye Druid? In Edinburgh? Alone?

Something certainly wasn't right. Skye Druids didn't normally leave the isle. They were the strongest there where their magic thrived and the elders kept the isle protected.

There was one other Skye Druid who had left the isle that Rhi knew—Aisley.

"Warrick will convince her to remain in Edinburgh," Thorn said, breaking into her thoughts.

Rhi focused on the conversation between Ryder and Thorn once more.

"One of you will have to stay with her at all times to keep the Dark away," Ryder said.

Thorn chuckled. "Have you seen her? That's no' going to be a problem. Shite. Even Warrick can no' take his eyes from her."

Their talk soon turned to all the modern amenities that Thorn was getting accustomed to. Rhi walked out of the computer room and searched the first floor for Con. She wanted to know why he would intentionally put a Druid in harm's way.

She could ask Ryder herself, or even go to Warrick or Thorn, but she was never one to pass up the opportunity to infuriate Constantine.

But her search gained her nothing. Con wasn't in the manor, on the grounds, or anywhere near the distillery. He was gone.

Rhi immediately teleported to Ireland and her queen's castle. She kept herself veiled and appeared in the throne room. It was empty, and since Rhi knew Usaeil wasn't off making a movie or doing a photo shoot, that meant her queen was in her room.

She strode to the door, intending to throw it open and catch her with Con. Her hand wrapped around the knob and turned.

But it wouldn't budge.

Rhi could blast it with magic, but she refrained. Barely. She knew Usaeil was having an affair with a King. Usaeil had never approved of Rhi's relationship with her King, and yet the queen was doing exactly what she'd criticized Rhi for.

If there was one thing Rhi couldn't stand, it was a hypocrite. It might take her some time, but she would find out who Usaeil was sharing her bed with. Rhi suspected it was Con. She just needed to see it with her own eyes.

The door began to rattle, and Rhi realized she was glowing. She quickly released the door and teleported away before her anger got the better of her and she flattened the castle to dust.

Warrick wasn't happy when Darcy demanded to return to her flat. He would rather they remain in her shop on the ground where there were few windows if the Dark did try to take her.

It wouldn't do for the entire city to see a dragon and a Dark fighting it out on the third floor of a building, or catching video of a Dark doing magic. Or worse—he or Thorn in dragon form.

But Darcy's argument about a bed and shower won out.

Warrick walked beside her. He was amazed at how quickly she made her way down the street. She was also cautious and watchful. Traits that would come in handy.

"Did you see Ulrik's future when you read his palm?" he asked.

Darcy shook her head. "It was odd, really. His future was blocked. The only other time that has happened was when someone had a choice to make that could determine their fate in opposite ways."

Warrick wondered if that determination would be if Ulrik killed Con or not. "His past was open to you?"

"Just about. If I had the time, I could've seen more. Ulrik was more interested in me unbinding his magic, so the longer I tried, the more of his memories were at hand for me to see."

"Which you did."

She glanced at Warrick, her expression unreadable. "I did. I saw what his woman did, and I saw what his friends did to him. There is pain inside that he's lived with for thousands of centuries. He doesn't even realize it's there anymore. It's what keeps him going, keeps him focused."

"It's what is ruling him," Warrick added.

"Exactly. I got a glimpse of what he was like before he was betrayed. The person he was, and the person he is now are night and day apart."

Warrick hurriedly switched to Darcy's other side when he saw a man coming toward her who had no intention of moving out of the way. The man bumped into Warrick before bouncing back and running into a light pole.

Warrick shot him a look without breaking stride. He turned back to Darcy. "Do you think if we welcomed Ulrik back at Dreagan that he could let go of the anger?"

"I don't think so. It's too ingrained in him now. He's past the point of no return."

"You knew this and still helped him?"

She rolled her eyes. "For the last time, yes. You've no idea how having some of his magic returned gave him a measure of peace. How would you like to have your wings clipped so you could never fly again?"

Warrick thought of Rhys and how Ulrik had combined his magic with a Dark's to curse Rhys. Those few weeks had nearly made Rhys lose his mind. Ulrik had endured such torture for thousands of years.

"He's trying to expose us to the world," Warrick said. "Ulrik has joined forces with the Dark and told a small section at MI5 about us. Those humans and the Dark have murdered and attacked other humans in an effort to show the world who we are."

Darcy's steps slowed as they reached the door to her building. "All of you wanted revenge on Ulrik for having to send your dragons away. You got it."

"It wasna revenge."

"Wasn't it?" she asked as she faced him. "Weren't you angry at Ulrik for being unable to control his rage and attacking the humans? Didn't each of you blame him for starting the war and the humans killing the dragons?"

Warrick started to shake his head, then he realized she was right. They had blamed Ulrik for all of it.

"Vengeance is a powerful motivator," Darcy continued. "Ulrik just wants what is his due. He blames all of you, but his focus is Con."

"You think Ulrik deserves his revenge?"

"I think Ulrik deserves to be who he is—a Dragon King who can shift and take to the skies once more."

"Even if it means your demise?" Warrick asked.

She glanced at the darkening sky. "Let's just hope that while Ulrik has been in human form that he saw a few of us who might have made him hate our race a little less."

Warrick waited until she was through the door before he whispered to himself, "Doona count on it."

CHAPTER TWELVE

Perth, Scotland

Ulrik went through every person who worked for him and ran a deeper background check on them. Now that he knew what to look for, he was able to spot whoever also worked for his uncle.

There were seven in total, and with each revelation, the more his anger grew and festered into hate.

Mikkel had put his hands into Ulrik's life more than he was comfortable with. Ulrik added a mark next to each of the seven names. He wanted to fire them, but that would alert Mikkel that he knew of his uncle's involvement.

Instead, Ulrik opted not to do anything. Let those seven others continue on as they were. Ulrik rarely told them much anyway, but now he would make sure not to tell them anything they could take back to Mikkel.

Ulrik put away the list and pulled out another. The next wasn't as extensive as he would've liked, but it was growing by the day.

Every time Mikkel let him into one of his many residences, Ulrik discovered more and more of the people working for Mikkel—and not just those at the houses. With a little eavesdropping and diligence, Ulrik was able to learn one name from the mercenaries Mikkel used. From there, it was easy to discover who the mercs were associated with.

He wrote several more names down from his investigation, adding any relevant information that could help him in the future.

One of the things he was working on was figuring out who Mikkel's inside man was with MI5. As far as the Dark, Ulrik wasn't concerned that they were united with Mikkel. Ulrik's alliance with them wasn't as deep—and that would benefit him in the end.

The Dark did favors for him, and he gave them information on the Kings. However, now he knew the Dark were taking that knowledge straight to Mikkel.

If he were the trusting sort, his uncle would have backed him into a corner. But betrayals were a hard lesson, and ones that were never forgotten. Trust wasn't something Ulrik could—or would—give anyone.

He pulled out another folder. This one listed all the mortals who worked for Dreagan. One of them was Mikkel's spy, and he was going to find out who it was. If there was one thing Ulrik had learned to do—and do well—it was to turn a potential snitch.

Money was always the motivator. Ulrik was prepared to pay triple what Mikkel had given the spy, but Ulrik would go one step further and ensure the mole was indebted to him in such a way that the mole would never betray him.

There was a flash in his mind and Rhi's face appeared as she teleported into his store. Ulrik closed the folders and tucked them into the drawer. Then he stood up from his desk and lifted his gaze to the second floor where Rhi stood looking at a painting of a noblewoman from the sixteenth century.

The first thing Ulrik noticed was the silent fury that swirled around the Light Fae. Her face was hidden by her position with her back to him as well as her long hair.

She stood still as stone in a thin shirt of soft taupe that draped sensuously over every curve to her hips. Her legs were encased in black pants tucked into tall black boots.

"Did you come back for another kiss?" he asked.

There was a long pause before she replied, "What would you say if I said I did?"

"I'd say you're too far away. If you want a proper kiss, you need to be beside me."

Rhi turned to face him, tempted to get closer and kiss him again. She had to know if Ulrik's kiss was as powerful as she remembered. But she was too irate to think about kissing right now. "I want to know what you want from me."

"I beg your pardon?"

Rhi sighed, her anger spiking again. She had to get it under control, and quickly. "You carried me out of Balladyn's prison because you want something. What is it?"

"I doona know yet."

She gripped the railing tighter and looked Ulrik over. His dark hair was loose, making him appear roguish. He was in a pair of jeans and a thin sweater. As always, he looked gorgeous.

"I'm tired of being used. Balladyn wanted to torture me and turn me Dark, and now he wants me in his bed. You want me for some untold thing whenever you decide to use it. Usaeil wants me at her beck and call and to know my every movement. Con wants to make sure I never step foot on Dreagan again."

"What do you want, Rhi?" His question was spoken in

a low voice as if she were some wild animal about to attack. Ulrik pulled his hands from the pockets of his pants and let them hang by his sides. He took a few steps toward the stairs. "Forget everyone else. Focus on you."

Forget? How could she when she was surrounded? Ulrik, Usaeil, Con, Balladyn, and Henry were just a few who sought something from her.

She closed her eyes, and immediately the face of her lover appeared. He was the only one who didn't want a thing from her.

Why did it continue to hurt so bad whenever she thought of him? Why couldn't the pain dim as everyone said it would? Thousands of years, and the pain was as fresh as the day he called an end to their affair.

"Rhi? Tell me what you want," Ulrik urged, his voice closer.

What did she want? She wanted *him* back. She wanted her Dragon King to love her again. She wanted to feel him next to her, to have his arms around her shoulders as he held her close. She wanted to see his smile, to look into his b—

"Tell me, Rhi. Who cares about the others? You're a powerful Light Fae."

She realized he was right behind her now. Rhi opened her eyes and saw that she was glowing. Everything around her was shaking. A vase fell off a pedestal and shattered, while books tumbled off the bookshelves. Teacups flew across the room to smash against the opposite wall.

Ulrik's arms were suddenly around her, comforting and gentle. "You've held it in too long. Let it out, Rhi."

She shook her head, even as her eyes filled with tears. "I can't."

"You can," he whispered, holding her tighter.

Rhi grabbed hold of his arms. She was exhausted from being pulled in so many directions. The lie she told herself and everyone else could no longer be spoken. She wasn't all right. She was so far from fine that it scared her.

Her chest ached, her throat closed up. Then the first tear fell. After that, the gates opened and they poured from her eyes.

The last one to see her cry was Balladyn. Rhi didn't want Ulrik to see her in such a weakened state, but it was his arms that held her and gave her the courage to see herself for the fraud she had become.

Rhi didn't know how long she cried. When her shoulders stopped shaking, she found herself still in Ulrik's arms with both of them sitting on one of the sofas near the bookshelves.

She leaned back against his chest, her hands still grasping his arms that hadn't loosened. Her head rested against his shoulder and she was pretty sure his sweater was wet from her tears.

"That was long overdue," he said.

She shrugged. "I hate to cry."

"You love to please people and to help them, but when are you going to realize that the only person who truly needs to be happy is you?"

Rhi turned her head to look at him. "Are you happy?"

"That probably isna the right word for me. Content. Aye, that's what I would use. I'm content. I willna be happy until I have all of my magic and I can shift again."

"You think you will?"

"I know it."

His certainty had her wiping her face of tears. She sniffed and let her head return to his shoulder. "I don't think I can be happy or content. I thought I was, and then Balladyn took me."

"You survived his torture and the Chains of Mordare."

"Did I?" She wasn't so sure anymore.

Ulrik's arms tightened a fraction. "You're sitting here.

You broke the Chains of Mordare, and you blew up his compound. Aye, Rhi, I'd say you survived."

"Perhaps."

"And now?" he asked. "Are you content?"

"I don't know anything anymore. Some days are good, and others are impossible to get through."

"Something set you off today."

Rhi stiffened as she remembered. "Usaeil has a new lover."

There was a beat of silence before Ulrik said, "Ah. I gather it's a King."

She nodded her head, unable to speak for a moment. "No one has seen him, but I think it is a King."

"Con?"

"I don't know. I tried to catch them together."

Ulrik shifted his arms. "Let it go, Rhi. What you had with your King is over."

"Are you over your woman and her betrayal?" she asked snarkily.

"Aye."

Rhi jerked out of his arms and turned on the sofa to look at him. "How?"

"I killed her soul."

She gaped at Ulrik. He was the only Dragon King who had the power to bring the dead back. It never occurred to her that he could find a soul and kill it. If the soul died, it could never be reborn.

"I see I've shocked you," he said and put an arm along the back of the sofa as he watched her. "It shouldna. You know what I am."

She most certainly did. But there were times she forgot. Like just a moment ago when he was holding her.

"How long has it been since you and your King were together?" he asked.

Rhi looked away, the tears returning again. "A very

long time, but not so long that I don't remember the taste of his kiss or the way he would look at me and smile."

"You'll never move on unless you let go. What you need is another lover."

She cut him a look. "Are you applying for the position?"

"Would you take me?"

"What can you tell me about Darcy Allen?" Rhi had to change the subject before she agreed to something that could make matters worse.

Ulrik's golden eyes narrowed a fraction. "I see you've been to Dreagan."

"Of course."

"Who did Con send?"

Rhi shifted to the opposite corner of the sofa so she could better see Ulrik. "How did you know he sent someone?"

"Because it's Con."

"Warrick and Thorn."

Ulrik didn't so much as twitch at the news. "Interesting combination."

"The Dark have attacked her."

At this, Ulrik's faced hardened. "Did they succeed in taking her?"

"Not with Warrick and Thorn there. Why are the Dark after her?"

Ulrik stood and walked to the railing. "There are many reasons the Dark might want her."

"But you know the real one." Rhi scooted to the edge of the sofa. "This is more emotion than I've seen from you in, well . . . ever. Is Darcy your mate?"

He flashed her a dark look. "Never again will I make that mistake."

"But she's significant." Rhi rose to her feet and walked to him. "How many Druids did you see before Darcy helped you?"

"Hundreds," he answered without hesitation. "Every one of them died as soon as they came in contact with the dragon magic."

With a wave of her hand, Rhi repaired all the damage in the store that she had caused earlier. "You should be guarding Darcy yourself then. Or at the very least, having a chat with Taraeth."

Ulrik grunted. "Darcy is more than capable of defending herself."

"Against the Dark?" It was Rhi's turn to grunt. "Keep telling yourself that. Besides, I figured you'd be concerned with her falling for one of the Kings and spilling all your secrets."

"She doesna know anything."

Rhi was willing to bet otherwise. Darcy was a Druid able to not just touch dragon magic, but reverse it, which suggested she knew more about Ulrik than he suspected. Why else would Con send Kings to her?

"She's from Skye."

Ulrik shrugged and pinned Rhi with a cold look. "Your point?"

"You know how powerful the Skye Druids are. Anyone who got their hands on her would have something special. Let's face it, the Dragon Kings aren't the only ones with enemies. You have them as well."

He turned sideways toward her, a slight grin turning up the ends of his mouth. "What do you know of my enemies?"

"Nothing. Yet."

All pretense of flirting disappeared. He straightened, one hand tight on her elbow. "Listen carefully, Rhi. Stay far away. You doona want to get involved in this."

He was deadly serious. Rhi wondered just what Ulrik was involved in. He killed and cursed as he wanted. The treachery of others had turned him cold and nefarious in ways that could never be erased.

"You asked what I wanted from you," he said. "I'll tell you. Keep Darcy safe. Doona let the Dark get her."

Rhi was going to help Darcy anyway, but Ulrik's plea made her curious. "I'll see it done."

"Rhi."

She halted mid-teleport and looked at Ulrik. "What?"

"Keep her out of the Kings' clutches."

CHAPTER THIRTEEN

Darcy tried to forget that Warrick was in the flat with her, but it was impossible. He was so tall and imposing that he dwarfed everything else.

But it wasn't just his physical appearance. Even in another room, she could sense his presence. He calmed her, made her feel as if nothing could harm her.

She wrung out her hair and stepped out of the shower to dry off. After she dressed in a pair of sweats and an oversized tee, she combed her hair and walked from the bathroom.

Warrick stood at the windows, looking out at the city. "If the Dark come, it'll be at night."

She looked past him to the inky sky and the lights of Edinburgh. "Even with you and Thorn here?"

"Depends on how badly they want you." Warrick turned around to her.

"All this because I touched dragon magic?"

"Ours is the most powerful magic on this realm. Nothing is supposed to be able to compare to ours."

Darcy padded to the kitchen area and stirred the soup

she was heating. "Would it help if I tell you that it nearly killed me?"

"Nay," he replied in a tight voice. "It doesna."

"I understand Ulrik better than you. Ulrik hates humans and doesn't care who knows. The other Dragon Kings must hate us, and yet you protect us still."

"There are those of us who detest mortals, but we made a vow. So did Ulrik."

"I think all the Kings have a case for not liking us."

He walked to the sofa and stood behind it to lean his hip back against it. "I wasna fighting you during the war. It was your ancestors and the decisions they made."

"Do you think it'll be any different if Ulrik releases the Silvers?"

Warrick scratched the back of his neck. "War is war no matter who is fighting or what time period. There is death and destruction, and both sides lose. Does this mean you're beginning to understand why we want to stop Ulrik?"

She reached for the bowls on the shelf and set them on the counter. Darcy dished out two servings and carried them to the small table between the living and kitchen areas. "No. I just like knowing what both sides are thinking."

"You heard our version of the story."

She set down the bowls and spoons, and then she went back to grab two bottles of ale. Darcy walked to Warrick and handed him one of the bottles. "I did. I'm not saying you were wrong in what you did, but I think it's gone on entirely too long. For every day that passes and Ulrik can't shift, his anger grows."

Darcy didn't realize how close she had gotten to Warrick until she looked up and into his cobalt gaze. He was mere inches from her. It grew difficult to breathe at his nearness.

Her chest rose and fell rapidly as her blood pounded in her ears. Then his gaze lowered to her mouth, and desire pooled low in her belly. She wanted his kiss with a desperation that made her knees go weak.

Then his eyes lifted. Their gazes clashed, held. There was no denying the sexual tension that filled the flat. It grew, expanded, with each breath leaving Darcy with chills racing over her skin.

Her lips parted expectantly when she saw his eyes darken, the desire blatant.

"I'm not interrupting anything, am I?" said a sensual female voice, with humor edging the words.

Warrick's nostrils flared as he pulled back from Darcy. "Rhi," he ground out.

Darcy whirled around to see a voluptuous raven-haired woman so gorgeous she could only gape at her.

Rhi lifted her hand from the back of the chair at the table and waved her fingers. "I'm guessing I did interrupt something. My bad," she said with a knowing grin.

Darcy looked to Warrick to find him glaring at the woman. Darcy then looked at the front door to find it locked. Her spells were still in place, and none of the alarms were going off.

She turned back to Rhi and pieced it all together. Black hair, silver eyes, and too gorgeous to be real. She was a Fae. She was also the one Warrick had told her about who'd had an affair with a Dragon King.

"How the hell did you get into my flat?" Darcy demanded.

Rhi's smile widened. She looked at Warrick and said, "Oh, I like her."

"Rhi," Warrick warned.

The Fae rolled her silver eyes and moved to the stove to sniff the soup. "Believe it or not, chica, I'm here to help you. What are you cooking? It smells delicious."

"Take mine," Darcy said as she handed Rhi the bowl. She watched Rhi take a bite and give an appreciative nod. Then Darcy said, "I need to know how you got in. I set up spells to keep the Dark out."

Rhi paused with the spoon halfway to her mouth. She frowned and turned to Warrick. "Didn't you tell her the difference between Light and Dark?"

"I did," Warrick said between clenched teeth.

Rhi shrugged and looked back at Darcy. "You'll need to forgive him. Warrick tends to keep to himself. In case he didn't explain properly, I'm Light Fae. All Fae have black hair, but the Dark have silver in theirs. The more silver, the more evil they've done. Then there's the eyes. Mine aren't red."

"Yeah, I got that." Darcy took Warrick his bowl of soup since he was obviously not going to sit down. Their hands brushed, and her stomach quivered wildly. "It doesn't explain why you're here."

"Doesn't it?" Rhi took another bite of the soup. "This is really good."

"It's a family recipe." Darcy didn't know why she kept being so nice. She wanted to order Rhi out of her flat, but for some reason she didn't.

Darcy reckoned it had something to do with Warrick being agitated at Rhi's arrival, but not in battle mode.

"Am I some beacon to the Fae?" Darcy asked Warrick. "Why do they keep coming?"

Rhi set down the bowl and faced Darcy. "You thought you could help Ulrik and not have everyone focused on you?"

"That was almost three years ago!"

It was the way Rhi frowned, a mixture of concern and wonder, that had Darcy swiveling her head to Warrick who was looking at her as if he'd just had the answers to the universe.

"I'll be damned," Rhi said softly.

Darcy looked between the two. "Someone please tell me what's going on."

"It was you," Warrick said and walked to set his bowl down on the table next to Rhi's. "You're the reason the Silvers moved."

If Darcy was confused before, she was sinking in a pit of puzzlement now. "Human needs an explanation, stat."

Rhi chuckled. "Oh, girl. We're *so* going to have fun."

Was it Darcy's imagination, or had Warrick just growled at Rhi? Obviously the Light Fae heard it too because she laughed harder.

Warrick ran a hand through his blond locks and sighed. "After what Ulrik's woman did—"

"What's her name?" Darcy interrupted.

Rhi cocked her head to the side. "Ulrik didn't tell you?"

"He refuses to speak it."

"Not surprising," Rhi said.

Warrick shrugged when Darcy looked at him. "Honestly, I doona think I ever knew her name. It wasna relevant."

"Well. That answers that," Darcy said, more to herself than the others.

Warrick cleared his throat and continued. "After the mortal's betrayal of Ulrik, Con feared it might happen again."

"Weren't there already Kings mated to humans?"

Warrick shook his head. "One or two, all of which died in the battle that split up the friendship between Ulrik and Con."

Darcy nodded in understanding. "So their mates died as well."

"Exactly. The other Kings who had mortal lovers pulled away from them. We had just sent away our dragons and so many others had died. We needed to disappear for a while."

"Which they did," Rhi added.

"We had to," Warrick said. "The humans couldna kill us Dragon Kings, but we didna want them to know that. We wanted them to think we left with the dragons. While we hid on Dreagan and set up a perimeter so that no mortal would venture onto our land, we combined our magic once more to ensure that we would never feel deep emotions for humans again."

Darcy was taken aback. "Ever?"

Rhi snorted loudly and tossed back her long black hair as she walked around the flat. "That was their plan. It worked for so many millennia that Con believed the spell would never be broken."

"But it was," Warrick said. "Two and a half years ago, the Silvers moved. We had them caged in our mountain, sleeping. They'd no' moved since we put them there. Then they did."

"Not long after that, the first Dragon King met an American and fell in love," Rhi said. There was a smirk on her face when she said, "No matter how much Con tried to put the spell back into place, it wouldn't work. Hal fell hard for Cassie."

"That moment changed everything for us." Warrick's cobalt gaze bore into hers. "It's the same time you unbound some of Ulrik's magic."

Darcy felt as if the world had been yanked from beneath her. Was she really the cause of a spell lasting thousands of years to be broken? Just because she wanted to help Ulrik? "I had no idea."

"No one did," Rhi assured her.

Warrick nodded. "We've never known until now what caused the Silvers to move and the spell to break."

Rhi came to stand beside Warrick, looking at Darcy, as she crossed her arms over her chest. "That's really going to make Con like her."

"Great." Darcy threw up her hands at Rhi's sarcastic

tone. "I did what I thought was needed. I'd do it again. Ulrik should be who he was born to be, not hindered because he made a mistake."

Rhi glanced at Warrick. "She's got a point."

"She doesna realize she's helping to destroy her world."

"And she's right here," Darcy reminded them, pointing to herself with both hands.

Rhi laughed as she walked to the couch and plopped down. "Love the view, Darcy."

Darcy didn't quite know what to make of Rhi. Why was the Light Fae there? She gave a shake of her head and got another bowl. Her stomach was growling when she ate her first mouthful.

Warrick grabbed the two bottles of ale and opened them. He brought one to Darcy as they stood in the kitchen leaning against the counter while Rhi flipped through channels on the telly.

"You know her well, don't you?" Darcy asked.

Warrick cast a quick glance at Rhi. "Aye. She's helped us out on many occasions. The Dark kidnapped a King and his woman. If it hadna been for Rhi, the mortal would've died, and Kellan would still be held by the Dark."

"Wow." Darcy peered around Warrick's shoulder to look at Rhi. She was dressed like a woman who loved clothes, and who knew what looked good on her. Darcy wished she could look that good in anything she put on, but the thought of Rhi being a warrior was what really made Darcy smile. "So she's not just a pretty face."

"Rhi is part of the Queen's Guard. It's an honor few get, and it shows what kind of warrior she is to have achieved such a distinction."

"I think I envy her."

"For the love of all that's holy," he whispered, casting a furtive look over his shoulder. "Doona tell her that."

CHAPTER FOURTEEN

Warrick worried about leaving Darcy with Rhi. It wasn't that he thought Rhi would turn on them. It was more that he was curious as to what she was doing there. Con would never have sent her.

There was a chance Rhys or Kiril might have told her, but then again, they would have let Warrick know she was coming.

The Light Fae was an asset, no doubt. He just wished he'd had a chance to talk to her privately and find out how she learned of Darcy.

"What are you doing out here?" Thorn asked and stepped from the shadows as Warrick exited Darcy's building.

Warrick sighed. "Rhi."

"She's here?" Thorn asked and looked at Darcy's windows. "I would've thought she would get as far from us as she could."

"She loves him. Love like that doesna just go away."

Thorn grumbled low. "Then I'd cut it out. She's only hurting herself by continuing to come around. If he wanted her, he would've made his move by now."

"He's an ass."

"Of the first order. I'm no' debating that fact. I'm simply saying what I would do in her position."

Warrick walked across the street and climbed the ladder up to the top of the building. Thorn was right behind him.

"When you see her, before you say anything stupid like that, you might want to remember that she helped save Kellan, Denae, Tristan, and Sammi. She was also there to help us battle the Dark with Isla and Laith."

Thorn held up his hands. "I get it, War. Rhi is a damned saint."

"I'm saying she puts her life on the line for us."

"And got caught by Balladyn in the process. Did it change her?"

Warrick ran a hand down his face. "In some ways."

"How many more centuries do you think she'll go before that love turns to hate?"

"Balladyn may have given her that push. Rhys caught her and Henry kissing."

"Henry? The mortal working for MI5?" Thorn made a sound at the back of his throat. "Did Banan no' talk to his friend?"

Warrick's gaze searched the streets for any Dark. "Of course, but a mortal can no' deny a Fae. I fear Henry may fall hard for her."

"Rhi's never messed around with mortals before."

"That we know of," Warrick added.

Thorn walked to the other side of the roof and peered over the side. "Did Rhi tell you why she's here?"

"I didna have a chance to ask her."

"But you're worried."

It wasn't a question. Warrick faced Thorn and nodded. "I am."

"Surely it's no' Balladyn."

Warrick faced Darcy's windows to see her and Rhi on the sofa talking. "I hope to hell it isna."

"So," Rhi said when Warrick finally left. "How are you doing?"

Darcy collected the bowls and rinsed them in the sink. "I'm fine."

"Riiiight," Rhi said. "Let's try that again. With honesty this time."

Darcy smiled and looked at Rhi. "I'm freaking the hell out."

"Better," Rhi said. She snapped her fingers and the kitchen was clean. Then she patted the sofa cushion next to her. "Come sit."

With nothing more to clean, Darcy walked to the sofa. "It wouldn't have taken me long to clean."

"Why do it at all? You've magic, chica."

Darcy took one of the accent pillows and held it against her as she sat down. "I was taught not to abuse my magic that way."

"It's magic! Use it, I say." Rhi's smile was wide, her silver eyes trained on Darcy. "Want to talk about what I interrupted earlier?"

Darcy ducked her head in the cushion. "No."

"Oh, come on," Rhi teased, laughing. "Your lips were nearly touching. Was that going to be your first kiss with War?"

Darcy looked up and nodded. "The first time I saw him was last night when he saved me from a group of Dark. I watched him battle them in the middle of the street stark naked."

"Oh, girl. You got to see the whole package right up front." Rhi rubbed her hands together. "I gather you approved."

Darcy put her hands to her hot cheeks. "It should be a crime for a man to look that good."

"Have you taken a look at any of the other Kings? They're all insanely gorgeous."

"True, though I've only seen Warrick, Thorn, and Ulrik."

"Trust me. They all make your mouth water."

Darcy licked her lips nervously. "I just found out about the Fae last night."

"And that's when they told you about me."

Her smile was still in place, but Darcy heard the slight edge to her voice. "They did. I wasn't expecting to meet you."

"There's a lot you don't know, Darcy."

Darcy rolled her eyes. "Apparently. Corann knows of you, doesn't he? And you know of him."

"You could say that," Rhi replied. "The Light have always had a connection to the Druids on Skye. You have visited the Fairy Pools, haven't you?"

"The tourist attraction?"

Rhi shook her head of black hair. "Nope. The real deal. If you return to Skye, you need to find it. I'll make sure you do, and then Corann will have to tell you all he knows."

That was something to consider, if Darcy was going back to Skye. But she wasn't. "You said there's a lot I don't know. Tell me. I want to know."

Rhi let out a deep breath. "I've known the Kings a very long time, and at one point I completely agreed with their decision regarding what they did to Ulrik."

"And now?"

The smile was gone. Rhi sighed loudly. "I can't imagine having my magic bound. In that instance, I feel Ulrik's pain. But don't let him fool you. Ulrik wants it all. He'll challenge Con, and he may well win. If he does, the world as you know it will vanish. There is nothing you mortals have that will kill a King."

"What about the Fae? Can they kill a King?" she asked.

Rhi's silver gaze studied her for long moments. "We seem to constantly be embroiled in a war. If we're not battling each other, we're fighting someone else. We came to this realm ages ago when we discovered humans. The Kings weren't happy."

"I bet not. First mortals, and then Fae."

"That was part of it. I'm sure Warrick explained why the Fae find this realm so exciting."

Darcy shifted, hugging the pillow tighter. "Us."

"The Kings were furious when they found out what the Dark—and the Light—were doing. We went to war with the Kings then in order to remain on this realm."

"They could've let you kill us. All their problems would've been solved."

"Ah, but then you don't know the core of who a Dragon King is." Rhi inspected the toe of her boot before she sat back. "This realm is their home. Whether they regret it or not, they made a promise to protect the other beings who also called this home—mortals."

"Warrick told me the Kings won."

"They did," Rhi agreed with a nod. "The Light took advantage of the Kings' momentum against the Dark and joined forces with the Kings. The Dark were beaten, but the Kings made a fatal mistake. They didn't push us out as they should have. Con believed the Dark would honor the pact to leave humans alone. But the Dark can never be trusted."

It was the perfect opportunity for Darcy to ask Rhi about her King lover. "Is that when you met your King, when you joined in the war?"

Rhi's smile froze in place. "Few have the nerve to even bring him up around me."

"I'm sorry," Darcy said hastily. "My curiosity often gets me into trouble. Neither Warrick nor Thorn would tell me his name."

"Is that right?"

Darcy quickly nodded. "They're protecting you."

"And him."

"I don't think so. I get the feeling Warrick and Thorn aren't happy about the situation."

Rhi smoothed a lock of hair out of her face and back into place. "For someone who doesn't know the story, you know an awful lot."

Darcy didn't hide the grimace from her face. "I apologize. It's a habit. I see things by reading palms and tarot, but there are times I can see other things if I look hard enough. Your story intrigued me."

"There isn't much of a story. We fell in love. I thought he was my entire life, but in an instant he changed his mind and ended the relationship without an explanation."

Darcy was in turns appalled and angry at the Dragon King who had done something like that to Rhi. "I've heard of a lot of douchebaggery, but this one takes the cake."

For the first time since bringing Rhi's King up, the Light Fae smiled. "I do like your way with words."

"You still love him, don't you?"

Rhi rose and walked to the door. She put her hands on either side of it, a soft glow showing beneath her palms. "I wish I could cut him out of my life like he cut me out of his. Perhaps one day."

Darcy watched as Rhi moved from the door to each window, repeating the same procedure. The Fae's magic was visible by the glow. All Darcy knew was Druid magic until she met Ulrik. Dragon magic was immensely powerful, but she had a suspicion that Fae magic was as well.

"Is that some kind of obstruction spell?" Darcy asked.

Rhi shot her a smile. "In a way. I'm hindering the Dark's ability to know if you're here."

"There has to be a way to keep them out."

After the last window was finished, Rhi turned to

Darcy, a troubled look on her face. "There is. We use it against our own, and it was to stay that way. Yet, I encountered it recently while helping another Dragon King, which means another Fae told our secret."

Intrigued, Darcy asked, "What happened?"

"Have you heard of Rhys?"

Darcy shook her head. "Is he a King?"

"Aye, and a close friend. Rhys is King of the Yellows. The Yellows were always known as the risk-takers, the hotheads, or daredevils. If there was danger, the Yellows were there."

"So Rhys has those characteristics, I presume," Darcy said with a grin.

"Which could be why we became fast friends. You're stepping into a war, Darcy, and you need to know specifics. The Dark are after a weapon to use against the Kings. It'll kill them."

"The Darks were beaten in the war with the Dragon Kings. Don't they know they'll lose again?"

"Not if they find the weapon. Ulrik is giving them information about Dreagan to get them onto the land and find the weapon. One of the tactics was taking a King and a human. Kellan didn't tell them anything, even when the Dark tortured Denae in front of him. I helped them get away, but it didn't stop the Dark from kidnapping another human to get to a King. Then a King went to Ireland to spy on the Dark."

An ominous feeling came over Darcy. "I gather it didn't go well?"

"The Dark sent one of their females to capture Kiril, but Shara fell in love with him. Still, both were captured by Balladyn. Rhys and Con went to Ireland to find Kiril, and during the breakout, Rhys was wounded."

"Warrick said only another King could kill a King."

"Exactly. Everyone expected Rhys's wound to mend,

but it didn't. Every time he shifted, the pain was immense. Essentially, the wound was tearing him in two. I was able to stop most of it."

"You can touch dragon magic as well?"

Rhi shook her head sadly. "I was able to help because Fae magic was used. Ulrik mixed Dark magic with his and used it against Rhys."

Darcy didn't want to hear any more. "Stop. Please."

"Remember when I said you stepped into a war? These are the specifics. I was able to give Rhys the opportunity to shift once more. When the mortal he was in love with got into danger, he shifted into human form. For her. But not even his love could help him deal with the fact that he couldn't return to his true form."

"Ulrik wouldn't do that," Darcy argued. "Ulrik can barely deal with it himself. The pain and frustration consume him. He wouldn't put that on another."

"He would. He did."

CHAPTER FIFTEEN

Darcy shook her head. She had experienced Ulrik's memories. She knew firsthand how he was tormented by what his fellow Kings did to him.

"It couldn't have been Ulrik," Darcy argued. "He labored for thousands of years to come to terms with the fact that he couldn't shift. It's torn him apart in ways no one could begin to fathom."

"He's the only Dragon King unaccounted for," Rhi said. "Con might be a world-class ass, but he protects the Kings. He found out where every King was during that battle, which left only Ulrik."

Darcy rubbed her hands over her face. "So everyone blames me since I was able to release enough of Ulrik's magic so that he could allegedly do this."

"You'll have to accept the fact that Ulrik is out for blood. He'll do whatever it takes to get what he wants."

"Killing Con?"

"That's part of it. He wants all of his magic and to be able to shift again. He wants to talk to his Silvers. Don't get me wrong. I know how amiable Ulrik can be when he wants. But he has an end purpose, and nothing will get in his way."

Darcy didn't want to talk about Ulrik anymore. She was having a hard time combining what Rhi was telling her with Ulrik's memories she hadn't just seen, but experienced herself. "You were telling me about a way to stop the Dark from entering."

Rhi regarded her with a knowing look, and then continued on with her story. "Ulrik sent two human men onto Dreagan and used Rhys's woman to do it. They shot Rhys in the head with a bullet laced with dragon magic. It wasn't enough to kill him, but it incapacitated him long enough for them to search the place they thought the weapon was."

"Tell me they didn't find it," Darcy urged.

"They didn't. Rhys called to me to help Lily. When I tried to enter the cottage, I couldn't. The symbols we used against other Fae were carved into the doorway."

"How did the Kings discover the symbols?"

Rhi smiled wryly. "It wasn't the Kings who carved them into the door. It was the two humans Ulrik sent."

Which meant Ulrik had found out about the symbols. Darcy began to feel sick to her stomach.

"I'm not comfortable with any being but a Light Fae knowing those spells," Rhi continued. "Yet, I may not have another choice but to show them to you."

"Why would you do that?" Darcy asked, confused. "Wouldn't that keep you out as well?"

Rhi nodded her head of long midnight hair. "Your magic is strong, Darcy, but not nearly powerful enough to keep out a Dark. Only Fae or dragon magic can do that."

"Then why hasn't Warrick used his magic?"

"He has. As has Thorn."

Darcy tossed aside the pillow as she scooted to the edge of the sofa. "Then that should be enough."

"Should be, yes." Rhi nibbled her bottom lip with her

teeth. "The thing is, I made a promise to keep you from the Dark. I owed a debt, and it's been called in. I can't fail."

"So you would use something that I could possibly recreate against you in the future?"

Rhi's silver eyes crinkled. "It appears so."

"Who would you do that for?"

"Ulrik."

If Darcy had been surprised before, she was floored now. She got to her feet and glared at Rhi. "Ulrik? The same Ulrik you've been trying to tell me is responsible for those horrible things?"

"The very one," the Light Fae said as she lifted a leg and half-sat on the back of the couch.

Darcy made a face while throwing her hands out in confusion. "Care to explain?"

Rhi sighed dramatically. "I was in a bit of a predicament recently."

"When Balladyn captured you?"

"Well," Rhi said in a haughty tone. "I see the Kings did fill you in on some of the less important things."

"I wouldn't call a Dark abducting you unimportant."

"Did Warrick tell you why Balladyn took me?"

Darcy gave a slight nod.

"Perfect," Rhi said, but her smile was too tight. "So you know he took me and why. Did they tell you what he did to me?"

Darcy fought the urge to take a step back. "Not really."

"Balladyn wanted me to turn Dark. Do you know what it takes to turn a Light Dark? You immerse them in a place where there's no sunlight, only darkness. You put the Chains of Mordare on them, which sends paralyzing pain running through their arm every time they attempt to do magic. And then you torture them. Endlessly."

Darcy backed up with every word until she came against the window, unable to go any farther. Until that moment, she'd had no idea of the pain Rhi kept so carefully hidden. She reminded Darcy so much of Ulrik that it was uncanny.

"Balladyn had me beat. I could feel the darkness taking over," Rhi continued. "Then he made me angry."

Darcy watched as Rhi lifted her arms out to her sides. They were glowing, as was her entire body.

"This I got from my mother. It's a very rare power for any Fae to have. I've kept it secret for a long time. You see, I can renew a dead realm. Or I can destroy one."

Darcy's respect for Rhi grew. "You destroyed the place Balladyn held you, didn't you?"

"Damn straight," Rhi said, the glowing gone in an instant. She had the confident look back in place, a mask she didn't intend to remove again. "Except I knocked myself out in the process. Ulrik carried me out."

"Ulrik? Was he part of Balladyn taking you?"

Rhi shook her head. "Ulrik sees opportunities and takes them. He likes having people in his debt."

"That can't be the only reason he helped you."

Rhi shrugged and stood. "We're both in a situation with Ulrik that puts us in a predicament."

"Is Ulrik your friend?"

"Friend?" Rhi barked with laughter. "Oh, chica. Ulrik doesn't have any friends. He trusts only himself, and he *always* has a backup plan."

"He warned me that I was in danger."

Rhi walked to her and tugged on a curl. "He still has need of you."

"That's what he said as well."

"Then don't look into any more than that. If he didn't still need you, he wouldn't have warned you."

Darcy snorted derisively. "If he didn't still need me, my life wouldn't be in danger."

"So true," Rhi said with a wink. "Now, tell me where

you got that red sweater I see in your armoire. I have to have it."

It was well past midnight when Warrick watched Rhi throw a blanket over Darcy, who had fallen asleep on the sofa. Rhi gave him a wave, and then in the next instant, she was standing beside him on the roof.

"Don't give me that sour look," Rhi admonished him. "Darcy was too wound up to sleep. I had to tire her out, and even then, it took a bit of magic to get her to sleep."

Warrick had to admit, he was glad Darcy was resting. The dark circles under her eyes indicated she was more stressed than she let on. "Thank you."

"You're welcome." Rhi winked. "Seen any uglies tonight?"

Warrick smiled despite himself. That's what Rhi always did. She had such a saucy attitude that if she wasn't irritating you, she was making you laugh. "Nay. I'm surprised after two attacks in two nights."

"That is interesting. Where's Mr. Thorny?"

Warrick choked on a laugh. "He's keeping watch on the back side. We make a round every twenty minutes."

"She's a smart one, Warrick."

He didn't even pretend that he didn't know who Rhi referred to. "Aye, Darcy is."

"She's quick and her magic is astounding. She didn't even know she used it against me."

Warrick jerked his head to Rhi. "What? When?"

"When I was talking to her," Rhi said as she glanced at her nails. "She felt threatened, which is what I wanted. The use of her magic was instinctive. That's very good, by the way."

He knew it was. He didn't need a Fae to tell him that.

"Oh, and I'm sorry for intruding on that kiss you were about to give her earlier."

"It's for the best." Warrick had been telling himself that for hours. Then he would look at Darcy and crave to taste her lips all over again.

"You really should practice your lies, handsome," Rhi said, shooting him an unapologetic look.

Warrick rubbed his temple. Rhi always had a way of getting beneath his skin with the simplest of words. The fact that he desired Darcy was all it took to exasperate him. "Rhi, please."

"I know, I know. You like to be alone. I'll leave as soon as I'm finished."

He stared at the Light Fae, waiting for her to continue.

She rolled her eyes and sighed dramatically. "I guess that means you want me to talk now. Fine. I've ensured no Dark can get into her flat."

Warrick frowned. "How?"

"I'm only telling you so you'll rest easier as long as she's in her home. I'd rather Con not know."

That's when he recalled the symbols from the cottage Rhys had destroyed. What Rhi didn't know was that there wasn't a full symbol found. All there was left were three bits of board with a portion of the symbols on them.

"There's the lightbulb," she said with a smile. "I knew you'd figure it out."

"You willingly gave Darcy that information?"

Rhi scrunched up her face in distaste. "I briefly thought about it, then put them up while she slept. I also hid them, so you'll never be able to find them."

"Thank you."

"Any time, sweets."

"But why?" Warrick shook his head and tried again. "You've always been there to help us, Rhi, but you've just stopped yourself from getting to her in the flat."

She let the smile drop from her face as she glanced at the window. "I can remove those symbols anytime since I put them up. If I tell you I just wanted to help, will you leave it at that?"

"Maybe. I get the feeling, though, that there's much more to your actions than liking Darcy's quips."

Rhi leaned over the side of the building. "Life gets so tedious at times. At least I know that I'll die one day."

Now Warrick was really worried. "Rhi?"

She laughed and straightened to face him. "You worry too much, War. Take my advice and kiss Darcy the next time you've got the chance. You never know when it'll be yanked out of your grasp."

He didn't know what to say. Warrick never had the right words in such a situation. He grew uncomfortable, unsure if he should offer her a shoulder or say something to take her mind off the one-sided love she carried.

"It's all right," she said with a soft smile. "I'll be fine. I got advice recently to just cut it out of my life."

"Who would tell you that?" Though he guessed it was her queen, Usaeil.

Rhi met his gaze. "The same person who asked me to keep Darcy safe—Ulrik."

CHAPTER SIXTEEN

Dreagan

Con looked at the files on his desk without seeing them. His mind was on other things. Or should he say, on someone else.

"What could possibly drag you away from the pile of paperwork?"

Con shifted his gaze to his door to find Kellan standing there. He noticed how Kellan's celadon eyes watched him carefully. "What could possibly be on my mind?" he replied acerbically.

"Hmm." Kellan shut the door and sat in one of the two chairs set in front of Con's desk. "You've been gone a lot, and you have an odd look on your face. Why do I think that doesna add up to you putting together an attack on the Dark?"

Con tossed down his pen. "We've all come up with dozens of different ideas on how to confront Ulrik and attack the Dark. All of it involves the mortals seeing us. If we wish to remain secret, that isna a possibility."

"Deflecting my initial question. No' a good sign."

"I'm no' deflecting."

Kellan raised a caramel-colored brow. "So that's how this is going to go?"

Con merely returned his stare. There was no way he would tell Kellan who he was thinking about or why. That was private. Nor would he divulge where he had been going when he left Dreagan.

"You're right," Kellan said. "We can no' risk the humans seeing us. The Dark doona care. If we attack, they'll draw the humans in."

"Exactly. I want nothing more than to take the fight to them, but it would be detrimental to us."

Kellan rubbed his chin as he contemplated something. "What if we drew them here?"

"They're idiots, but no' so much as to willingly come to Dreagan."

Kellan smiled. "Ah, but they're willing to do anything to find the weapon."

"I doona like the idea of them on our land in any capacity."

"No' even Rhi?"

Con chose to ignore his comment. "There's a chance the Dark could get away and find the weapon."

Kellan twisted his lips. "No' only was it hidden well, but they wouldna know it was a weapon if they saw it. Just to be safe, one of us could guard it in case the Dark actually grow a brain."

"Like Balladyn?" Con said the name with distaste. "To think that at one time I considered him an ally."

"Balladyn is someone we need to keep an eye on. He's dangerous."

"Verra dangerous. Taraeth I doona worry about, but Balladyn is another matter entirely. He used to come to Dreagan regularly."

Kellan stretched his legs out in front of him and crossed

one ankle over the other. "Aye, but he didna see anything of importance."

"Because I doona trust any Fae."

Kellan snorted loudly, shooting Con a scathing look. "That's no' true. And we both know it."

For him to argue the point would bring up things Con would rather keep to himself. So he ignored Kellan. Con rose from his chair and walked to the sideboard to pour two glasses of whisky. He turned and handed one to Kellan. "If we brought the Dark here, we would have to take down the spells we put in place to keep them out."

"It would be risky for sure. Now, if we had the complete symbols found on the cottage door frame that would keep the Fae out, we could put those with the weapon so we could all fight the Dark."

"Rhi willna give those to us, and I willna ask for them. Our magic will have to be enough to keep the Dark away from the weapon. It's the mortals I'm more concerned with. Ulrik is using them more and more."

Kellan swallowed his drink of Scotch. "And at odd times too. I can no' figure out what he's thinking."

"That's easy. He wants revenge."

"Which is pointless until he has all of his magic."

Con tossed back the whisky and gently set the glass down on his desk. "We have his Druid now. She willna be helping him."

Kellan straightened in his chair. "You're no' seriously considering holding her as a prisoner, are you?"

"What she doesna know willna hurt her."

"You're messing with fire, Con. She touched our magic and lived. That should tell you right there she's special and no' someone to disregard easily. Besides, do you really think Ulrik will let us have her?"

Con opened his mouth to respond when the door was flung open and Denae walked in.

"Surely I didn't hear y'all right," Denae said in her thick Texas accent as she let her anger show. "Darcy is a person. She has rights. She's not an object to be fought over."

"Denae," Kellan began.

She put up a hand to stop him and speared Con with her whisky-colored eyes. "Y'all have some gall."

"Whether you want to admit it or no', she's a pawn in this game," Con stated.

Denae rolled her eyes. "All because she was about to undo what you put in place."

"What we all put in place," Kellan corrected his wife. "It wasna just Con."

Denae dropped her hand, shaking her head as she did. "If y'all think Darcy is just going to let you 'take' her, I think you're going to be sorely mistaken. Didn't your time with the Warriors and Druids tell you anything about the Druids?"

"She's got a point," Kellan told Con.

Con looked at the mates. "Warrick and Thorn will do what they must to keep Darcy from returning to Skye."

"Which makes her rely on them." Kellan lifted a shoulder. "It could make her see us in a good light, but if she ever feels trapped, I doona think the outcome will be good."

"Warrick and Thorn will keep her there," Con said again.

Kellan harrumphed. "You obviously doona know Warrick. He's a guardian, Con. He'll protect her from any danger—even us."

"Warrick is a Dragon King. He knows how important it is to stop Ulrik. He'll do what's right."

Kellan slid his hand against Denae's, their fingers twining. "Let's hope you're right. I doona want to fight the Druids as well."

Neither did Con. They had enough enemies, but he had to do what he had to do—regardless of who it angered.

* * *

"What do you mean she protected my flat only?" Darcy asked in outrage.

Warrick looked at Thorn for help, but Thorn shrugged, telling Warrick he was on his own. Warrick turned back to Darcy who stared at him impatiently. He shifted his feet. He hated situations like this. No matter what he said, it wouldn't be enough. If only he had a silver tongue like Rhys.

"Hello?" Darcy said, her brows lifted.

Warrick opened and closed his mouth. He released a breath. "I told you all I know. Rhi did it while you slept, then hid them so they couldna be used again."

"That's great for my flat, but what about this place?" Darcy asked, her arms spread wide, indicating the shop.

"Rhi left before I could ask. At least you have one place to go that you know the Fae can no' intrude."

All the anger deflated right out of her. "True," she grumbled. "I was just hoping to protect the shop as well. It sucks that I can touch dragon magic, but I can't keep a Dark out of my space."

"That is rather odd," Thorn said, his face scrunched with confusion.

Darcy shot him a withering look. Warrick stepped between them when he saw Thorn's grin. It was just like Thorn to want to irritate Darcy.

"We'll add our magic to yours," Warrick told her. "We can keep the Dark off Dreagan. We'll keep them out of the shop."

That seemed to satisfy her, and for the next thirty minutes, the three set up the spells, each overlapping the other to make them stronger.

By the time they finished, Darcy was ready to get to her plants. Warrick didn't follow her. He remained in the front with Thorn.

"I doona like that there were no Dark last night," Thorn said.

Warrick glanced toward the back where Darcy was. "Aye. No' a single one even scoping out the place."

"They know we're here."

"Which means there was another hiding and watching the other night."

Thorn's lips flattened. "The next attack will come soon."

"One of us needs to stay with Darcy at all times while the other keeps his distance."

"Agreed," Thorn said. "I'll stay close enough to help, but far enough away that the Dark willna see me."

Warrick was more than happy to stay close to Darcy. "Perhaps I can convince Darcy to return to her flat before dark."

"Good luck with that," Thorn said with a laugh. "That woman is as stubborn as they come."

She was all that and more. That's what drew Warrick to her. That and the fact he *wanted* to be with her. When he couldn't stand to be with anyone for very long, that spoke volumes about her.

"Has she mentioned returning to Skye?" Thorn asked.

"Nay. I get the feeling she'll go back only if she doesna have another choice."

"So we arrived in time." Thorn scratched his jaw. "Interesting."

Thorn saw conspiracies everywhere, so Warrick didn't pay him any mind. "She doesna realize what kind of man Ulrik has become."

"Why would she? He's done nothing to her."

"No' yet."

Thorn's lips twisted. "No' until she unbinds all his magic."

"It's been nearly three years since she first helped him. Why has he waited to have all of his magic released?"

"Perhaps she can no' do it."

Warrick shook his head. "Nay. If that was it, he wouldna care if the Dark took her."

"Then maybe he's scaring her into helping him."

That was certainly a possibility, and one he didn't like in the least. "I'll ask her."

"Ask me what?" Darcy questioned as she came into the front of the store.

Thorn leaned a shoulder against the wall. "We want to know why you've no' unbound all of Ulrik's magic yet."

Her fern green eyes moved from Thorn to Warrick and back to Thorn. "The first time I touched the dragon magic within Ulrik I was knocked unconscious for an entire day. The second time, it shot me across the room, banging my head against the wall."

"You didna stop though," Warrick said.

"No. I kept going. I saw flashes of dragons whenever I touched the magic, and I was intrigued. It took months and dozens of tries before I was able to touch the magic and finally help Ulrik."

"Then what?" Thorn pressed. "Why did you stop?"

"Because it nearly killed me."

CHAPTER SEVENTEEN

After Darcy's revelation, Warrick was stopped from replying by her first client of the day. Thorn disappeared out of the back unnoticed, and Warrick quickly ducked behind the curtains to the back before the client could see him.

The lights were dimmed in the store. Warrick kept the lights in the back shut off, and it allowed him to watch Darcy throughout the day.

She was warm and friendly to everyone who walked into her shop whether they were regulars or people off the street. Darcy had a way about her that set others at ease instantly.

He was captivated by her. By the way she tilted her head as she listened to her customers, by the way she gently ran her fingers over their palms, and how her forehead furrowed slightly when she saw something in her readings she didn't like.

Not that she told her clients. That's the first thing Warrick noticed. Darcy was careful never to spill too much information. She kept things vague, letting the customers decide what step to take next in their lives.

Some of her clients were easier than others. Warrick saw her shoulders tighten with two different customers. After the first one left, Darcy rested her head on her arms on the table. After a moment, she rose and walked to the back with him. She opened the small fridge she had tucked next to her desk, the light from within illuminating her haggard expression.

"What is it?" Warrick asked.

Darcy drank the entire bottle of water before she turned to him, clicking on the desk light. "I saw an accident coming soon. It'll claim her life."

When it happened again, Warrick didn't bother to ask. He knew Darcy saw something terrible. It affected her deeply, and he couldn't imagine how hard it was for her not to tell them. When the last client left, he decided to ask her. He came out of the back as she locked the front door and flipped over the sign so it showed CLOSED.

"Why do you no' tell them what you see?"

Darcy pushed away from the door and returned to the table where she put away the stack of tarot cards. "I made that mistake once. I thought it was my job to help people and steer them away from danger."

"And it's no'?" he asked, confused.

"No."

"Then why do you think you have the ability to read their palms?"

She sat heavily in her chair and shook her head. "I don't know. I've asked myself that thousands of times. The first time I told someone they were going to die, they averted disaster on multiple occasions. Every time they would return to me and want me to read their palm again so I could see what was coming next."

"Did you?"

"Yes," she replied softly. "It got so bad that the person wouldn't leave the house until I did a reading. Eventually, death comes for all of us. And it did for this person as well, no matter how hard they tried to divert it."

Warrick didn't know what alerted him that the person had been someone close to her. "You knew this person well, didn't you?"

"It was my mother."

"I'm sorry."

Darcy shrugged and tossed the empty bottle in the recycling container. "It was a hard lessoned learned."

"Is that why you left Skye?"

"One of several reasons. I couldn't lie to my family, but neither could I keep to myself if I saw bad things coming for them."

Warrick felt the uncontrollable need to pull her into his arms. It wasn't something he did. Ever. Showing affection was something he saw people do, but never did himself. "I'm sorry."

As soon as the words left his mouth, he heard how meaningless they were.

Darcy met his gaze and attempted a smile. "Thank you."

"You carry a great burden, and yet you face it every day by having this shop. Why?"

She took a deep breath, some of the tension releasing from her shoulders. "Because I help people. Sure I see their deaths or their significant others cheating. I can nudge them in the right direction without coming straight out and telling them."

He'd seen proof of that earlier. "Mortals come here for answers."

"No, they don't," she said with a laugh. "They think they want them, but trust me, they really don't. If I told my first client today that her husband was cheating on her and she would walk in on him in a week's time, she would be outraged."

"But she asked you specifically if her husband was faithful."

"The fact she's asking means that she already suspects, but she's hoping she's wrong. She doesn't want to be right, and she was praying I tell her differently."

Now Warrick understood. "So you don't tell her definitively either way."

"Exactly. With enough clues, she'll figure it out and find him with her neighbor. So it all works out in the end."

"Amazing."

A pleased smile pulled at her lips. It wasn't every day that he caused someone to smile, so Warrick enjoyed the moment.

There was a nudge against his mind from Thorn. Warrick immediately opened the link. *"Aye?"*

"We've trouble. The Dark kind."

Damn. Warrick was hoping they would stay away for good. *"Where? How many?"*

"I'm moving around to the back now, hang on." A moment later, Thorn said, *"Shite. The bastards have a plan this time. There are ten of them, War. They've surrounded the shop."*

"We can take ten."

Thorn's grunt was loud. *"And who is going to watch Darcy? We're no' at her flat. Our spells are strong, but between Darcy and trying to keep the humans from discovering our battle in the middle of the streets—"*

"I know," Warrick interrupted. *"Our spells should keep the Dark out of the shop. Do you think we could get Darcy to the flat?"*

There was another pause before Thorn let loose a string of curses. *"No' likely. It looks as if they've set up on the route she uses to walk home. Just in case we get past the ones at the shop, we'll have more waiting for us."*

"Which means they're probably at the flat as well."

"That's my guess. I can call more Kings."

"No' a good idea. If the Dark see that many of us, they could possibly start a war right on the streets of Edinburgh."

Thorn growled low in his throat. *"We should've ran those assholes out when we had the chance. If we doona want to make a run for it or call more Kings, then our only other option is to remain here."*

"And hope they doona try to test our spells."

"I'll keep watch out here."

Warrick frowned, because he knew Thorn too well. *"Doona be an idiot and try to fight them on your own."*

"I wouldna dream of it," came the sarcastic reply.

"Thorn!"

"I'm no' daft, War. I'll curb my need to spill Dark blood and watch the fuckers tonight."

In other words, Thorn couldn't guarantee the same once dawn came. Warrick closed the link and focused on Darcy.

"Where did you go?" she asked. "You looked by turns concerned then angry, and I know you weren't listening to me because I called your name twice."

Warrick walked past her to the conservatory and clicked off the lights. He checked the spells, making sure they were all still in place.

"You're freaking me out," Darcy said from behind him.

He faced her then. "Have you slept here before?"

One auburn brow rose. "No. Why are you asking?"

"We have a wee bit of a problem."

"A wee bit?" she repeated. "It can't be wee if it means I can't leave the shop, and that's exactly what you're implying, isn't it?"

Warrick walked to her and gently grasped her arm to guide her back into her office area. Once there, he reluctantly released her. "The Dark are here."

"Here?" she asked in a voice that wobbled slightly. "We put up spells."

"Aye, and it should keep them out."

"But I can't get home, to the one place I know they can't reach me."

"I'm afraid so."

"How many are there?"

Warrick knew where she was headed with the question. "Too many. There are ten surrounding this building, and there are more on the way to your flat. We'd never make it."

"They are persistent."

Her quip didn't hide the fear he saw in her fern green eyes. Warrick didn't want her frightened. He wished to see her smile back, to see her gaze alight with mischief.

"I guess it's good I didn't eat all of my sandwich for lunch," she said with a tight laugh. "I'll split what's left with you."

Warrick waved away her words. "There's no need. I'll be fine."

"And if we're here for days?"

"No' going to happen," he promised.

That made her relax. "Good to know. So. What do we do?"

"Anything you want other than going outside."

"Just when I was looking forward to a hot bath and my bed," she said with a grin.

Warrick looked at her mouth at the mention of her bed, his balls tightening as he recalled how close they'd come to kissing. If only Rhi hadn't arrived, he would know how sweet Darcy tasted.

"How did you know about the Dark outside?" she asked.

Warrick tamped down his desires and focused on her words. "The Kings have a mental link. We can converse that way."

"Do you get tired of always having someone in your head?"

"We have the ability to keep our minds shut, and only allow another in if we want."

"Nice," she said with wide eyes. "Do you have the ability to know who is trying to talk to you?"

Warrick found it hard to believe that he not only didn't mind talking to Darcy, but that he wanted it to continue. He enjoyed her responses, and liked trying to figure out how she might respond to something. The fact that she kept surprising him was only a bonus.

"Aye," he answered. "All dragons spoke mentally until the Kings were able to shift."

"It's all so fascinating. A little scary, but intriguing."

His spirits dampened a bit. "So I frighten you?"

She stared at him a moment before she gave a shake of her head. "The idea of the Dragon Kings, a wee bit," she said, using his words from earlier. "But not you."

They were just two steps apart, each on a side of the tiny office. He couldn't remember the last time he'd wooed a woman. When he wanted to fulfill the needs of his body, he visited a brothel.

Darcy was unlike any human he'd ever encountered. She was smart, vivacious, and considerate. She smiled at him, laughed with him, and didn't so much as bat an eye when he grew uncomfortable trying to find the right words.

She was obstinate, tenacious, compassionate, and sexy as hell.

It wasn't just her beauty that captivated him, it was her mind and her conversation. She had charmed him from the first moment they spoke, and he hadn't been able to look away since.

He wanted her. Desperately.

He craved, he hungered.

He yearned.

All for her.

Their gazes were locked, the air thick with desire. Warrick closed the distance between them. He rested one hand on her waist and the other around her back.

Her lips parted slightly as her hands came to rest on his chest. He lowered his head slowly, her eyes drifting shut just before their lips met.

CHAPTER EIGHTEEN

Warrick bit back a groan of pleasure when her tongue skimmed against his lips. He tilted his head and deepened the kiss, their tongues dueling, mating.

Her taste was more tempting than he thought possible. He had to have more. His arms tightened as the kiss intensified, sizzling and burning him until he was aching to have his way with her. He groaned when her hands slid into his hair, her nails lightly scraping his scalp as she pressed her body closer.

Warrick pressed her against the wall of cabinets and ground his throbbing cock against her. She was panting, her hand clinging to him as she rocked her hips in response.

It was his undoing.

Need pounded through him, demanding he fill her. He tried to pull back, to clear his head some, but she wouldn't release him.

Then her hand skated beneath his shirt. Her palm rested against his tat on his right side. Whatever thoughts he had of walking away vanished.

Darcy was floating, soaring. Warrick's kiss was sensual,

carnal. It aroused her, inflamed her. His touch was just as wickedly delightful. His hands stroked her back, her butt, holding her tight, as if he couldn't fathom releasing her.

She never wanted the kiss to end. It was too good, too . . . perfect.

A sigh escaped her when the kiss deepened. As soon as she felt his arousal pressed into her stomach, she clutched him, her own body responding wantonly.

Desire pulsed, throbbed low in her belly. It intensified with each kiss, each touch until she was trembling with it.

His hand moved over her shoulder and slid down her side, pausing to cup her breast. Darcy gasped as a fresh wave of need hit her.

When his lips traveled down her neck, she dropped her head back. His hand massaged her breast before his thumb stroked over her nipple. Instantly her breasts swelled as the peak hardened through her shirt and bra.

Suddenly, Warrick lifted his head. Darcy struggled to open her eyes and think through the fog of desire. She gazed into his cobalt eyes, her stomach clenching at the longing she saw reflected there.

"There's a Dark at the back," he whispered.

Darcy was so frustrated that she wanted to scream. Why couldn't they have a few minutes of privacy? If it wasn't Rhi popping in, it was the Dark after her. "Tell him to go away. We're busy."

A sexy grin pulled at Warrick's lips. "Gladly."

She dropped her forehead to his chest. After a few deep breaths, calming her heart and her body, she lifted her face to his. It was hard to think with his hand still on her breast, and her lips swollen from his kisses.

"Perhaps he'll go away."

Warrick sighed and gave her a soft kiss. "I need to check."

If Darcy didn't hate the Dark before, she did now. She

waited until Warrick disappeared into the conservatory before she touched her lips and closed her eyes.

Romantic and dreamy were never two words she used with any man she attempted to date. Yet, Warrick embodied both of those terms to perfection. He might not have meant the kiss to be romantic, but it was. From the way he held her gaze, to the determined look in his eyes before he strode to her and wrapped his arms around her.

She opened her eyes to find Warrick watching her. His cobalt gaze blazed with need that made her knees weak.

"There's another at the front door," Warrick said in a voice laced with desire.

Not once in her life had Darcy wanted to thumb her nose at danger and rip the clothes off a man, but she was contemplating that very thing.

"Stay here," Warrick ordered and walked to the front, clicking off the dimmed lights as he did.

The minutes ticked by with Warrick remaining near the front door as the Dark tested the spells again and again. Darcy was sitting at her desk with Warrick dividing his time between the front door and the back.

The night dragged on as the Dark continued to attempt to get through the spells. Darcy looked at her hands, wishing she could make them glow like Rhi and evaporate the Dark.

Darcy wanted to stay awake. It's not like she was completely helpless. She was a Druid. She had magic with which to defend herself. She almost told Warrick that on one of his trips back and forth from the front to the back, but then she recalled how the Dark affected her.

It made her think about the desire she still felt toward Warrick. It was profound, meaningful, and acute. The feelings went soul deep, unlike those she felt around the Dark Fae.

With the Dark, desire was there, but it was forced upon

her, not something she felt herself. It overwhelmed and overpowered, subduing her. She didn't think about the Dark, only of easing her body. Whereas in Warrick's arms, she wanted to touch him, to please him as much as she wanted his hands on her.

Even knowing that, she wasn't sure she could withstand the Dark. Their magic was potent, and their will to take her staggering.

It was scary to think the Dark had been around and she hadn't known it. For all she knew, she'd walked past a Dark using glamour before and was just lucky enough the Dark hadn't paid her any attention.

Darcy bit back a giggle when she thought of all the humans worried about being attacked by aliens when their world was inhabited by Dragon Kings and Fae, and had been for thousands of years without the humans ever knowing it.

Her eyes eventually grew heavy in the darkness of the room. Apparently Warrick had some type of night vision, because he didn't stumble once around chairs or cabinets.

She yawned and rested her head on her arms. Her eyes burned she was so tired. Darcy decided to close them for a moment, but she wouldn't sleep.

Warrick watched Darcy drift off to sleep. In some ways he was glad. It was difficult to be so near her after their scorching kiss and not pick up where they left off. But there was the matter of the Dark.

They tested the entire building, looking for weaknesses in order to break through the spell and get to Darcy. Luckily, there weren't any for the Dark to find. That didn't make Warrick rest any easier, however.

It just meant that the Dark were devising another way to get to Darcy. Luckily, the following day was Sunday, and Darcy didn't open the shop. If need be, they could remain there.

All Warrick needed to worry about was getting Darcy food. Thorn couldn't help, because he needed to remain hidden. They wanted the Dark to think Warrick was the only one who had remained behind to guard Darcy.

Warrick rubbed his eyes with his thumb and forefinger. It went against his code to sit back and not kill the Dark. The fact they remained alive grated his nerves.

He gave Thorn a mental nudge, and waited for Thorn to open the link. *"Are they still there?"*

"Aye," Thorn answered. *"They're also still circling the building. I think they finally realize they can no' get to you."*

"Depending on how many remain at dawn, we might be staying here."

"That's what I would suggest. The Dark are looking for trouble, War. If they see one of us, this entire city will get to see a battle. As much as I want to kill these twats, even I think it would be a really bad idea in daylight."

Warrick had to agree. *"Especially in the middle of Edinburgh."*

"How is Darcy holding up?"

"As well as can be expected. She finally fell asleep. I hope she stays that way for a while."

There was a beat of silence before Thorn said, *"You kissed her."*

"What?" Warrick was so shocked by the comment he didn't know what to say in response.

Thorn chuckled. *"I knew it!"*

"You doona know anything."

"It's a good thing you're in there with her then. How long has it been, War?"

Warrick closed off the link. He checked the front and

the back before he returned to Darcy. It didn't feel right unless he was with her.

Mikkel walked into The Silver Dragon. He glanced around, then made his way to the back where the hidden staircase led to the upper floors where Ulrik lived. He really needed to tell Ulrik to find a more secure place, but then again, it made his nephew easy to find.

"It's rather late," Ulrik said from above him.

Mikkel paused and looked up to where Ulrik kept the books and more expensive relics in his antiques store. "Night is the best time to conduct business."

Ulrik didn't respond. He stared for long minutes before he gently closed a great tome of a book and returned it to its wrapping and removed his gloves. "What is it you want?"

"I found your Druid."

"That's nice."

Mikkel wasn't deterred by Ulrik's flippant response. "I've sent the Dark after her."

"That was rather stupid. I would've brought you to her had you but asked. Now you'll bring the attention of the Kings to her, and they'll begin to wonder why I would have the Dark go after her."

"You worry too much."

Ulrik returned the book to its glass case. He descended the stairs and released the leather strap holding his hair back at his nape. "Perhaps. But you're getting reckless. You want the Kings' attention solely on me, which is what we agreed. It's becoming difficult to do that when you go after someone I wouldna harm until I had everything I wanted from her."

"Ah, yes. Your magic." Mikkel didn't bother hiding his smile. "You're still without much of it. It took you a long time to find the Druid, didn't it?"

"I see you're no' trying to hide your intentions."

"Why should I? You need to know where you stand in this relationship. I'm the Dragon King now. I'll be the one to rule the Silvers."

Not a muscle moved as Ulrik returned his stare. "We already covered that."

"Removing Darcy Allen will cause you to remember your place," Mikkel said.

"It should've been done another way. You've brought Kings to Edinburgh."

"A King," Mikkel corrected. "The other is gone. Only Warrick remains."

Ulrik walked to his desk and wrote something in a log book. "Interesting."

"What do you know of him?"

"That he works alone. Always. He doesna do well with others."

Mikkel smiled, rubbing his hands together. "Then we don't have to worry about any more Kings showing up."

"The Dark might try and take Warrick," Ulrik said as he faced him once more.

"Let them try. If they're that stupid, it's their own downfall."

Ulrik's gold gaze was unmoving. "Why send the Dark after Darcy? Why no' just have her killed?"

Mikkel had expected this question. Ulrik hadn't become King of the Silvers for nothing. If Mikkel was to remain a Dragon King, Ulrik could never have his magic returned. "To prove a point to you."

"That you can kill someone?" Ulrik asked in a bored tone.

"That I control things. The Dark and I made a pact. They're doing my bidding."

Ulrik slid his hands into his pants pockets. "The Dark can no' be trusted."

"I never said I trusted them."

"So this attack is all for my benefit."

Mikkel chuckled. "I know you, Ulrik. I know how your mind thinks. Doona even attempt to oust me. I'm in charge now—and always." He walked to the door, but paused when he reached it. "Besides. There's nothing you can do without your Druid."

CHAPTER NINETEEN

When dawn came, the Dark didn't leave their posts. Warrick at least knew they couldn't get to Darcy, which allowed him to relax a little.

He gently lifted Darcy and set her on the floor so she wouldn't have a crick in her neck. She rolled to her side with a sigh. After he covered her with a blanket, he sat in the office area with her. But that wasn't enough.

After much internal deliberation, Warrick lay down beside her. A few minutes later, he rolled onto his side so he faced her back. Then she scooted back as if seeking his warmth.

He clenched his jaw at her nearness and her shapely bottom rubbing against his groin. Need rose swiftly within him again, but there was also a feeling of rightness as they lay together. He draped an arm over her, bringing her even closer.

Warrick tried to pretend that he didn't notice how good it felt to have her against him, or how his breathing began to fall in time with hers. But there was no denying that he liked the feel of Darcy next to him, that he craved her like no other.

How odd it felt to not wish to be alone. Warrick didn't just eagerly fall into conversation with her, he found himself actually starting them. He wasn't sure what to think now that he didn't long for the assignment to end so he could return to his solitude.

No, he feared something much greater—the time when he might have to return to Dreagan without Darcy.

And that shocked him as nothing else could.

Darcy stretched her arms over her head as she rolled onto her back. She felt the heat beneath her, proving that someone had been lying with her.

Warrick.

She sat up, looking around. The last thing she remembered was sitting at her desk. It didn't take much for her to realize he'd moved her to the floor. Then he lay down with her.

Darcy smiled at the thought. If only she had been awake to enjoy it. Though she wondered why he wasn't still with her. Now that would have made for a great way to wake up.

She rolled her neck from side to side working out the stiffness. Darcy then stood and peeked into the front of the store where she found Warrick standing at the door looking out while rain fell.

"How did you sleep?" he asked without turning around.

"Better than I expected."

He shifted toward her then. "You needed the rest."

"How are things?" she asked, motioning outside with her hand.

"The same," he said with a frown. "They've no' left."

Darcy blew out a frustrated breath. "Figures."

"Thorn is making his way to your flat now. He'll let me know if the Dark are still there as well."

When he once more faced the door, Darcy turned on her heel and walked back into her office area. She saw the pot of freshly brewed coffee and grinned. Warrick was certainly surprising.

She stepped into the bathroom and turned on the light as she shut the door. It wasn't until she saw herself in the mirror that she gaped in dismay, embarrassed to see her hair sticking out everywhere.

Darcy pulled her hair free of the ponytail and tried to tug the curls back down, but her hair had a mind of its own. She wet her hands and dampened her hair, which helped some. She then pulled it all back and quickly braided it to hide most of the crazy curls.

She splashed some water on her face and patted it dry. After smoothing down her clothes, Darcy walked out of the bathroom to find Warrick holding a cup of coffee.

He handed it to her. "I've got bad news."

"What is it?" she said, wrapping both hands around the cup after she accepted it.

"The Dark are at your flat."

Darcy took a sip of the hot liquid and let his words sink in. "In other words, we're not leaving anytime soon."

"There are several reasons why I doona recommend that. First, there are too many Dark for Thorn and me to battle and keep you safe. We could bring in more Kings, but that would only make things worse."

"I gather it has something to do with the Dark."

"The Dark doona care if the mortals know of them. They flaunt themselves in Ireland just as they are, and the humans doona even realize they live so close to such evil."

There wasn't going to be enough coffee in all of Edinburgh to help Darcy deal with this news. "You think they'll do the same here."

"I know they will. If we try to fight them, they'll no' keep it secret as we do."

Darcy shrugged, knowing there was only one option.

"Then we stay. The rest of the world doesn't need to know of the Dark or the Kings. It would cause panic and chaos."

"And be exactly what Ulrik wants. The problem is that there isna food here for you. You didna have enough yesterday. I can no' let you go without food."

"Yeah, I'm not all about starving."

His crooked grin made her smile with pleasure. Lord, the man had no idea how tantalizing he was. With just a lift of his lips, he made her body rush with warmth—and need.

"I've a feeling we'll need Thorn as a diversion later, so I doona want the Dark to realize he's still here. I'll be leaving to bring back food."

Darcy gawked at him. "Are you nuts? They'll go after you."

"Nay. They'll remain, thinking you'll be an easier target alone."

Well that made sense, in a twisted kind of way. "And do you think they'll just let you back in without a fight?"

"Oh, I'm counting on them trying to stop me."

Darcy shuddered at the rage in his eyes and his voice. There was no doubt, Warrick wanted blood, Dark Fae blood. And he was going to get it.

She recalled how he'd said Ulrik mixed his magic with the Dark to hurt Rhys. There was a chance that Warrick could be hurt the same way. Just the thought of that happening sucked all the warmth from her body.

"I'll leave out the front," Warrick continued. "Give me a list of what you need from your flat and what food you'd like. When I return, I'll come in the back. That way it's less likely for the humans to see us if there is a fight."

Darcy snorted. If. Not likely. There would be a fight. The Dark weren't going to let Warrick back in to her shop easily. If only she didn't need to have food, or if she could use her magic to conjure food.

"I don't want you to go."

His cobalt gaze softened. "I'm a Dragon King, lass. I can no' be killed."

"Except by another King. Or one who mixes their magic with the Dark, which could do serious damage."

"Aye. There's that chance."

Darcy shook her head in amazement. "Is it the fact that you're immortal and unstoppable that gives you such confidence?"

"I'm a dragon."

He said it as if it explained everything, and she guessed it did. Warrick was unlike any man she knew. He was quiet and taciturn one moment and amenable and tender the next.

Right up until he kissed her.

Then he was passionate and intense.

The man was a roller coaster of responses. And she loved every moment of it.

There was a split second where she almost asked to read his palm so she could look to see if she saw the outcome, but she held back. She knew better than to want to look at those closest to her. It never turned out well.

"A list," Warrick urged.

Darcy sat at her desk and set her mug of coffee aside. She scanned her desk looking for a piece of paper to write on. "I can do without stuff at my flat."

"We doona know how long the Dark will surround us."

That drew her up short. Her head whipped around to look at him. "What? Are you telling me they could remain out there for days?"

"Days. Weeks. Months. Aye, that's exactly what I'm saying."

She closed her eyes as her heart plummeted to her feet. This couldn't be happening to her. All her life she knew she was more powerful than those around her.

Not once did she fear anything, because she knew she had her magic to use as a defense and offense, if needed. She thought herself untouchable, if she were honest—pretty much what Warrick thought of his kind.

The difference was, Dragon Kings *were* untouchable. Her Druid magic might help her against other humans, but it did nothing against the Dark or the Kings.

"You'll no' go through this alone."

Warrick's voice, deep and strong, came from beside her. His promise was freely given, and it did help ease her mind somewhat. But she wasn't just thinking of herself. She was thinking of the mortals around her as well as the Kings.

Darcy opened her eyes to look up at Warrick. "You don't know me. I've helped one of your enemies, and yet you would put yourself in harm's way to protect me. I don't understand it, but I'm immensely grateful."

There was a flash of . . . was that regret in Warrick's gaze? Darcy frowned and got to her feet even as the emotion she spotted faded away.

"What was that?" she asked.

Warrick didn't look away, but he tensed. "What?"

"That look," she pressed. "As if you're hiding something."

Warrick turned his head to the side and let out a long breath. After a moment, he faced her once more. "We've been honest with each other, aye?"

"Yes. I'd like that to continue."

"You willna like what I have to say."

She shrugged. "You didn't like hearing me talk of Ulrik, but you did it anyway. Just tell me."

"Con wants all the information you have on Ulrik. Thorn and I were to convince you to remain in Edinburgh so we could get it."

For a heartbeat, she could only stare at him, her mind

a whirlwind of confusion. "Wow. And I made your job that much easier by refusing to return to Skye."

She clutched her stomach. And to think she'd almost made love to Warrick. He didn't care for her. He was using her.

"I would still be here protecting you even if you didna unbind Ulrik's magic."

She laughed, the sound hollow even to her ears. "That makes everything better. I trusted you."

"And I've done nothing to make you doubt that trust."

"No?"

His face hardened. "Nay. We agreed on sharing information, and I've helped keep the Dark from you."

"So I would be grateful and tell you everything about Ulrik as well as turning against him."

"He's evil!" Warrick shouted.

Darcy shook her emotions ran so high. She couldn't decide if she was angry or disappointed or hurt. Each emotion tried to swallow her whole. "At least he was honest about why he came to me. He told me up front what he wanted me to do and what he would give me in exchange."

"He's killed."

"And you haven't?"

A wall came down over Warrick, his eyes turning cool as he became aloof. "I didna lie to you."

"You played on my desires, which is worse. I want you to leave."

The shock of her words showed on his face for an instant before he hid them behind his mask of indifference. "You'll face the Dark alone?"

"I've been alone for seven years. If this is the end, then it's the end. I'm a Druid from Skye. I won't go down without taking a few of them with me."

CHAPTER TWENTY

West Coast of Ireland
Light Fae Court

Rhi remembered the first time she walked into the queen's court. It was in the palace on the Fae realm, and she'd stood with her brother, Rolmir.

Every Fae—Dark or Light—fell for her brother. He'd had the looks of a Fae, yes, but he had something else as well. It was a spark of something bright and omnipotent. It drew people to him continually.

That might have given most Fae a superiority complex, but not Rolmir. He remained humble and genuine right up until the end. And by his side, always, was Balladyn.

Those two swept through a city, leaving broken hearts in their wake. While Rolmir shone with allure, it was the secrets Balladyn kept that drew women to him. He was mysterious, steadfast, and stubborn.

Remembering that day brought back more memories of Balladyn. Rhi tried to stop them, but the floodgates were open.

There were so many recollections with Balladyn. He

and Rolmir were so close that her parents considered Balladyn a son. Which is why she thought of him as a brother.

How did she never know he loved her?

It was the whispers around her that brought Rhi back to the present. She stared at the white and gold walls of the antechamber outside of Usaeil's throne room. Rhi turned her head to the group of ladies-in-waiting who were staring at her, whispering behind their hands.

Gah. She hoped she was never so . . . annoying.

Of course, Rhi knew she was a magnet for gossip after being taken by the Dark and getting free. She used it as an excuse to stay away from the castle, but Rhi could only ignore Usaeil's command so many times before the queen's fury exploded.

Rhi stood alone against the wall. As the only female in the Queen's Guard, Rhi was regularly called on for missions Usaeil thought needed a feminine touch. Usually, Rhi looked forward to such assignments. This time all she could think about was Balladyn, her promise to Ulrik, and Darcy.

The doors to the throne room opened and another of the Queen's Guard walked out. His black hair hung to his shoulder, and his silver eyes searched the chamber until they came to rest on her.

Rhi wasn't surprised it was Inen. He was Usaeil's favorite. At one time, Rhi thought the two of them might get together, even though it was forbidden for the queen to marry one of her guards. Which Rhi always thought was silly. Usaeil was queen. She could make the rules.

"Stupid rule," Rhi mumbled.

Inen raised a straight black brow. "Did you say something?"

"Nope. Is it my turn?"

His eyes narrowed, making his face look even more hawkish. With his hand resting on the hilt of his sword strapped to his waist, he walked to Rhi.

The fact he was coming close enough to keep their conversation between the two of them didn't bode well. Inen normally didn't care who heard what he had to say. He had one main objective—protecting Usaeil.

"It took you long enough to get here," he whispered in a callous tone.

Rhi wasn't bothered by his words. "I've duties as a special envoy, and I protect Usaeil in other ways."

"How did you protect her when you let Balladyn kidnap you?"

She felt the spike of anger rumble within her. Rhi pushed away from the wall and moved until they were nose to nose. "I didn't *let* him do anything, you imbecile."

"Didn't you?" he asked haughtily, his lips pulled back in a sneer. "Everyone knew Balladyn was in love with you. Did you think remaining around the Kings would make him forget?"

"Well. It seems like someone has been following me." Which seriously pissed her off. Perhaps it was time she walked away from the Queen's Guard. No one had ever done it before, but then again, no other Fae had been through what she had.

Not to mention, she had some . . . issues . . . to deal with.

Inen returned her stare. "I did what I was told."

"As any good dog will."

His nostrils flared and his grip tightened on the sword. She'd hit a nerve. Chalk one up for Rhi. Which wasn't easy to do with Inen. Nothing bothered him unless it involved Usaeil.

She mentally did a little happy dance at his reaction.

"Next time, don't keep her waiting."

The threat wasn't veiled, and it nearly set Rhi off again. "I answer to her. And *only* her," she added as she shouldered past him.

Rhi walked into the throne room and saw Usaeil sitting on the white throne. She rose, her deep blue dress hugging her curves and falling to her ankles.

Usaeil was barefoot, her long black mane flowing free as she walked down the steps to Rhi. There was no smile on her queen's face. "Where have you been?"

"About."

"That's not good enough, Rhi. You're part of my Guard. I need you here."

Rhi cocked her head to the side. "Really? You've never needed me here before on a daily basis. What's changed?"

"You."

Ah. So her time to get her shit together had come and gone.

"You've nothing to say?" Usaeil asked, a frown puckering her brow.

Rhi shook her head. "I'm doing what I've always done."

"That was before you were taken by Balladyn. That was before you became different."

"Different? Hmm. I tell you what. Put any Light through what I went through and see if they could come out of it without turning Dark. How about Inen? Do you think your favorite Guard would survive? That would be a big fat no."

Usaeil's lips were tight, a sign of her displeasure. "That's not the point, Rhi. We're all glad you made it out."

"Are you? I'm not so sure. You want to confine me after having me followed."

"I think I've been too lax with you through the years. I'm your queen. You need to treat me like one."

"Then act like one," Rhi retorted. The outburst was loud, echoing around the spacious throne room. "Stop gallivanting around as a human movie star and start paying attention to your people."

Usaeil slashed her hand through the air between them. "I have my people in my thoughts at all times."

Rhi was tired of ignoring the larger issues and bowing down to Usaeil. She made a sound at the back of her throat. "Really? That's rather hard to do when you're off for months at a time making some stupid movie. How can you be here to tend to daily business and grievances while off doing your own thing? You want to stop me from doing my thing while you continue doing yours? Not going to happen."

The queen was momentarily stunned into silence. When she drew in a deep breath, her wrath was visible. "I'll not have you question me."

"And I'll not have you question my loyalty. If I wanted to go Dark, I'd have taken Balladyn up on his offer the other day." The worry that flashed over Usaeil's face made Rhi chuckle. "Guess your little dog, Inen, wasn't able to keep up while trailing me."

"Enough, Rhi."

She shook her head. "No. It's not nearly enough. Tell me, my *queen,* did you know the Dark are amassing? Did you know that they're moving all over the world? I can see by your expression filling with concern that you didn't. It's something you might want to think about the next time you leave our people for a photo shoot. I'm not so sure they'll follow a queen who's never around into battle with the Dark again."

Rhi turned on her heel and walked toward the door. She reached it and paused. Then she looked over her shoulder at Usaeil. "If I'm to be followed or confined to this castle, then I quit the Queen's Guard."

She didn't wait on Usaeil's response. Rhi shoved open the doors, and as soon as she stepped into the antechamber, she teleported away.

Usaeil snapped her fingers, shutting the throne room

doors at once. She walked back to her throne and slumped in the high-backed chair. "Well? What do you think?"

Constantine opened the door to her private chamber and leaned against the jamb. "I think you just lost your most valued warrior."

"I know," she said dejectedly. "I was right to worry though. I knew Balladyn wasn't done with her."

Con crossed his arms over his chest. "You should've waited to see what she would do. Following her was a smart move, but Inen should've kept his mouth shut. Rhi would never have known otherwise."

"Inen has an issue with Rhi. He wants to be the best, and he knows as long as she's around, he's not."

"He's no' even close," Con said with a chuckle.

Usaeil shot him an annoyed look. "Don't let Inen hear you say that. He's devoted to me, and I don't want that to change."

"By having Rhi followed, you've caused a wedge to come between two of your Guards. If you're no' careful, Usaeil, your entire group of Guards will fracture."

"And you would know that better than anyone," she retorted angrily, because she knew he was right. And she hated the fact he was correct and that she'd made a grave mistake.

Con lifted one shoulder in a shrug. "Aye. I would know. It took everything I had to bring the Kings all back together."

"All but one." Usaeil sighed loudly. "Is Rhi going to be my Ulrik?"

"Quite possibly."

She rose and glared at him as she began to pace. "That's not what I wanted to hear."

"I thought we agreed on truth."

"By the stars," she exclaimed and threw up her hands in defeat. "You take everything so literally."

Con merely looked at her, showing no emotion. But she knew how to bring those emotions out in him easily enough.

He tracked her with his eyes. "Rhi has changed. She's gotten stronger both mentally and through her magic."

"I know." It was the first thing Usaeil had noticed. She only hoped Rhi and the rest of the Light hadn't.

"Are you worried?"

Definitely. "Not in the least. I've been ruling my people for many millennia. Just as you have."

"So you think she might challenge you for the right to be queen?"

Damn, but he was perceptive. "She's too angry right now."

"She met Balladyn. How many more meetings between them before she turns Dark or challenges you? Either outcome willna be good. You doona want Rhi to turn Dark and join forces with Balladyn."

"I know Balladyn."

"Nay, Usaeil. You *knew* him. He's Dark now, and he's much worse than Taraeth. It willna be long before he kills Taraeth and takes over ruling the Dark. If you think you have your hands full now, wait until then."

She hated when others tried to tell her how to think or rule. "Don't you have enemies you need to keep an eye on?" she snapped.

Constantine pushed away from the doorjamb and walked to her. "You're the one that asked me here. Remember?"

Did she ever. She put her hands on his chest and tore open his shirt. "Remind me again."

CHAPTER TWENTY-ONE

Warrick was furious, his emotions in a jumbled heap after his conversation with Darcy. He threw open the door to Darcy's shop and walked out into the rain. Just as he had expected, the Dark didn't stop him. They didn't even show themselves. They knew he knew they were there.

There was a pounding in his mind from Thorn. Warrick briefly thought about refusing to open the link, but he wasn't at all sure Thorn wouldn't make a scene to get his attention.

"What?" he asked calmly once the link was open.

"What? What! *Is that all you have to say?"* Thorn shouted. *"What the devil are you thinking?"*

"She's in a temper, and she needs food."

There was a brief pause before Thorn asked, *"You think she's in a temper because she needs food?"*

"Aye." At least he hoped that was the case. Warrick shook the water from his face. *"I've seen it before. Humans get . . . testy when they're hungry."*

"So do I, but I'm no' going to go flying over Edinburgh Castle and grab me a snack from the hundreds of tourists there."

Warrick kept walking and ignored the rain, making mental notes of where he spotted Dark Fae hiding on his route.

"Well?" Thorn urged. *"Are you going to tell me what Darcy is in a snit about?"*

"She thought I was foolish to want to leave with the Dark waiting."

Thorn chuckled. *"Ah. A lovers' spat, aye?"*

"We're no' lovers." But did he ever wish they were.

"She'll understand when you bring her back food. Then she'll thank you."

"I'll no' be talking to her."

"Come again?"

Warrick sighed as he entered a co-op and grabbed a basket. He walked through the narrow aisles and began tossing food into the basket in his hand. *"I told her what Con wanted."*

"For the love of . . ." Thorn trailed off. *"You're no' right in the head, War. No wonder you stay to yourself. Lasses have to be handled delicately, and certainly lasses like Darcy. Her world has gone sideways. Now she isna going to trust you."*

"She's already said as much. She ordered me out of the shop."

"Shite. What a mess. Why did you tell her?"

Warrick reached the last row and put in several types of bottled drinks and ale, then went to the cashier to pay. He tossed down some money, not bothering to count it as he walked out with the basket and all. *"I felt she deserved to know the truth."*

"While we're trying to tell her what a bad guy Ulrik is? That doesna work to our benefit."

"It's better to tell her now rather than later."

"Later you could let Con deal with her. Now, she's our problem."

Warrick didn't see her as a problem, and he certainly didn't want Con to "deal" with her at all. *"You're keeping your distance, remember? I'm the one who will be fixing this muck up."*

"Good luck with that, War. You're going to need it. By the way, how much longer are you going to be?"

"I'm headed to her flat for some clothes. Why?"

"You might want to get back here. The Dark are beginning to close in. You'll have a hell of a time getting back inside the shop if you wait much longer."

Warrick let out a curse and turned toward Darcy's shop. He began jogging down the street, splashing in puddles in his hurry to return to Darcy. It was difficult not to let the dragon loose and take to the skies. He knew he could reach her quickly then, and douse the Dark with some dragon fire in the process.

Nothing but a dragon could survive dragon fire. It burned hotter and longer than anything else in all the realms. And the Dark knew it.

It wasn't the knowledge that the mortals would freak at seeing him in his true form that stopped Warrick from shifting. It was the fact that he knew the Dark couldn't get to Darcy in her shop.

That alone kept him calm enough to return to a slow walk so as not to draw too much attention to himself. "Rhi," he said as he walked. "If you can hear me, I need your help with Darcy."

It wasn't often that Warrick asked for help, but he wasn't too proud to do it. Darcy was the one who needed the food. He could take care of himself.

"Rhi," he said again, a little louder.

Still the Light Fae didn't appear. Not that he expected her to. She only seemed to answer to Rhys.

Warrick lengthened his strides as he saw more and more Dark the closer he got to Darcy's shop. He was halfway there when he noticed how the Dark began to surround him. Warrick paid them no attention as he continued on his way.

"Going somewhere, Dragon?" taunted one Dark.

Warrick gripped the handles of the basket tighter. He didn't slow, didn't turn and punch the idiot. But he wanted to.

"Forget it," shouted another Dark. "The Kings are afraid to fight us in front of the humans. They want to stay hidden."

There was a snigger from yet another Dark. "Hidden? Hell, the best place to live is out in the open so the mortals fear you. Hear that, Dragon?"

"The humans will know of them soon enough," said another.

Warrick was close enough that he could see the door to Darcy's shop. He hoped she wasn't watching, because things were about to get ugly.

He gave a mental nudge to Thorn and said, *"Stay hidden. No matter what, keep an eye on Darcy."*

"We should've called in other Kings."

Warrick didn't have time to respond as he was blasted in the back with magic. It crackled over his back, making his skin burn.

He waited for the magic to wear off, then he carefully set the basket of food down and turned to face the group of Dark. Warrick counted eleven of them. That didn't even take into consideration the others who circled the building.

"If you wanted my attention, all you had to do was ask," Warrick said.

"As if you'll fight us."

Warrick didn't know which of them said it. He looked from one set of red eyes to another. All had silver in their hair, but it wasn't as thick with silver as older Dark who had done more evil. "I'll gladly fight."

"Here? Right," came the sarcastic reply.

"How about the smartass who keeps mouthing off stepping forward. I'll deal with him first."

Darcy hated being mad. She hated feeling deceived as well. As irritated as she was at Warrick, she knew he could've kept the information about Con's plans to himself.

She had reacted harshly and quickly, but she needed time to herself. All she could think about with Warrick near was his mind-blowing kisses and the way he set her body ablaze with desire.

At this point, she wasn't sure who the bad guy was anymore. Was it Ulrik? Was it Con? Was it all the Dragon Kings?

She ground the heels of her hands into her eyes. Her stomach was nauseated from lack of food, and the added cup of coffee loaded with caffeine hadn't helped. She really needed to look into decaf.

Darcy didn't know what made her get up and check the magic as Warrick had done countless times. She felt along the walls to sense how their magic was holding up. As far as she could tell, it was all still in place.

She glanced out the back, and didn't see anything but rain. It wasn't until she went to the front that she spotted the group of men through the rain. They had black and silver hair of varying lengths, and were all standing in the street.

They seemed to be surrounding someone. It took some ducking and weaving, but she finally saw who it was.

"Warrick."

Her heart pounded wildly in her chest as her blood iced. He didn't seem the least bit concerned that there were over a dozen Dark Fae focused solely on him.

Then she heard his voice muffled through the glass of

the door. "How about the smartass who keeps mouthing off stepping forward. I'll deal with him first."

Darcy winced as several of the Dark looked at each other with smiles, as if they had been waiting for just such a suggestion.

A tall Dark Fae with his hair in a Mohawk that was now falling down due to the water walked through the crowd and faced off against Warrick. The Dark looked him over. "What's one King going to do to us?" he asked with his arms wide, indicating the other Dark.

Warrick waited until the laughter stopped. Then he said, "You mean besides kick your ass?"

That's all it took to send the Dark into a fit of fury. A large ball of magic formed in the Dark's hand before he reared back and threw it at Warrick.

Warrick ducked and rolled, coming up in front of the Dark. He punched the Dark with two swift jabs before he grabbed him by the neck and lifted him.

The Dark tried to gather more magic, but Warrick moved too quickly. Warrick knelt on one knee and slammed the Dark onto the ground, splitting his head open on impact.

Darcy covered her mouth with her hand and stepped back. She knew Warrick was strong, but she hadn't realized just how much until then. After holding her so gently, those same hands could end a life in the blink of an eye.

Warrick stood, his look daring the Dark to attack. For one heartbeat, two, nothing happened. Then, with a shout from a Dark, the battle began in earnest.

Darcy tried to keep an eye on Warrick, but she lost him in the crowd. She grasped the window, rising up on her tiptoes to get a glimpse of him. But there were too many Dark.

She screamed and fell back when a Dark Fae suddenly appeared before the window. He reached for the handle of the door, then bellowed and fell back holding his hand. He ran off, two others taking his place.

Darcy forgot about Warrick as the Dark began to hurl magic at the spells she, Warrick, and Thorn had put into place. She knew the minute her spells cracked under the onslaught. She felt the tremor shake through the entire building.

All that separated her now from the Dark was dragon magic.

CHAPTER TWENTY-TWO

The rain began to fall harder, thicker. The dark gray clouds obscured the sun, making the morning appear as if it was dusk. Darcy was grateful for the weather. Otherwise, there was no doubt mortals would see Warrick fighting the Dark.

Her chest rose and fell rapidly as she tried to figure a way out. The fact there wasn't one only ramped up her fear.

Darcy ducked behind the table. It wouldn't save her, but she wanted to stay out of sight of the Dark. The problem with that was that she could no longer see Warrick. And that wasn't going to work.

She peered over the top of the table and around the crystal ball to find Dark Fae still stood at her front door blasting the shop with magic. Warrick couldn't be seen through the throng of Dark, but movement out of the corner of her eye drew her attention.

Darcy looked to the left and spied something on the roof across the street. It was Thorn. He looked over the side to the ground where a few Dark lingered.

Then Thorn jumped off the four-story building to land behind the Dark. In less than a heartbeat, he killed two. A moment later, three more were dead.

Darcy wanted to cheer when Thorn ducked into an alley right before a Dark turned and saw him. She sent up a prayer of thanks. Not just for her, but for Warrick as well.

He had told her Dragon Kings could only be killed by another King, but he never said anything about being injured by the Dark. She had the distinct feeling that the Dark could do some damage to him.

If only she could help.

Darcy dropped her head back and inwardly kicked herself. "Of course I can help. I'm a Druid. From Skye. What the hell is wrong with me?"

She knew the answer—the Dark. They scared her as nothing else could, and she hated them for that. She loathed them for making her forget she was a Druid. She detested them for feeding off humans. She reviled them for how they'd forced their seduction on her the other night.

With her eyes closed, Darcy called to her magic. She heard the drums and chanting of the ancestors as she felt her magic build higher and higher.

As her magic grew, her inner strength did as well. She stood and opened her eyes to the Dark at the front door. Then she walked around the table, her hands clenched into fists.

The two Dark Fae smiled when they saw her. They thought she was coming to them. Fools.

Before Darcy could release her magic, the door flew open, ripping it from one of its hinges. She twisted away, her arm raised to shield her head.

The sound of rain hitting the concrete filled the area. She lowered her arm and looked back to the front to see the door bent inward and off to the side.

"Are you ready for us?" one of the Dark asked, his red eyes looking her up and down.

Darcy lifted her lip in revulsion. "You'll never get your hands on me."

"We'll see."

She saw more dead Dark littering the ground thanks to Thorn. The fact the Dark couldn't find out who was doing it made her smile. But that quickly died when she tried to look for Warrick again.

"The Dragon King won't be able to save you," said the second Dark, his Irish accent so thick she almost couldn't understand him.

Darcy rolled her eyes. "Don't you ever shut up?"

He sneered and hurled magic at her. She jerked, expecting it to hit her, but it slammed into dragon magic at the door and splintered.

Would hers be stopped as well? Only one way to find out. Darcy spread her fingers and threw her arms out in front of her, releasing her magic as she did.

It sailed through the doorway and slammed into the two Dark, knocking them on their asses.

Darcy didn't stop there. She threw blast after blast. The two were able to deflect most of them, but the ones that landed kept knocking them backward.

With each hit, Darcy grew more confident. She was determined to do her share against the Dark and not stay huddled in a corner waiting to be saved. She was a Druid, for goodness sake. She needed to act like one.

If only she could get a glimpse of Warrick. He must still be doing damage, because the group around him hadn't moved away. Why would they though? They'd managed to catch a Dragon King twice before. Why wouldn't they try again?

Darcy renewed her blasts of magic. She was not going to be responsible for Warrick being taken by the evil shits.

Thorn was doing his fair share of taking out Dark Fae, but he had to be stealthy about it and remain hidden. Which meant he couldn't take out as many as he wanted. Still, he was doing enough damage that those around Warrick began to take notice.

When the two Dark Darcy was fighting ran off, she shifted and began focusing her magic on Warrick's group. It didn't take long for them to turn to her.

That's when she got a glimpse of Warrick. He was still fighting. It made her smile—and breathe easier.

Until she realized the Dark were now fixated on her. Darcy squared her shoulders. Whether the dragon magic held around her shop or not, she was going to stand as a Druid and show the Dark what she was made of.

Thorn dashed from the shadows, throwing her a smile before he grabbed a Dark and wrenched his head 180 degrees. Darcy winced and gathered her magic once more.

Warrick was on his hands and knees in the rain. He tried to rise, but the blows of magic had taken a toll. His arms, unable to hold him, gave out so that he pitched forward onto the cobblestones. His limbs were going numb while the rest of him burned as if acid had been poured on him from the Dark magic.

"I've got you," Thorn said and dragged him off the streets into a narrow alley. "Damn, War. You look awful."

"Oh good. I look better than I feel."

Thorn set him against the wall and squatted beside him. "The few Dark that remain have hidden. They'll be back. With more."

Warrick shook his head. More was not good. More meant that the odds of the humans seeing them grew exponentially. He still wasn't sure how mortals hadn't noticed them, but he was thankful of the rainclouds and the rain for aiding in that fact.

Warrick dropped his head back against the building as his body began to heal. "How did you do?"

"I killed several. Wanted to kill more," Thorn said with a grumble. "But I stayed hidden as we discussed. It worked. They didna know where I was, or if Darcy was the one killing them."

Warrick's gaze jerked to Thorn. "What? What do you mean they thought Darcy was killing them?"

Thorn grunted as he shot Warrick a look. "Did you forget she was a Druid?"

"Nay. Well. Maybe." He briefly closed his eyes. "It doesna matter. Tell me what happened."

"There were two Dark trying to get to her. They broke through her magic. She stood and faced them, War. You should've seen her. It was . . . impressive."

For Thorn to say such words was something to be sure. Warrick wished he could've seen her. He could only imagine Darcy standing there with her green eyes narrowed and trained on the Dark as she used her magic.

"She was a sight," Thorn said.

"Where is she now?"

"Still in the shop. She knows better than to attempt to leave."

Thank the stars. "I got food. I need to get it to her."

Thorn pushed him back when he tried to sit up. "I'll get it to her. You stay here and rest. You took a great many hits of magic, War." Thorn frowned as he looked him over. "I'm surprised you're still conscious."

"Me too."

It wasn't the first time Warrick had taken hits from a Dark. He'd taken many in the Fae Wars, but this was the first time he had been beset by so many Dark at once. He tried to count. In the end, there had been twenty Dark he faced at once.

But he knew why he kept fighting. Darcy.

During the battle with the Dark, he tried to use his

power of protection, but he hadn't had a chance to get past the Dark to do it.

A mistake he wouldn't make again.

Warrick watched Thorn use the shadows, buildings, and cars to remain hidden as he gathered what remained of the groceries Warrick had gotten. There wasn't much, but it would be something for Darcy.

He closed his eyes when Thorn went to the back of the shop. Darcy was safe and soon to have her belly full of food. Warrick had done his duty. It wasn't nearly over, but he could rest for a bit.

It was just a few minutes later before Thorn returned. He sat beside Warrick, a peevish look on his face.

"What?" Warrick asked, suddenly worried. "Is Darcy all right?"

"She's more than fine," Thorn grumbled.

Warrick forgot the pain and sat forward to face him. "What's that mean?"

"She wouldna stop asking questions about you. Apparently I didna satisfy her, because she's demanding to see that you're all right, despite my telling her that you were."

Warrick smiled. He wasn't surprised by Darcy's words. She might be angry, but she held a great amount of empathy within her. "Is that so?"

"Aye. Go to her, mate, because I willna be going back without you."

"Is she scared?"

Thorn's eyes grew large in agitation. "Scared? Did you no' just hear what I told you?"

"Mortals sometimes mask their true feelings with others."

"Is that so?"

Warrick leaned back against the building once more. Damn. Had he let too much slip? His brethren wouldn't understand his fascination with the mortals. "Or so I've been told."

"By who?" Thorn asked. "You doona like being around anyone. Except, apparently, Darcy. It seems you're content to remain with her for hours."

"We're here to protect her."

"That we are, but you usually want to take the position farthest away from everyone. No' so this time."

Warrick shrugged. "She's interesting."

"And quite pretty. That explains why you want to remain around her, but you've still no' said how you know so much about the humans."

No matter what Warrick said, Thorn wasn't going to stop questioning him until he was satisfied with the answer. There wasn't time for that kind of debate, and Warrick wasn't keen to sit there that long either.

"You've always been riveted by them."

Warrick's head swung to Thorn. "What?"

"It's no' a secret, War. You tried to hide it, sure, but we saw how you watched them."

"You've been asleep," Warrick said, disgruntled that he hadn't kept his interests to himself as he originally thought.

Thorn glanced out to the street. "For only three centuries. You liked your solitude, but that didna mean the rest of us didna look out for you."

"I know," he answered roughly. He wasn't comfortable talking about such things. The way Thorn wouldn't meet his gaze, said he wasn't happy about it either. "We look out for each other."

"Aye, but you forget that when you go off by yourself."

"I doona," Warrick argued. "I stay to myself because I'm never sure of what to say, and when I do talk, most times I say the wrong thing."

Thorn turned his head back to him. "I'm no' condemning you for your choices."

There was more to his words, the meaning going much deeper than Warrick's choices. He wondered what Thorn was alluding to, but he knew better than to prod. Thorn would never reveal anything.

It was odd to realize that other Kings knew what he had been about. Warrick had assumed they didn't care when he went off by himself. It seems he was wrong about a great many things.

"Aye, I find the mortals interesting. Their choices, their stupidity, their brilliance. All of it intrigues me."

Thorn's dark eyes held no censure. "You've been studying them a long time. How is it you didna hold the hate within you as most of us did?"

"I doona know. Every time I tried, the humans would do something miraculous or malicious, and I would need to know why."

Thorn ran a hand through his long, wet hair. "Your knowledge may be what gets us out of this bugger of a situation. So, War. Tell me how I get the humans' attention away from this area so you can get Darcy to her flat."

CHAPTER TWENTY-THREE

Darcy looked at the food delivered by Thorn and wasn't sure if she could eat. She was in knots after what happened, and not even Thorn's assurances that Warrick was fine helped.

Of course Thorn would tell her Warrick was all right. But if Warrick wasn't hurt, why didn't he bring the food?

"Because you told him to leave, that's why. Idiot," Darcy told herself.

She swiped a hand to shove the hair back from her face and sighed. She had taken her hair down twice. Now she was alone again. Not completely alone. Warrick and Thorn were near, but Warrick wasn't with her. All because she'd let her anger get the better of her.

Darcy brought the food into her office and placed it on the desk. She couldn't sit. She had to occupy her body somehow to keep her mind off what had occurred.

With nothing else to do, she made her way into the back and tended to her plants. It did nothing to help as it usually did. Her hands were working but with tasks she could do in her sleep. Which left her mind free to wander.

And all she could think about was her words to Warrick, him walking out, and then the Dark arriving. She grew ill recalling how they had surrounded him.

Darcy finished with the plants and returned to the front. The rain had yet to let up, and the spray was getting into the store. She tried to lift the door, but it was too heavy for her. Undeterred, she released just enough magic to help her not just right the door, but set it in place. It wouldn't close, but it kept most of the water out.

Next, she gathered the crystals that weren't broken and set them in a box in her office. Once that was done, she began to clean up the mess.

When Darcy finished, she looked up to find only an hour had passed. At least she'd had sixty minutes of not worrying. It wasn't a lot, but it was enough to give her a bit respite.

Darcy looked at the shattered window on the door hoping for some glimpse of Warrick. She didn't get one. Not only was the rain coming down too hard to see more than a few feet from the door, but the dark skies cast shadows everywhere.

Storms like these were a common occurrence, and they didn't keep people from going about their business. They kept their heads down and hurried from place to place.

Humans weren't the only ones walking about however. Her gaze snagged on a Dark here or there. Just her luck they wouldn't go away. Most likely they would return with more. Would she survive another encounter?

Would Warrick and Thorn?

Darcy was about to turn away when she saw a woman hurrying past the front of her shop bump into a Dark. Darcy shouted to get the woman's attention, but one look into the Dark's red eyes, and the woman was his.

They walked off together, the Dark shooting Darcy a smug smile.

She prepared to send a blast of magic at him, but

stopped as she remembered the woman. There was a chance Darcy could hit her and kill her. Was that better than the poor woman having her soul sucked out by a Dark?

By the time Darcy came to the conclusion that it was, the couple was out of sight.

She was so distraught by what she'd seen that she couldn't move. Darcy stared, unseeing, into the rain thinking of what the woman would endure.

Darcy then spotted two college-aged girls come splashing down the sidewalk. Only one had an umbrella, but they were too busy having fun and seeing who could get the other the wettest to notice the danger fast approaching.

Three Dark made a beeline for them.

"Hey!" Darcy shouted. "Those guys are dangerous! Do you hear me?"

When the laughing girls kept coming her way, Darcy yanked open the door and moved forward until her toes hit the threshold. She cupped her hands around her mouth and yelled, "Hey! Keep away from the guys!"

The girls finally stopped, their laughing dying instantly. They looked from Darcy to the three Dark who approached them.

Darcy held her breath, hoping the girls would realize how perilous the situation was. "Please," she whispered. "Walk away."

Instead, the girls were soon giggling again. One sauntered off with a Dark while the other two pushed the second female against the front of Darcy's shop and began to kiss her. Darcy covered her ears as the girl's sighs grew louder and louder. The only way Darcy could help the girl was by going out of the shop and away from the dragon magic that protected her.

She contemplated it for a minute. The Dark weren't going to give up, and the longer she held out, the more humans they would take.

Darcy took a step back and shut the door. The Dark were going to take the people regardless. They had been doing it for centuries, and they weren't about to stop now just because she gave herself to them.

With her heart heavy, she walked to her office and leaned against the wall. She slid down to the floor and simply stared off into nothing.

If only it was a dream. What spurred all of this almost three years after she unbound Ulrik's magic? Why would the Dark just now be coming after her? None of it made any sense. Why not do it when she first helped Ulrik? Why wait?

She knew it wasn't Ulrik after her. Why would he tell her she was in danger only to send the Dark?

It wasn't the Dragon Kings either. They wouldn't protect someone they wanted dead.

The Fae? There was that option. It could be the Light who weren't happy she helped Ulrik, but why would they care? And if it was them, why was Rhi assisting her? Because Ulrik asked her to?

Darcy shook her head as her thoughts jumbled. She had no idea what was going on between Ulrik and Rhi, and she didn't think she wanted to know.

As for the Dark? Again, why would they wait three years to come after her? Unless it was in retaliation against Ulrik for something.

The only other possibility was that there was another player no one knew about. Which was ludicrous. The Dragon Kings knew all the participants in this war. If there was someone else, Warrick would have told her.

No closer to figuring out anything, Darcy leaned her head back against the wall and closed her eyes. How quiet the shop was without Warrick.

It wasn't as if he ever talked a lot, but his mere presence changed everything. All these years she'd never minded the quiet. Why had that changed after Warrick?

* * *

Warrick stood in the rain watching the front of Darcy's shop. He too had seen the Dark walk off with two females. Thorn killed one while Warrick took the other. As for the two remaining Dark and the girl, he wasn't going to stand by and watch them suck her soul away out on the street.

Warrick stalked from the shadows to the Dark. He tapped the one kissing the girl's neck on the shoulder. The Dark looked over and frowned. He nudged the second Dark who was on his knees trying to yank the girl's wet pants down.

"Get away from her," Warrick demanded.

The two male Darks laughed as they stood facing him.

Warrick was eager to end more Dark. "You've broken the pact signed by Taraeth and Con several times over. You will be removed from this realm."

"Good luck," the Dark on the right said with a sneer.

The one on the left chuckled. "You know nothing, Dragon."

Warrick slammed his elbow into the Dark's face to his right. He wrapped his hand around the throat of the one to his left and squeezed. He shoved the Dark back against the corner of the building where Thorn was waiting in the alley.

Thorn grabbed him from behind and dragged him into the darkness.

Warrick saw the hilt of a dagger in the Dark's waistband. He grabbed it and plunged it into his throat. The Dark's eyes widened in fear a moment before the life faded out of them. With no other choice, Warrick half-carried, half-dragged the Dark into the alley where Thorn was standing over the other Dark Fae.

"No' that I'm no' enjoying ridding the realm of Dark," Thorn said. "But I'd much rather do it in our true forms."

Warrick dumped the Dark next to Thorn's and nodded. "I agree. That willna happen until we get out of the city."

"Which we can no' attempt with Darcy."

Warrick ran a hand down his face. His body had quickly healed from the Dark magic he'd endured, but he was weary. And the fear wouldn't shake loose. For every Dark they killed, three more seemed to take their place. Who but Taraeth or Balladyn would have that kind of pull?

They stopped talking when Thorn helped the young girl to her feet and gave her a nudge to the alley entrance. "The robber has been dealt with. Go find your friend."

The female looked around confused and stumbled out into the street. Warrick waited until he saw her and her friend walk back the way they had come.

"What about the first mortal?" Warrick asked.

Thorn came to stand beside him. "She got away quick enough when she saw the Dark lob a ball of magic at me."

"Damn."

"She willna say anything. She was undressed when I interrupted them."

Warrick cut his eyes to Thorn. "Let's hope no'."

"What are you going to do about Darcy?"

Warrick turned back to the Dark. "What about her?"

"She needs you."

"She told me to leave," Warrick argued.

Thorn grunted loudly. "For someone who's studied mortals as long as you have, you know nothing about women."

"And you do?" For some reason, Thorn's comment really annoyed Warrick.

"She was angry, but she didna really want you to leave."

"You didna see her face or hear her voice. She most certainly wanted me to leave."

Thorn glanced down at the dead Fae. "We've got two immediate issues to deal with."

"And they are?"

"Getting rid of these ugly buggers."

Warrick blinked the water out of his eyes from the rain. "And the other?"

"One of us needs to be back in there with Darcy."

Warrick thought of their kisses, of the heat and desire and need that being near her caused. His cock hardened just thinking of pulling her into his arms for another kiss.

"I take that look to mean you'll be headed back into the shop," Thorn said with a knowing grin.

Warrick shoved him in the shoulder.

"That's a definite aye," Thorn said with a laugh. "I'll do my best to keep the Dark away and give the two of you some . . . alone time."

Warrick swallowed hard.

Alone. With Darcy.

Already his hands itched to feel her soft skin. Whether she wanted him with her or not, he was going to be by her side until this fiasco was over.

He started to walk to the back entrance when Thorn called his name. Warrick turned back to him. "What?"

Thorn gave him a dry look and pointed to the Dark.

Warrick was so caught up in thoughts of Darcy he'd forgotten about the dead Fae.

CHAPTER TWENTY-FOUR

Ulrik was used to wearing a façade. He had a different one for every aspect of his life. There were times that he forgot who he really was buried under so many different identities.

But that didn't make being summoned any easier to swallow.

Ulrik stepped into the dimly lit restaurant on the outskirts of Glasgow and stopped so that he could slowly survey the inside.

"Hello, sir," said a high-pitched feminine voice.

Ulrik lowered his gaze to look at the young blonde. She smiled brightly, her gaze raking over him not so subtly. He lifted his eyes back to the occupants of the restaurant. "I'm meeting someone."

"Oh, yes," she said, her brogue becoming thicker. "He's expecting you. Please follow me."

Ulrik should've known Mikkel would have alerted the hostesses of his arrival. Because it never entered his uncle's mind that he wouldn't come.

For now, that's exactly what Ulrik wanted Mikkel to

think. But there would come a time when their positions were reversed.

Ulrik followed the blonde, glancing at her ass as he did. His attention was snagged by the alcove he was taken to. He spotted Mikkel sitting comfortably with one arm resting along the back of the curved booth while his other lay next to a stemless glass of wine.

When the hostess stepped aside, Ulrik spotted the woman with his uncle. She was a stunner with her dark hair falling in big curls to the tops of her shoulders. She wore a low-cut shirt that showed off her assets so that Mikkel couldn't take his eyes off her breasts.

So much for a business meeting. Ulrik was about to turn and leave when the woman's gaze slid to him. The exact color of her eyes couldn't be garnered in the dim lights, but it didn't matter. He recognized her.

Ulrik looked at Mikkel. It was obvious by the way his uncle let his fingers brush her shoulder that he was completely captivated. It was also obvious that Mikkel didn't have a clue that his companion was a Dark Fae using glamour.

There was a flash of surprise and fear in the Dark's gaze when Ulrik returned his attention to her. If she was here, that meant she had been sent by Taraeth.

"Ulrik," Mikkel said when he noticed him. "Glad you could finally join us. Sit," he ordered as he grabbed the bottle of wine and filled a new glass before topping off the Dark's.

Ulrik was curious as to why the Dark was there, and even more interested in why Taraeth would send her. That was the only reason he slid into the booth.

Mikkel was across from him, and the Dark sat in the middle but closer to his uncle. Which was fine with Ulrik. He recognized the Dark from being in Taraeth's court. Unfortunately, that was all he knew.

"I found this beauty sitting alone at the bar," Mikkel said as he gazed at the Dark. "I couldn't imagine such a woman being by herself. So, I invited her to my table."

"Is that so?" Ulrik said and met her gaze once more.

Her hand shook slightly when she brought the wine-glass to her lips. She drank deeply before she smiled at Mikkel.

"She's rather shy, I think," Mikkel said. "I hope you won't mind us cutting our meeting short. Why would I want to talk business with her next to me?"

"Why indeed." Ulrik's mind was already running through the Dark he knew who he could contact and ask what was going on.

Depending on the reasons for the Dark being sent to Mikkel, Ulrik might not get any answers.

Unless he went to Taraeth himself.

It wasn't optimal, but Ulrik wasn't ruling that out as a possibility. He couldn't care less what happened to Mik-kel. If the Dark wanted to take him, then Ulrik wouldn't stand in their way. It would be one less foe to worry over.

"I called in a favor," Mikkel said in his British accent. "However, it isn't going to plan."

By the tone Mikkel used, the problem was a Dragon King. Which meant this was about Darcy. "I warned you that you were bringing unwanted attention where there shouldna be any."

"And you know why I had to do it."

Back to this again. Ulrik rested both hands atop the table, but didn't bother to reach for the glass of wine. How many times were they going to go over this? "You didna call me all the way here just to tell me of the problem."

"How perceptive of you."

Ulrik waited for Mikkel to elaborate. The silence stretched as his uncle leaned closer to the Dark and whis-pered something in her ear that had them both smiling. By the way the female licked her lips in anticipation, it was about sex.

Ulrik thought he was going to be sick.

If Mikkel wasn't going to tell him what he wanted, then Ulrik wasn't going to stay. He started to rise.

"We're not done."

Every muscle in Ulrik's body locked. It went against everything that he was to take orders. It would be so easy to reach across the table and rip out Mikkel's throat with his bare hands. But that was to come later. For now, Ulrik must hide his anger and strength and pretend once more.

It took every last shred of Ulrik's control to tamp down the need to kill and relax his muscles. Only then did he return his gaze to Mikkel. He didn't sit back, but remained on the edge of the booth.

Mikkel smirked. "That's what I thought."

Ulrik's vision went red with fury. How did he ever think he could act the fool and bow down to Mikkel? It was impossible.

Yet he had to think of the end goal. The first step was protecting Darcy. Thanks to the Kings watching over her, that was one problem he didn't have to worry about.

Nor did he concern himself with Darcy siding with the Kings. She wasn't just the most powerful Druid he knew, she also had a mind of her own. Darcy made her own decisions, which meant she was rarely swayed in any one direction.

That was the first thing Ulrik had learned about her. He didn't try to convince her he was in the right. In fact, he didn't say anything. All he did was ask her to free his magic. Darcy made the decision to help him, and to continue helping him.

The few times she asked questions, he answered. She wasn't interested in his past—or his future. He suspected she wanted to see if her magic was capable of helping him.

Of course, she hadn't realized how perilous it was until after the initial attempt.

Ulrik's second step would be to kill Mikkel.

Then . . . Con. There were a dozen ways Ulrik had thought about attacking Constantine. Any of them would work, but it wouldn't be easy. Con knew he was coming. It was a battle that was many millennia in the making.

Ulrik drew in a deep breath and slowly released it. He focused on Mikkel and waited as his uncle continued to flirt with the Dark Fae. The female was good. Not once had she looked Ulrik's way since he came to the table. She kept her focus solely on Mikkel, slowly seducing him with her smiles and flirtations.

Mikkel leaned back and took a sip of wine. Once he'd replaced the glass on the table, he turned to Ulrik. "I want you to end my problem. For good."

Ulrik felt the weight of Mikkel's stare. His uncle thought he had him by the balls. Just one more instance that Mikkel underestimated him.

He stood and adjusted his suit jacket. "Consider it done."

Taraeth rotated his left shoulder. There was just a stump left after Denae had used a Fae sword and chopped off his arm. Taraeth snorted. A Fae sword. The sword belonged to Rhi.

The same Rhi who Balladyn had captured and attempted to turn Dark. Though Balladyn assured him that Rhi would come to them and become Dark, Taraeth had his doubts.

Rhi was stronger than Balladyn realized. And she still held the love of a Dragon King within her.

The one crucial mistake the Dark made in coming to Earth was in misjudging the Kings. None of the Dark, especially the idiot who had led the Dark into war with the

Kings, realized how formidable they were. Every Fae—Dark and Light—assumed their magic was even with the Kings' or greater. How wrong they had been.

The Fae learned their lesson well. It was one of the reasons once Taraeth took over as king that he didn't attack the Dragon Kings.

They were a hindrance. More than that, he'd had to watch his back since he aligned with one and helped another on occasion.

His intention had been to refuse Ulrik. Until he met with him. It only took one look for Taraeth to see the hate Ulrik had for the Kings. If there was one who could bring down the Dragon Kings—it was Ulrik.

There was a knock on the steel doors of his private chamber. Taraeth walked to the door and opened it to find one of his guards.

"Ulrik is here to see you," replied the Dark.

Taraeth smiled and walked from his chamber. He turned the corner to a corridor where he spotted Ulrik standing in front of a painting of the capital city of the Fae realm.

"Every time you come, you stare at that painting," Taraeth said as he stopped beside him.

Ulrik lifted one shoulder in a shrug. "I find it hard to believe with everything I know about the Fae that both the Light and Dark once lived together."

"That was a very long time ago."

Ulrik turned away from the picture and faced Taraeth. "You doona seemed surprised that I'm here."

Taraeth chuckled. "I'm never surprised by your visits, as infrequent as they are. You come to me with unusual requests that only further both of our interests. PureGems has given us a glut of humans with which to satisfy us."

"Ah, but I wasna the only one with my hand in PureGems, was I?"

Taraeth had wondered how long it would take Ulrik to piece things together. "So, Mikkel finally came to you."

"How long have you known?" Ulrik's face was completely devoid of emotion, just as his voice was.

It was enough to make Taraeth wary. Ulrik might have his magic bound by the other Dragon Kings, but as Ulrik proved—things could change. "Long enough."

"What is your reasoning in sending a Dark to seduce my uncle?"

Taraeth hadn't seen that coming. He might not want to like Ulrik, but it was hard not to when he was as devious as a Dark. "Her glamour is too good. There's no way you saw through her magic, nor would she tell you who she is."

"I recognized her from your court."

At least Taraeth knew that Ulrik couldn't see through glamour like Kiril could. Damn Dragon Kings and their magic.

Then Ulrik's comment registered. In the thousands of millennia since the Fae came to Earth, Ulrik had been at court only a half dozen times. That made Taraeth realize that there were few things Ulrik didn't see, and even fewer that he forgot. It would behoove Taraeth to remember that.

"Why did you send her to Mikkel?" Ulrik asked again.

"I wanted to see if your uncle could spot one of my best."

"Liar."

It was said without heat, but a hardness came into Ulrik's golden eyes. Taraeth tried another approach. "He gave me a promise, and then didn't fulfill it."

Ulrik turned on his heel and started walking away.

Taraeth frowned. "Ulrik?"

But the Dragon King didn't stop. Taraeth wasn't sure if Ulrik was going to alert his uncle or not. Either way the female needed to be warned.

CHAPTER TWENTY-FIVE

Darcy jumped at the sound that came from the conservatory. She got to her feet, her heart pumping wildly. Then a tall form came into sight.

"Warrick," she whispered.

Her smiled died before it got going when she let her gaze run over him. Blood splattered his shirt, or what was left of it. It was torn and ripped so that it barely hung on his shoulders.

His gaze was direct, unblinking as he stared at her as if he hadn't just been in a battle with the Dark Fae.

Without thinking, she ran to him looking for wounds. She gently moved aside his still wet shirt in case there was a wound beneath, but all she saw was skin and the black and red ink of the tat.

Then she recalled what he was and his immortality.

Darcy dropped her arms and met his cobalt gaze as she remembered the fear that had consumed her not that long ago. "They surrounded you, and then I couldn't see you."

"The fight wouldna have lasted that long had I been in dragon form," he said matter-of-factly.

"I was scared out of my mind, and you make a joke?"

"It isna a jest. In my real form, I could do much more damage."

She shuddered, recalling Ulrik's memories and the sheer size of some of the dragons. She turned away, embarrassed for letting her emotions get the better of her. "Of course. I forgot."

"Were you worried for me, lass?"

She halted and looked over her shoulder at his softly spoken words. He actually sounded surprised. "Yes."

After everything she had said to him, he'd returned to the shop, to her. There was no anger in his visage or his voice, as if her harsh words never happened. He add risked his own life for her. Though he was immortal, there was no doubt the Dark could do damage to the Kings.

"I'll get you out of Edinburgh if that's what you want," Warrick said. "Damn Con and what he has planned for you."

Darcy was so taken aback that, for a moment, she couldn't find any words. "I thought Con wanted information."

"If you give it, then Con will have it. But I willna keep you here with this many Dark just so Con can have some tidbit on Ulrik."

"Even if that tidbit might be the difference in Con winning over Ulrik?"

Warrick rubbed his hand on the back of his neck and sighed.

Just as Darcy had thought. "Ulrik is gaining in this war, isn't he? You need information to win."

"There's a chance that even if I get you to Skye, the Dark will attack you there."

She snorted. "They could try."

"You've never faced the Fae, Darcy. You doona know what it means to fight them. As powerful as Skye magic is, it isna enough to keep the Dark out."

Could Darcy bring such repulsive terrors to Skye? To her family? Just to save her own ass? No, she couldn't. Regardless of how scared she was, this fiasco couldn't reach Skye.

"Can the Dark hurt you?"

Warrick made a face, confusion marring his features. "They can no' kill us."

"But they can hurt you?"

"Aye."

It felt like someone kicked her in the stomach. "You were injured out there, weren't you?"

"I'm fine."

But he wasn't before. All she had to do was look at his clothes to see how vicious the battle had been. He'd stood alone against the Dark while being bombarded with their magic.

How many wounds had he sustained that healed before he came to see her? She inwardly cringed just thinking about it. And she was the one who sent him out because of her anger.

"So their magic can harm you?" she asked.

"It can weaken us, and they can also make it to where we can no' shift into dragon form for a while."

"What else?" She didn't know how she knew there was more, but she did.

Warrick blew out a harsh breath. "During the Fae Wars, they captured two Kings. Both lost their minds. We had to kill them."

Darcy's legs grew weak. She grabbed hold of the edge of her desk to keep standing. The thought of Warrick being captured and tortured by the Dark made her sick to her stomach. That couldn't happen to such a proud, powerful man. "I don't want that to happen to you."

"It willna."

She stared at him, aghast. "I'm sure the two Kings they captured thought the same thing."

Warrick shrugged, as if it happened every day. "It's part of being who we are."

"You and Thorn should leave before neither of you can."

It was his turn to look at her as if she'd sprouted wings. "You can no' be serious."

"I am. I'm not going to bring this," she said, gesturing to the front where the Dark were, "to Skye. I'm also not going to be responsible for the Dark taking you or Thorn."

"Remaining here is our decision. No' yours."

Darcy shook her head in dismay. "You have no idea how it felt to watch them surround you as you stood out there alone against them. I thought you were gone!"

Her words hung in the air for long moments as they stared at each other. Warrick's cobalt eyes were bright, his gaze intense.

All Darcy could think about was his kisses. The rest—Con, Ulrik, the Dark, the elders on Skye, and even her family—faded away.

"I promised I would keep you safe. I'll no' leave until you are."

Darcy rushed to him, throwing her arms around his neck as she planted her lips against his. He enfolded her in his embrace, holding her tight as he tilted his head and parted his lips. A low, deep moan rumbled his chest as they kissed. She slid her hands into wet hair and sank into the kiss until she was living, breathing him.

It didn't take long for the flames of desire to overtake them. Darcy was teased by the bits of his skin she felt against her from his torn shirt. She reached between them while they kissed and ripped his shirt in half. There was a smile on his lips as he let it fall to the floor.

Their kisses became heated, frantic as they sought to get closer to the other. With a flick of his hand, he unbuttoned her jeans and had them unzipped. Then his hand was down her pants cupping her sex.

Darcy gasped for breath as he kissed across her jaw and down her throat as his fingers began to lightly stroke her through her panties.

She clung to him, her breath locked in her lungs at the force of desire that tightened low in her belly. His tongue was hot against her skin, his lips soft.

In the next instant, his hand was gone, leaving her squeezing her legs together to hold back the tide of need that enveloped her.

Her shirt was pulled over her head so quickly she had no idea what he was about. There was a ripping noise as her bra followed. Then he jerked her against his chest, skin to skin.

She looked into his eyes and recognized the same longing, the same yearning she felt within herself. He bent, grabbing her bottom, and then stood. With her legs now wrapped around him, he claimed her mouth in a wild, fiery kiss.

Darcy didn't have long to wonder where he was going as he began to walk. He leaned over, holding her firmly with one hand as he swiped her desk with the other, clearing it of everything.

He pressed her against the top of the desk, his thick arousal rubbing against her already swollen sex. He rocked against her several times before he pulled back, ending the kiss.

"I need you, lass," he whispered.

Darcy opened her eyes to find him over her. "How fast can you get out of those clothes?"

A grin started right before he straightened and kicked off his boots while pulling down his pants. Darcy wasn't having as much luck with her own attire. She only got one boot off in the time it took him to get undressed.

He yanked off her other boot. Then he grabbed her jeans and pulled. For him, they slid right off, leaving her in nothing but her black silk panties.

His gaze wandered over her, beginning at her feet and working upward. As soon as his eyes landed on her breasts, her nipples hardened. He smiled in anticipation as he stepped between her legs once more.

Then he lightly ran the pads of his fingers up her legs to the juncture of her thighs. At her sex, he paused and skimmed his hands over the silk. Then one hand moved upwards to her breasts where he circled one nipple with a finger before moving to the next.

She hoped he would ease her suffering and touch her when his mouth came down on her other nipple. Darcy gasped, her back arching as he suckled the tiny peak hard. At the same time, one of his hands returned to her sex. He shoved aside the silk and mercilessly, ruthlessly teased her clit until she was shaking.

The orgasm slammed into her unexpectedly, the force of it taking her breath. Her mouth opened on a silent scream as her body jerked and pleasure poured through her.

Just when she thought it might end, Warrick knelt between her legs. Her body was still pulsing from the orgasm when he ripped her panties in two then slid his tongue over her clit.

The pleasure was almost too much. She tried to scoot back, but Warrick had both hands on her hips, holding her in place. With his hot tongue teasing her flesh, she was soon writhing as another climax took her.

Then he was over her, his big body pressing against her as the head of his arousal slid inside her. Darcy spread her hands over his chest as he slowly entered her, stretching her, filling her.

She lifted her legs so that they wrapped around his waist. When he was fully seated, he bent and kissed her passionately.

Darcy was floating on a cloud of pure passion. Everywhere he touched, Warrick was leaving a mark on her, forever changing her. She could feel it through her skin and muscle, through bone and into her soul.

It was as if he was altering her. And she welcomed it.

He pulled out of her and thrust. In and out he moved, fiercely, powerfully. Each time he went deeper, plunged harder.

Soon sweat moistened their skin, allowing their bodies to glide against each other smoothly. Darcy tightened her legs, urging him onward.

His hips jerked as he moved faster. Their breaths were ragged, their bodies in a rhythm as old as time. Her fingers gripped him as desire tightened low in her belly. Then he buried himself deep and stilled.

To Darcy's surprise, another orgasm swept her along with Warrick. It was just as powerful as the first, pulling her into a whirlwind of passion, pleasure, and . . . everything Warrick.

It seemed like hours later when she was finally able to open her eyes. She found Warrick staring down at her with a look of awe that made her stomach clench and her lips tilt in a smile. He pulled out of her and lifted her in his arms until he had them situated on the floor. Darcy snuggled against him, using his chest as a pillow.

Sex with Warrick was sublime. No one had taken her to such heights before, and she was certain no one but Warrick ever would again.

Her life was in shambles, but she had something solid and real to hold onto.

She had Warrick.

CHAPTER TWENTY-SIX

Warrick's world had been turned upside down by the soft touch and passionate kisses of one obstinate, beautiful mortal.

He stared at the ceiling, going over every moment of their lovemaking. The violent, uncontrollable need to claim her had pushed him as nothing else ever had. He almost regretted taking her so fast.

Almost.

A smile pulled at his lips as he remembered the fire in her fern green eyes. Her nails had scoured his skin, her legs had clamped tight even as she urged him faster with her heels.

Her abandon, her unabashed need only drove him wild with longing. When it came to Darcy, the control Warrick always seemed to readily have evaporated. He was feral, untamed. Brutish.

And she reveled in it.

She didn't care when he said awkward things. Warrick frowned as he realized he'd carried conversations with her more than he ever had with anyone else in such a short period of time.

Her beauty might have first snagged his attention, but her sharp mind—and even sharper tongue—kept him on his toes and thoroughly engaged. She was as tempestuous as a stormy sea, and he wasn't always sure how to navigate the waters. But he wanted to learn.

Warrick felt her breath tickle his chest as she let out a sigh in her sleep. He wasn't a fool. There had been too many Kings who had found mates lately for him to not consider Darcy was more than a quick tumble.

There was just one hitch.

Warrick didn't want a mate. He didn't want the worry, fear, or nervousness of having a woman mated to him. Regardless that she would be immortal, the simple fact was that she could die if he was killed. The war they were in was enough to bring that realization home.

Not to mention, he saw how Kellan, Rhys, and the other mated Kings reacted when a threat came to Dreagan. It was natural for a King to protect. Add in the element of a mate, and things went haywire.

Even if he did take a mate, she wouldn't be safe from the Dark. The Kings might have spelled themselves never to feel any love for a human all these centuries, which is the only reason the Dark hadn't taken a mate from a King. However, it was just a matter of time before they tried it.

The wild idea of claiming Darcy as his mate to save her from the Dark halted instantly at that insight. The Dark wanted Darcy dead. Though he wished to know who'd sent the order for her death, Warrick was more concerned with keeping her alive.

The Dark's attack earlier proved that they were more than willing to let their war spill over into the human world.

Warrick opened the telepathic link and called Con's name. It didn't take the King of Kings long to answer.

"Do you have information on Ulrik?" Con asked.

Warrick was surprised at the burst of anger that he felt. Was it the battle with the Dark? Was it having Darcy in his arms and her taste on his tongue? *"In case you wanted to know, Darcy is still alive."*

"I didna have any doubts. What information have you gleaned?"

"None."

There was a long stretch of silence. Then Con said, *"None? Why?"*

"Perhaps because we've been battling the Dark all day."

"You've never been one to talk a lot, Warrick, but apparently you have something to say. So out with it."

Warrick held Darcy tighter as she slept. *"There is more than Ulrik in this battle, Con. Keep that in mind."*

"I have."

"Nay. You're blinded by your hate. The fact that your first question was about what Darcy might have shared regarding Ulrik instead of asking if she was still alive or how Thorn and I were holding up against the Dark is telling."

"Then tell me what happened."

Warrick wasn't deceived. Con was placating him, and it infuriated Warrick. *"I did. I was attacked."*

"That's no' a surprise. The Dark will attack you to get to the Druid."

"Thirty of them? Out on the streets? With only the rain to hide us?"

There was a pause, and Warrick could practically see Con frowning.

"Thirty?" Con asked.

"That were just the ones who surrounded me and were visible. There were more that I couldna take time to count."

"When did this happen?"

"A few hours ago."

"And you're just now telling me?" Con shouted.

Warrick hadn't been thinking of reporting to Con. His thoughts had been centered on Darcy. *"Aye."*

"You were wounded."

It wasn't a question. *"As I said, they surrounded me when I tried to return to Darcy's shop. I blocked most of their magic, but some got through."*

"At least they didna take you."

"They didna want me. They were too focused on Darcy. She was inside the shop watching. They hurt me to get her to come out since Thorn and I used magic on her building and the Dark couldna get to her."

"How is Thorn?"

At least that was one thing Warrick didn't have to worry about. *"Thorn has remained hidden. The Dark doona even know he's here. It's allowed him to kill them without being seen by the others."*

"I didna have any doubt."

"You should also know that the Dark didna just attack us today. They went after humans as well."

"They know we protect the mortals," Con said. *"They'll try to divide your attention between the Druid and the mortals. Perhaps I should send Kiril and Rhys back to Edinburgh."*

"I doona think that would be a good idea. The Dark were blatant in their attack today, and that was just with me. If they knew Thorn or any other Kings were here, I'm afraid we wouldna be keeping our secret from the humans any longer."

"The Dark are that intent on taking Darcy?"

"Aye. They busted through her magic quickly enough. It was only our dragon magic that held them."

"Then they willna stop until they have her. It's just a matter of time before they get to her."

"Unless she's on Dreagan." Warrick had no idea where that thought came from. Once said, however, he knew it was the only place for Darcy.

His mind was going through how to get her to Dreagan when Warrick realized Con hadn't uttered another word. That's when Warrick comprehended that if Darcy was at Dreagan, she would be at the mercy of Con, and he would pester her for any and all information about Ulrik.

"Perhaps you're right," Con said.

Warrick closed his eyes. *"You need to know now that Darcy willna give us anything on Ulrik."*

"She sides with him?" Con asked coldly.

"She doesna side with anyone. Ulrik didna try to turn her to his side. The fact we are makes him look good, and doesna shed us in a pleasant light."

"Have you learned anything from her?"

"I know she saw his memories."

"Saw?"

Was that a note of anxiety in Con's voice? *"Aye. She saw what happened when we banished him and bound his magic."*

"Of course Ulrik would willingly share such things."

"He had no idea. He still doesna. Darcy saw more than that as well."

"It looks like the best place for the Druid is on Dreagan. Get her here as soon as you can."

Warrick knew it was the only safe place for her, but that didn't mean Darcy would readily go. Even with sixty thousand acres, it was still a sort of prison. Not to mention there was Con.

But all of that paled with the knowledge that she would be out of reach of the Dark.

"Warrick?" Con asked.

"I heard you."

"But?"

"Nothing." There was no point in asking Con why he wanted Darcy at Dreagan. Warrick knew it was because of her association with Ulrik, and the fact she'd seen Ulrik's memories.

"I'll see you soon then," Con said and terminated the link.

Warrick opened his eyes to stare at the ceiling again while he tried to figure out a way to give Con limited access to Darcy. Every plan fell apart, because Con wasn't the only King who wanted to bring Ulrik down. Warrick would be up against most of the Kings.

It put him in a difficult place, because he didn't want to help Ulrik. Yet in order to protect Darcy, Warrick was doing just that.

Rhi knew she was going to get shit from Thorn and Warrick for not coming when they called. She would take whatever they had to say, because they couldn't know where she had been.

She was still veiled when she found Thorn on the roof of a building across the street from Darcy's shop. Rhi dropped the veil and squatted beside Thorn.

He jerked his head to her and glared. "You're a little late."

"It's called fashionably late," she retorted and tossed her hair over her shoulder dramatically. Anything to keep him from asking what she had been doing.

Thorn grunted. "Whatever. We could've used your help when the Dark attacked."

"Again? How many this time?"

"I stopped counting at forty-eight."

Rhi met his dark gaze, her stomach falling to her feet. He wasn't just angry that she was late. He was pissed because something had occurred. "What happened?"

"Last night the Dark arrived and surrounded the shop

and set up along Darcy's route home so that we couldna get her out."

Now Rhi felt badly for not ensuring the shop was as protected as Darcy's flat. "I'll make the shop safe."

"We already have," Thorn said icily.

Rhi looked down at the shop to see the door precariously hanging on one set of hinges and one of the windows busted. "It seems to have worked."

"Aye. Right up until Warrick left to get Darcy food. The Dark began attacking the shop, and when Warrick returned, they went after him."

"Where is Warrick?" she asked as worry set in.

"With Darcy." Thorn kept to the shadows as he rose and jumped from one rooftop to another. "Do you think I'd be the only King here if the Dark took him?"

Rhi followed Thorn, deftly landing on her four-inch heels. She once more sidled next to Thorn and followed his gaze to a small group of Dark who stood staring at Darcy's shop.

"Was Warrick injured?"

Thorn shrugged. "Nothing a bit of time couldna heal."

"You're angry with me."

He turned the full force of his fury on her then and looked her up and down as if she was the lowest of the low. "I suppose you only come when Rhys calls. It's a good thing the Dark were no' interested in kidnapping another King, Rhi, because thirty of them surrounded him, pounding Warrick with their magic."

"I'm sorry."

"Doona tell me," he replied irritably. "You need to say that to Warrick."

Rhi immediately teleported away.

Thorn rolled his eyes. "Just another reason why the Kings should cut all ties with the Fae. They can no' be trusted."

CHAPTER TWENTY-SEVEN

No matter how Warrick looked at it, there was no other way to ensure that Darcy was kept out of the Dark's hands than to take her to Dreagan. He wasn't so sure she was going to agree, however.

It wasn't just her life on the line either. There was the fact that the Dark were walking the streets of Edinburgh, and the Kings had yet to do anything.

Warrick gently turned Darcy onto her other side and rose. He pulled on his jeans, buttoning them as he walked to the front of the store and looked out the windows as dawn lightened the sky. Two Dark Fae stood on the opposite side of the street staring at him. Their smug smiles made him itch to wipe them from their faces. Forcefully.

If something wasn't done as retaliation, then the Dark would know they could come into Scotland any time they wanted. It was bad enough they roamed far and wide in Ireland.

Scotland was the land of the Dragon Kings.

Warrick grabbed the broken door and swung it open. He

ignored the bite of glass in his bare feet as he stepped across the threshold.

There was a forceful push against his mind as well as Thorn's voice shouting his name. Warrick opened the link. *"What?"*

"I know that look. Whatever you have planned, count me in. I'm sick of watching these fuckers think they can do whatever they want."

Just what Warrick was hoping Thorn would say. *"Con wants me to bring Darcy to Dreagan."*

"I know. Con told me to make sure that I do whatever it takes to help you."

"I willna force her," Warrick stated.

"Neither will I."

Warrick didn't question Thorn. He knew Thorn was a man of his word. *"The Dark are no' supposed to be in Scotland. They've had the run of Edinburgh for too long already."*

"It'll mean leaving Darcy on her own."

"Our magic will hold."

"You really want to take that chance?"

Warrick sighed heavily. He didn't, but it went against everything he was to allow the Dark to get away with such atrocities.

"I didna think so," Thorn said. *"There's no rain today, War. We can no' fight them now."*

"They'll attack again."

"That's what I thought all night, but they didna. What are they waiting on?"

That was a good question. War turned his head to the left and spotted another three Dark. When he looked right, he saw five. How many more were at the back and hiding along the street?

The only way to get Darcy out was by flying her to

Dreagan, which meant taking a chance of someone in the city seeing him.

"Darcy can no' stay here another day. We have to do something," Warrick said.

Thorn gave a wry laugh. *"Good luck with that, mate. She leaves that building, then you might as well say farewell, because you'll never see her again."*

"I can use my power."

"Your protection?" Thorn asked. *"It could work. Have you ever held it up under the onslaught of Dark magic?"*

"I've never needed to."

"You'll be taking a chance, War. If your power fails and Darcy is taken, will you be able to live with that?"

"Nay, but I doona see another alternative. We get to Darcy's flat, and then we think of a way to Dreagan."

"You mean you'll talk her into going to Dreagan," Thorn said with a laugh.

Warrick severed the link in the middle of Thorn's laugh. He turned and walked back into the building.

Darcy woke shivering, and realized instantly that Warrick was no longer beside her. She sat up, feeling the slight pulling between her legs. A smile broke as she remembered their lovemaking.

She rose and looked around for her clothing. Her jeans and shirt were salvageable, but her bra and panties were done. With her clothes in her hand, she walked into the bathroom and closed the door. Darcy winced when she looked in the mirror.

"It could be worse," she said as she tugged on some curls.

She splashed water on her face and patted it dry. Then she dampened the hand towel and wiped herself down. She was soon shivering and grabbed a fresh hand towel to dry off.

A hot shower sounded heavenly. At least she had the small powder room in which to freshen up. Darcy remembered the pair of sweats she kept for the times she worked with the plants. She rose up on her tiptoes and opened the cabinet door to pull them out. If she survived this, she was going to add underwear to the stash.

After her shirt was back on, she fished out the toothpaste and toothbrush she always kept at the shop and brushed her teeth.

She valiantly tried to use her fingers to comb through her curls, but her hair was too knotted to do any good. The frizz didn't help either. With no other choice, she pulled it into a messy bun and pinned it in place.

A quick look in the mirror showed that she was at least presentable, even if she felt odd not having any panties on. Darcy opened the door and stepped out.

She expected to see Warrick, but he wasn't in sight. A quick look in the back showed that he wasn't there either. She then went to the front and found him inside staring out the broken window.

"I hope I didna wake you," he said without turning to look at her.

There was something about the way he was standing that set warning bells off in her head. She followed his gaze to the two Dark across the street. "You didn't," she answered. "What's going on?"

Before he could answer, her stomach gave a loud rumble.

"There isna much left of the food I gathered for you yesterday, but I know Thorn brought it to you. You should eat."

She wasn't fooled by the change of subject. "I'll eat if you tell me what's going on."

"Get the food. Then we'll talk."

Darcy didn't think there was a man alive as stubborn as Warrick. She pivoted and immediately winced when something pierced her foot. She stopped and leaned a hand against the wall as she lifted her injured foot. There was a small shard of glass buried deep in her foot.

"You should be more careful," Warrick said as he bent over her foot and gently removed the glass.

"You're barefoot." As soon as it came out, Darcy knew how petulant it sounded.

One side of his mouth lifted in a grin. "Aye, so I am. Let's get our shoes on."

Darcy was still looking for a boot when Warrick walked to the back. She was on the floor, slipping on her shoe when he returned with the broken plastic basket of food. She grabbed it from his hand and opened a bottle of water. After downing half of it, she tore open a bag of cookies and stuffed one in her mouth.

That's when she glanced up and found him watching her with a strange look on his face. "What?" she asked around the cookie.

"I like watching the joy on your face."

It wasn't the first time she'd caught Warrick watching her as if studying her, but this was the first time he gave any sort of explanation. She found it . . . endearing.

Darcy swallowed her bite. "We're not so different than you."

"Och, but you are," he said. "You've seen Ulrik's memories. You've seen us in our true forms."

"Yes. I'll admit that you all are terrifying. But in human form, you're like us, right?"

"In some aspects, I suppose we are."

"Then why do you look at me like that?" she asked.

He glanced at the floor and shrugged. "From the moment humans arrived in this realm, I've been fascinated by you."

"I'd think we're pretty boring," she said with a laugh.

"There are some who are brilliant, as well as amazingly talented."

"Like who?" she asked not expecting to get an answer of someone she knew. But she should've known better.

Warrick reached for another bottle of water. "I particularly liked Leonardo da Vinci. His ideas were extraordinary."

Darcy watched his eyes take on a faraway look as if he were remembering something. "Da Vinci? *The* da Vinci?"

"Aye," Warrick said, affronted. "I wouldna lie. I kept my distance for a while, but he was just too interesting. We struck up a friendship of sorts."

"Did he know what you were?"

Warrick looked away. "He had a verra sharp mind. I didna realize that the times he seemed to ask mundane questions that he was actually learning me."

Darcy's eyes went wide. "Are you telling me he figured it out?"

"He guessed I wasna human," Warrick said and sat in her office chair. "It didna take him long to figure things out from there."

"What did Con say?"

Warrick laughed, his cobalt gaze meeting hers. "He didna know."

"How many others did you get to know?"

His smile dropped as he sat back. "No' many. With more and more humans populating the realm, it grew more difficult to hide who we were. Then when technology came and now with everyone walking around with a camera on their mobile phones, we really have to be careful."

"You have Dreagan."

"That we do. It's no' just our home. It's our refuge." He paused, his gaze intensifying. "It's also one of the few places a Dark Fae can no' get into."

Darcy knew where he was going with this. Two days ago, she would have flat-out refused his offer. Now? Well, after the battle yesterday her mind had been changed about several things.

"Dreagan, huh?" she asked.

"You'd be safe. The Dark couldna reach you there."

She nodded, knowing it was the only option left open to her. "What do we do?"

"You mean, you'll come?"

The surprise on his face almost made her laugh. "Am I that difficult?"

"You just know your mind."

"In other words, I'm difficult."

His smile was back, making the corners of his eyes crinkle. "You doona hear me complaining."

If he continued to be so charming, there was no way Darcy wouldn't fall for him. A Dragon King.

A dragon!

She'd seen a glimpse of him in the dark, but she couldn't wait to see him in the day.

"First," Warrick said. "We need to get you to your flat."

CHAPTER TWENTY-EIGHT

Rhi stood at the edge of the lake against a tree, but it wasn't the water she was looking at. It was the cottage. Phelan was tending to a plant near the porch and had yet to notice her. Aisley was sitting in the sun reading a romance novel.

Rhi hated to disturb them, but she knew any more Dragon Kings in Edinburgh would mean an all-out war. As a Fae, she shouldn't care if the mortals knew there were Fae and dragons on the realm or not.

But as an ex-lover to a Dragon King, it became ingrained in her to keep their secret.

Even when she didn't want to.

Rhi pushed away from the tree and started walking toward the couple. She only got a few steps when Phelan's head turned her way.

There was a flash of gold as his skin shifted as he released the primeval god within him until he recognized her. He sat on his haunches with a smile. "Rhi!"

Aisley lowered her book and got to her feet as she waved.

"Hey, stud," Rhi said as she reached Phelan.

He stood and enveloped her in a hug. "I doona like that look on your face," he whispered.

Rhi pulled back and met his blue gray gaze for a moment before Aisley reached them. Rhi gave the Druid a quick hug.

Aisley looked between her husband and Rhi. "What's going on?"

"A few things," Rhi said.

Phelan threw down the hand shovel so that it landed blade first in the dirt. "Does this call for liquor?"

Rhi's shoulders dropped. "Probably."

Aisley was the first to step up onto the porch. "I'll get the glasses," she said as she entered the house.

Phelan stopped Rhi when she tried to follow. "Are you all right?"

She knew he was asking because he cared. How Rhi wished she could lie without feeling extreme pain. "I'm working on it."

"Is it Balladyn?" he asked with an angry twist of his lips. "I really hate that son of a bitch."

"He wants me."

"Of course he does. You're a powerful Light Fae."

Rhi licked her lips. "No, stud. He *wants* me."

"I know that too," he said softly. "Do you care for him?"

"I did. At one time, he was all that I had. He was my best friend."

"But are there deeper feelings?"

Rhi shrugged, having asked herself that same question. "I'm not sure."

"And your King lover?"

She looked away. Every time he was brought up, it was a fresh wave of pain all over again.

"Will you tell me who he is? I'd like to punch him. Repeatedly."

Rhi laughed, even as her eyes filled with tears. "I think I'd like that."

"You won't tell me his name, will you?"

She shook her head and blinked the moisture away. "No."

"Why?"

"It's my way of trying to pretend that I'm over him, that I don't still love him with everything that I am. That I don't need him every moment of every day no matter what realm I'm in."

"Have I met him?"

Rhi might not be able to lie, but she could refuse to answer a question.

"If you ever change your mind and want me to deck him a couple of times across the jaw, just whisper his name in my ear," Phelan said as he put an arm around her.

Rhi let him lead her onto the porch. When she looked up, Aisley was at the door, a sympathetic smile on her face.

She didn't even care that Aisley had overheard the conversation. Aisley and Phelan shared everything. There were no secrets in their marriage. They'd learned the hard way how secrets could destroy. It had cost Aisley her life. Good thing she had been a Phoenix, or Phelan wouldn't have her now.

Once inside the cottage, Rhi took the overstuffed chair in a dark blue and deep purple plaid. She accepted the glass of whisky from Aisley. Rhi didn't even ask if it was Dreagan, because she knew it was.

"So," Aisley said as she sat beside Phelan on the sofa and tucked her legs beside her. "What brings you to see us?"

"There's a Druid in a bit of a bind."

Phelan frowned. "Where?"

"Edinburgh," Rhi answered. She took a sip of the

whisky and answered the next question she knew they would ask. "She's from the Isle of Skye."

Aisley and Phelan exchanged a look. "Skye," Aisley repeated, concern pinching her lips.

Rhi watched the play of emotions cross Aisley's face. She hadn't been sure how Aisley would react knowing that Darcy came from the same isle as she did.

"What kind of trouble is she in?" Phelan asked, his fingers curling around Aisley's hand.

Rhi pressed her lips together. "The absolute worst kind. The Dark Fae are after her."

"What?" Aisley cried.

"Her name is Darcy Allen, and she left Skye seven years ago," Rhi explained. "She's smart and is quite potent in the magic department."

Phelan's frown was growing by the moment. "That wouldna bring the Dark to her door."

"Nope. That would be Ulrik." Rhi tossed back the rest of the whisky as the two digested her information. She set the glass on the table next to her and crossed one leg over the other. "Ulrik has been visiting Druids for centuries looking for one who might be able to unbind his magic."

Aisley let out a breath. "How did we not know this?"

"Does it matter?" Phelan asked. He sat forward, resting his elbows on his thighs. "Go on, Rhi."

She eyed them both before she continued. "Every Druid Ulrik visited who attempted to touch dragon magic died. Everyone, that is, except Darcy."

"Shite," Phelan murmured.

"Exactly," Rhi said. "She wasn't just able to touch the dragon magic binding Ulrik's, but she was able to undo enough of it that Ulrik had some of his magic returned."

"She's the only one?" Aisley asked, a frown marring her forehead.

Rhi nodded. "Yes. We're not sure who sent the Dark after her, but they don't intend to let up anytime soon."

"Who's watching over her now? Just you?" Phelan asked.

Rhi glanced away, wondering if she should've done more to help Darcy. Rhi had been too intent on her own misery to think of anyone else, even after Ulrik asked her to watch over Darcy. That wouldn't have happened before her torture with Balladyn.

"Rhi?" Aisley called.

She mentally shook herself and focused on the couple. "Two Dragon Kings are there. Warrick and Thorn."

"I doona know Thorn." Phelan scrubbed a hand down his face, his blue gray eyes boring into Rhi's. "I barely know Warrick."

"The Kings are the Kings," Rhi said with a shrug. "What do you want me to tell you? Thorn recently woke. He likes to walk close to danger, which is what makes him so good in battle situations."

Aisley put both feet on the floor and clasped her hands together in her lap. "And Darcy? How is she doing?"

"She's still alive. The Dark broke through her magic protecting her shop easily enough. If Warrick and Thorn hadn't added their dragon magic, I'm not sure she'd still be there."

Phelan rose and made a round of the living room, as he thought things over. "How many Dark are there?"

"A lot. Thorn said he stopped counting at forty-eight."

"Forty-eight?" Phelan asked as he halted and shot her a look. "The last time I saw that many, we were in Ireland."

Rhi swiped her hand through her hair. "I know. That doesn't even count the many Thorn and Warrick killed. Warrick is with Darcy while Thorn remains hidden. The Dark think there's only one King in the city."

"Then Con should send more," Aisley replied angrily.

"He can no', sweetheart," Phelan said. "The more Kings there, the more the Dark bring this war out into the open. Then all the work the Dragon Kings did to stay hidden will be for naught."

"And Ulrik gets what he wants," Aisley said with a nod.

Rhi had the uneasy feeling that something was about to change in the world. She wasn't sure about Ulrik. One moment he seemed to be one thing, and then in the next, he was the epitome of malicious.

He hadn't just cursed Rhys, but he'd had Lily killed. Then brought her back. Now he might be responsible for sending the Dark to Darcy, only to ask Rhi to watch over the Druid and ensure that she remain alive.

Whoever it was that wanted to expose the Kings might very well get their wish soon. There was no way the Dragon Kings would allow the Dark to so flagrantly flaunt themselves in Scotland without some kind of battle.

The Dark had to know that.

Because if the Kings didn't retaliate, then the Dark would know they could do whatever they wanted and go wherever they wished.

That would bring about another war.

"Are you all right, Rhi? You look a little green," Aisley asked.

Rhi blinked and looked from Aisley to Phelan. "I thought I knew who the bad guys were. What if I don't?"

"We've all known the enemies are the Dark, the small group of MI5, and Ulrik." Phelan folded his arms across his chest. "There's no doubt another group or person out there aligned with one or more of those groups, but they're small players if we doona know of them yet."

Phelan was right. It all made sense. It all fit neatly together. Why then couldn't Rhi dislodge the sick feeling that there was something they were missing?

"Let's get Darcy free of the Dark before we turn ourselves into knots over the bigger picture," Aisley said.

Rhi winked at Aisley. "Smart thinking, flame girl."

"With that many Dark, we're going to need more Druids," Phelan said. "And Warriors."

Rhi held up her hand to stop him. "Wait. Right now, the Dark aren't focusing on the Warriors. You bring that many there, and you're asking for trouble."

"What did you expect when you came to us for help?"

She really hated when Phelan was right. "Fine, but keep the gods tamped down as best as you can. I'm seriously going to kick your ass if the Dark figure out you're half-Fae. You don't want to know what they'll do to you, Phelan."

"Message received loud and clear." He shot her a grin. "Now get out of here and keep an eye on Darcy. We'll be there soon."

Rhi told him the address and started to teleport away when Aisley pulled her close for another hug.

"Be safe," the Druid whispered.

"Always."

"We see the Light within you."

Rhi pulled back, shaken by Aisley's words. "Are you sure? Or is it just that you think you see it?"

"It's there," Phelan said. "Just as bright as before."

Rhi wasn't so certain anymore. She teleported away before she gave herself a closer look.

CHAPTER TWENTY-NINE

The more Warrick thought of taking Darcy out of the shop, the more he wondered if it was a terrible idea.

"Stop worrying," Darcy said as she nudged his arm with her shoulder. "It'll be fine."

He raised his brows as he looked away from the broken door to her. "Fine? It's going to be anything but."

"I'm trying to make myself believe it'll be all right," she told him. "Can't you just pretend with me?"

Warrick shook his head. "Nay. You've encountered a few Dark, but you've no' seen what they can do in a group."

"It's not that far to my flat. We can make it. I refuse to spend the rest of my days in this shop. I've had to cancel all of my clients for the next week because I didn't want them walking so near the Dark."

"Maybe we should wait another day." Warrick had never doubted his power, but he hadn't been in such a predicament before either.

Darcy turned to face him and scrutinized him. " Everything you've done has helped me so far. There's no reason to believe this protection bubble thing you can do won't as well. You've used it before, right?"

"Of course." As if he would try something new while her life was in jeopardy.

"Then it'll be fine."

Unless the Dark surrounded him like they did the day before. Warrick wasn't certain his power could remain up and surround Darcy if he was knocked flat again. He'd managed once before long, long ago, but he had been in dragon form then.

"I'd rather do this at night," he murmured.

Darcy glanced out the window to the two Dark Fae who remained on the opposite side of the street. "I just wish my magic could do more damage. If I can touch dragon magic, why can't I do more against the Dark?"

"A verra good question." He'd been wondering the same thing. Her magic should be strong enough to do more damage to the Dark. There was something wrong, but Warrick couldn't put his finger on it.

Darcy blew out a breath. "If I stand around any longer, I may chicken out completely."

"That might be the wisest decision."

"It's because we're in the city, isn't it?"

He turned his head to her. "What is?"

"The fact you're not completely kicking some Dark Fae ass."

Warrick found himself fighting a smile, despite the gravity of the situation. "Aye. If we were in the country away from all the people, Thorn and I would've shifted to fight them."

"But you can't because humans might see you here." She lowered her gaze and sighed forlornly. "The longer we wait, the more Dark will come. I've seen eight more already this morning."

"They were farther down the street," he lied. He didn't want her to know that he and Thorn had also noticed the new additions.

Darcy smiled as she lifted her gaze to him. "Nice try, but you're a terrible liar."

Warrick took her hand and pulled her to the back so the Dark could no longer see them. "I want to have at least two routes planned out. The most direct route is the one you use all the time. The Dark are there and waiting for us."

"So we need a different one," she said with a nod of understanding. She reached her desk and picked up a pad of paper and a pencil from the floor.

Warrick vividly recalled taking her on the desk. His cock twitched, hungry for her again. He fisted his hands to keep from yanking her against him for a kiss and let her draw a map of the area.

"We have many options," Darcy said as she drew. "Some are easier than others."

Warrick knew Edinburgh well. He was already devising routes while she marked the streets and talked about intersections, various hills, and numbers of people.

"Here," Warrick said, pointing to a street two over from where they were now.

Darcy followed the line of the street with her eyes. "It could work. It's a side street, so there won't be as many people on it as the main roads. However, it's one of the longest routes. What about this one?"

He looked to where she pointed and trailed her finger across the map to her flat. "It's short, but there are many intersections. I doona want to be stopping for a light, nor do we dart out in front of traffic and bring attention to ourselves."

"You're right," she said with a twist of her lips. "Other than flying, what choice do we have?"

Warrick suddenly smiled. "I can no' believe I didna think of it sooner."

"What?" she asked.

"We can no' take to the skies. But we can go underground."

Darcy's eyes widened in excitement. "Of course! The city was built atop another. There's an entire city beneath us, not to mention the sewers and other tunnels."

"I'll still no' be able to shift, but it'll keep the humans from seeing us."

"Looks like we found our way," she said with a smile.

"I need to check in with Thorn and let him know what we've planned. We also need to find the quickest way beneath the city."

She shooed him away with her hand as she picked up her laptop and set it back on her desk as she sat. Darcy began typing something into the search engine, her attention thoroughly absorbed.

Warrick turned away and moved back far enough so that he could still see Darcy. Then he opened the telepathic link. *"Thorn?"*

"Aye," he answered. *"Are we ready?"*

"No' yet. We've found another way to get to her flat."

"If it involves anything other than the damn street, I'm all for it."

Warrick smiled at his comment. *"Good, because we're going underground."*

"Where are we going in at?"

"Darcy is looking that up now," he said as he glanced at Darcy.

Thorn let out a string of curses. *"You might want to hurry up. Another ten Dark just arrived."*

"I wanted to wait until dusk, but it doesna look like that'll be possible."

"Nay."

"I found something," Darcy said.

Warrick walked to her. *"Hang on, Thorn. Darcy might have found something."*

"You're doing that mental talking thing again with Thorn, aren't you?" Darcy asked, one eyebrow raised.

"Aye. Show me what you've found."

She pointed to the screen and the map of the underground that filled it. "There are three choices. One is a manhole cover just out front of the shop. Since the Dark are there, that's probably not the wisest choice."

"And the others?"

"There's an alley two streets over with a door that leads to the hidden city. It's narrow and the streets are major tourist destinations. Which leaves this one," she said, pointing to another manhole cover on the street behind her.

Warrick gave her a smile. "We've found our way in. We'll need to go soon. There are too many Dark here for them to sit back and no' attack."

"Got it."

"Thorn, our way in is in the street behind the shop. Can you get the manhole cover off before we get there?"

"Aye. How are you going to get Darcy there?"

Warrick glanced at her and then at the back of her shop. The conservatory with the top of all glass made it easy for him to get a look at the building behind hers. *"We're going up. I'm going to take her on top of the building behind hers."*

"I'll be waiting. Good luck."

Warrick was still looking at the building when Darcy came to stand beside him.

"We're going up that, aren't we?"

He looked at her and nodded. "I hope you're no' afraid of heights."

"That's not my issue. It's the climbing part."

"You'll be hanging on to me. I'll be doing all the work."

She put her hands on her hips and looked from him to the building. "I like the way you think."

"Good, because we need to go now. The longer we wait, the more time the Dark have to mount their attack."

"They'll see us."

He glanced behind him to the front. "Aye. They'll come after us too. I'm hoping to be beneath the city when that happens."

"Holy crap," she said and swallowed hard.

Warrick held out his hand. "Do you trust me, Darcy?"

She looked from his hand to his face. Then she put her hand in his and said, "Yes."

"Ready?"

"Warrick!" Thorn's voice shouted in his head.

She smiled nervously. "Yes."

"It's Ulrik!" Thorn bellowed.

Warrick paused and turned to the front of the store at the same time someone stepped on the broken glass.

"Wh—" Darcy started to say.

Warrick put a finger to her lips to silence her. "It's Ulrik," he whispered.

Darcy nodded, a frown furrowing her brow.

"Darcy?" Ulrik called from the front. "Tell the Dragon King guarding you that I mean you no harm."

Warrick wanted to believe him, but he wasn't sure of anyone anymore.

"He did warn me I was in danger," Darcy whispered. "It'll be all right." She stepped back and said, "Ulrik, we're in the back."

Warrick watched as Ulrik walked through the curtains to Darcy's office area. With the doors open to the conservatory, Ulrik saw them immediately.

"Warrick," Ulrik said. "I knew Con would send you."

He bowed his head in greeting to Ulrik. "Is that so?"

"You always did have the cool head. Who's with you?"

"I'm alone."

Ulrik smiled, though it didn't reach his gold eyes. "Now I know you're lying. There's always at least two Kings in situations like this. Is it Ryder? Darius? What about Dimitri?"

In that moment, Warrick realized that Ulrik knew it was Thorn with him. "What do you want?"

Ulrik threw him a flat look. "Why else would I be here? You know Darcy. You know what she's done for me. She's the one who gave me part of my life back."

Warrick eyed Ulrik as he walked to the doorway of the conservatory and leaned against the doorjamb. His hands were in his pants' pockets, his black suit jacket open to reveal a white shirt beneath.

"So you walked through all the Dark?" Warrick asked.

Ulrik shrugged, his gaze shifted to Darcy. "I need her to remain safe."

"Why didn't you tell me it was the Dark coming for me?" Darcy asked. "If it hadn't been for Warrick, I'd have been taken that first night or the second."

Ulrik's lips flattened. "Then it's a good thing Warrick was there."

Warrick moved closer to Darcy. "Why are you really here?"

"I told you. I'm here to help. I assume you have a plan to get Darcy out?"

Darcy nodded. "He's taking me to Dreagan."

"Of course he is," Ulrik said as he pushed away from the door. "What's the plan, then?"

CHAPTER THIRTY

Darcy knew Warrick wasn't particularly happy at Ulrik's arrival, but she was ecstatic at the extra help. She smiled at Ulrik. "Thank you. We accept your help."

Warrick tensed beside her. He had his own motives for not trusting Ulrik, but Darcy didn't share those reasons. In all the time she had known Ulrik, he had done nothing to put her in danger.

In fact, he'd warned her there was something approaching. It didn't go unnoticed by her that he had yet to explain why he hadn't told her it was Dark Fae coming for her. She would address that later.

Ulrik eyed Warrick. "Is it the fact that I'm willing to help that has you looking constipated?"

"You forget. I know who you really are," Warrick said.

"You think you know."

Darcy got between them and looked at Warrick. "Whatever you think of Ulrik, we need him."

"It's no' a smart move," Warrick said, never taking his gaze from Ulrik. "He'll betray you."

"He needs me."

"She's right," Ulrik said. "She's the only Druid who can

touch dragon magic. Why would I do anything other than save her?"

Warrick shook his head as he turned away in disgust. "Keep your false words. Darcy doesna need to hear them."

Darcy sighed and looked at Ulrik. She trusted him. She also trusted Warrick. It was only with her magic that she saw Ulrik's memories. He'd told her a little about the Dragon Kings, but nothing that compared to reliving those memories.

As for Warrick, she'd given him her body. They had been in close proximity for a couple of days. The few times they talked had been easy and open.

The same couldn't be said for Ulrik. He was an incredibly private man, but she understood why. Ulrik didn't trust—anyone.

But he needed her. That was her one advantage.

"Say the word, and I'll leave," Ulrik told her.

She knew firsthand how vicious the Dark were. Thorn was out there but keeping a low profile until the last possible moment. No matter how Warrick and Thorn felt, they were going to need Ulrik's help to get her out.

"The Dark let you walk in without bothering you?" she asked him.

Ulrik nodded once. "I know them."

"So you didn't send them after me?"

He made a face. "Darcy, what would that gain me? I've searched for ages for a Druid to unbind what my so-called friends did. Every one of them failed until I found you."

"Do you know why they're after me?"

"Because you helped me. Ask yourself who that angers?" he asked and looked pointedly at Warrick.

Warrick snorted loudly. "You're forgetting in your time away from Dreagan that we doona associate with the Dark."

"Ah, but you associate with the Light."

Darcy was immediately wary. "I thought you sent Rhi to help me."

"So I did," Ulrik said succinctly.

A muscle clenched in Warrick's jaw.

"Ah," Ulrik said with a cocky grin. "It bothers you that she's willing to help me as well as you. What else did you expect when I carried her out of Balladyn's dungeon?"

"I expected her to remember who you are," Warrick said.

"A Dragon King who had his friends betray him?" Ulrik said, a dangerous look flashing in his gold eyes.

"You started a war."

"The humans killed dragons, War. Or have you forgotten that?"

"Nay," Warrick said tightly.

Darcy felt the tension escalate. She had to do something. "Look, I know the two of you don't particularly like each other, but right now that needs to be put aside."

Ulrik raised a brow as he looked at her. "What's it to be, Druid? Do I go, or do I stay?"

"Stay," Darcy said without looking at Warrick.

Ulrik unbuttoned his black suit jacket and removed it. Then he carefully folded it and laid it on the table. Next, he reached up and gathered his long dark hair behind him and wrapped a leather strap around it.

"The plan?" Ulrik urged.

Warrick blew out a breath and glared at Ulrik. "If at any time I think you'll betray Darcy, I'll kill you."

"Ah. The obvious threat. Now, can we get on with it? I'm sure Darcy would like to get in some fresh clothes and eat properly."

Silence stretched as Warrick continued to stare at Ulrik. At this rate, she would never leave the store. Darcy hoped she was making the right decision about Ulrik. If not, she would find out soon enough.

"We're going underground," she said.

Ulrik looked at her and nodded approvingly. "A good plan. I know how the Dragon Kings doona want the mortals to know they're around."

"And you want to expose us," Warrick stated.

Darcy speared him with a stern look that he didn't even glance at her to see. She then focused back on Ulrik. "The best entrance is on the street behind us. Warrick wants to climb up the building instead of trying to run through the streets."

"A wise choice," Ulrik said. He walked to the back of the conservatory and looked at the building. "It isna too high, but the stone is smooth. It'll be a tough climb for you, Darcy."

"I'll be carrying her," Warrick replied.

Ulrik glanced at Darcy. "Probably for the best."

"Yeah," she said as she looked at the building. "I'm not exactly a climber."

Ulrik turned and faced Warrick. "Perhaps I should carry her."

"And let you spirit her away?" Warrick stated in annoyance. "I doona think so."

"He has a point," Darcy said. "The Dark want to fight a Dragon King. If you go out there and take their attention off me, then that would give us enough time to get up the building."

Warrick ran a hand through his hair. "I'd like it better if Ulrik was the decoy."

"But they willna fight me," Ulrik pointed out. "It's either you or Thorn."

Darcy wished there was another way, but she couldn't think of one. And she wanted out of the shop before the Dark attacked again.

"I need to talk to Thorn," Warrick said and strode to the front of the store.

Darcy watched him, wishing she could help relieve some of his worry.

"I'm surprised you accepted my offer of help."

Her eyes shifted to Ulrik who was rolling up the sleeves of his dress shirt. "Why? I know they told you about me."

"I knew about you before them." Though she hadn't known all of it.

Ulrik raised a dark brow. "How is that?"

"I was inside your mind."

His gaze went hard for a fraction of a second. "What did you see?"

"A lot. I know and understand why you are the way you are. However, there are two sides to every story. I listened as Warrick told me his."

"And?"

She shrugged and pulled off a dead leaf from one of her plants. "Both of you are right and wrong."

"It's no' that simple."

"No bad situation is. You are too angry to see their side of the story, and they're too stubborn to see yours. So you both gather hate around you and use it as a shield. Hate destroys from the inside out. It hardens the heart and maligns the soul."

Ulrik closed the distance between them. He got so close she could see the darker ring of gold around his eyes. For once, he let her see the anger that sizzled just beneath the surface.

"They brought this war onto themselves."

"Can you understand why they were angry at you?"

He gave her an annoyed look. "Were?"

"You know what I mean," Darcy said with a roll of her eyes.

"Have you ever loved someone, Darcy?"

The change in topic and Ulrik's soft voice threw her off guard. "My family."

"Nay. Have you ever fallen in love?"

Warrick's image instantly flashed in her head. "Not the kind of love you're talking about, no."

"You give everything to that person. Every shred of your soul, every breath that leaves your lungs. You trust them implicitly. You share everything with them. They are your entire world."

She swallowed hard, chills rising on her arms, because she could tell how deeply Ulrik had loved his woman. It was so tangible, so physical that it brought tears to her eyes.

Ulrik took a deep breath and slowly released it. "Now, imagine that same person betrays you. They stomp all over the love you gave them, proving that they never cared. They were using you."

Darcy could no longer hold his gaze. She looked down and sniffed.

"That would tear any being in two, be they human, dragon, or Fae," Ulrik said softly.

She glanced up at him to see his gaze was directed elsewhere. It gave her time to look at him and see past the indifference he showed the world. The problem was, there was only callousness and nothing resembling anything close to kindness.

"You survived it."

Ulrik smiled coldly. "If you believe that, Darcy, you're more naïve than I believed."

She rubbed her hands over her arms. "If the humans discover the Dragon Kings, all of the Kings will be hunted—including you. They can hide on Dreagan. Where will you go?"

"They can have Dreagan," he said through clenched teeth. Then he slid his gaze back to her. "Would you want to be with the people who turned their backs on you? Banished you? Bound your magic so you couldn't be the very thing you were born to be?"

"No," she answered honestly.

"Neither do I."

"Con asked you to stop killing the mortals."

Ulrik lifted one shoulder casually. "I wanted every trace of your kind wiped from the realm. I didna want to look at you again and be reminded of what happened."

She knew in that instant his feelings for humans hadn't changed. As soon as she unbound the rest of his magic, he would wipe the Earth clean.

"You're no' going to inquire if I still feel the same?" he asked into the silence.

"It's obvious you do."

His head tilted to the side slightly. "Had you known this before, would you have unbound my magic?"

Darcy didn't need to look to the doorway to know that Warrick was there. How much of the conversation had he overheard, she wondered?

"What I know is that this world needs the Dragon Kings."

CHAPTER THIRTY-ONE

Thorn looked down at the shop with distaste. He still couldn't believe what Warrick had just related to him. Ulrik was going to help them.

This could be the one thing that helped to mend old wounds.

Or it could all go up in a shit storm of lunacy.

Thorn might like to ride the wave of foolhardiness more times than not, but he hadn't been one who sided with Ulrik and killed mortals.

Not even when he wanted to burn a few humans with dragon fire himself. A vow was a vow. Thorn wasn't even one who hated mortals.

They were a huge pain in his ass, but they were part of the realm. The dragons were saved, even if they were on another realm now. Sitting around and bemoaning the fact that they were gone, or even hating the humans that were around now for something their ancestors did seemed stupid.

What was done was done. The mortals had their uses—particularly the females. Thorn smiled. A great amount of time had passed since the last time he sampled a willing woman. He couldn't wait until this shite with the Dark was over so he could enjoy himself a bit.

The smile died as his thoughts once more returned to Ulrik. Con had awakened every Dragon King because of the threat Ulrik posed to their way of life.

That in itself was enough to make Thorn conscious of the risk they were taking in including Ulrik in their plans. For Warrick's sake, Thorn hoped Ulrik was as good as his word.

If not . . .

Thorn wouldn't want to be Ulrik.

The plan was going into action in less than ten minutes. The way the Dark Fae gathered around Darcy's shop made him wonder if they shouldn't go sooner.

Thorn fisted, then flexed his hands. He was ready to kill more Dark. The fuckers were like fleas. You killed one and a hundred took its place. How he despised them and their use of the mortals.

He yearned to shift into dragon form and rain fire down upon the street, setting the wankers ablaze. It would be a fitting end to such scum.

As gratifying as that would be, Thorn held himself in check. Even if no other King admitted it, he knew it was a matter of time before the mortals discovered what they were. Until then, he would continue to keep his identity a secret and play by the rules set down so long ago.

It made Thorn yearn for the days when the mortals weren't so many. Then they could get the Dark to follow them to a secluded piece of the country and settle things once and for all.

Even during the Fae Wars, it was everything the Dragon Kings could do to keep the mortals from discovering everything. It was one of the reasons Con accepted the truce. There had been too many close calls, and Con feared their exposure.

It would've been the perfect time for Ulrik to strike. It was a good thing he hadn't had his magic then, because he would've succeeded.

Thorn hunkered low and made his way to the other side of the roof. He leapt across to the next building and walked the steep roof. As he was about to get set for Warrick to exit the shop and distract the Dark, one appeared in front of him.

"I knew there was another of you around," the Dark sneered.

Thorn smiled, eager for a fight. "It took you idiots long enough to realize it."

"But we have now."

He looked at the Dark with his red eyes glowing and his short black hair streaked with thick stripes of silver. "Are we going to talk all day or fight?"

A ball of magic swirling black and silver appeared between the Dark's hands. Thorn wasn't about to wait on him to throw it. He took two steps, put his foot on the side of a chimney, and launched himself at the Fae.

Thorn knocked the ball of magic away and slammed his shoulder into the Dark, knocking them both off the roof to the ground. He was up first and pressed his knee into the Dark's throat while he used his foot to keep one of the Dark's arms flat.

The Dark gasped for air and tried to throw magic at Thorn with his free hand. Thorn reached behind his back and pulled out the small blade he always kept hidden. It was a Fae blade, one made in the Fires of Erwar.

Thorn lifted it over his head as the Dark's eyes went wide as he recognized it. Thorn plunged it into one of the Fae's eyes and twisted.

He yanked it out and wiped it on the Dark's shirt before he stood and sheathed the dagger once more. Soon, the blade would feel more Dark Fae blood upon it.

Warrick was disappointed in Darcy's answer. He felt for sure that she finally saw Ulrik for who he really was, and yet she still wanted his help.

She was right. The world needed the Dragon Kings. The humans had no idea the monsters the Kings kept from them.

If only she said she regretted helping Ulrik, or even that she wouldn't do it now with all that she knew. Which meant she knew more about Ulrik than she let on.

That bothered Warrick more than he wanted to admit. He wished he knew what she saw in Ulrik. That might help him handle the situation better. As it was, Warrick was seriously considering pummeling Ulrik.

"Verra diplomatic, Darcy," Ulrik said as he turned to Warrick. "Wouldn't you say, War?"

Warrick shifted his gaze to Darcy. "It's almost time. Are you ready?"

"No." She gave a short laugh. "I've always fallen back on my magic in situations like this. I've never encountered anyone who my magic didn't affect. I'm not sure what to do."

He walked to her and stopped just short of touching one of the auburn curls that escaped her bun. Warrick could feel Ulrik's gaze on them, and he wouldn't let Ulrik know there was more going on between him and Darcy. "Your magic is strong. You're the first Druid to touch dragon magic. Remember that. The Dark have weaknesses. They often underestimate their opponents. Doona let them do that to you."

"Right," she said, nodding.

"Keep your magic at the ready."

She kept nodding, but Warrick saw the fear in her fern green eyes.

Ulrik gave him an impatient look when Warrick glanced at him. Warrick wished he was the one taking her up the building, but he had to be the decoy.

"I'll see you at the manhole," Warrick said.

As he began to turn around, Darcy grabbed his arm to stop him. Then she rose up and placed her lips on his. Warrick forgot about Ulrik as he wrapped his arms around Darcy and held her tight as he savaged her mouth in a rough, desire-driven kiss.

When he was able to pull back, her lips were swollen and a small smile was visible.

Warrick tugged on a curl that brushed her cheek. "Be safe."

"You too," she whispered.

It was harder than Warrick expected walking away from her. Thorn knew to keep an eye on them. Warrick didn't trust Ulrik to do as he promised, and Thorn would be there to stop him from whatever Ulrik tried.

Thorn wasn't exactly happy with his request, but Warrick didn't care about being left behind. He cared about Darcy and getting her to safety.

Once Darcy was at Dreagan, Warrick was going to find out why Rhi was helping Ulrik, and why she didn't protect the shop as she did Darcy's flat. There was too much not adding up properly for Warrick. Someone wasn't who they said they were, and someone was playing both sides.

Warrick paused at the front door and used his power to put a bubble of protection around Darcy. Then he walked out of the shop. He waited for a taxi to drive past before he walked across the street to the two Dark Fae who had been eyeing him all day.

He slammed a fist into the one on the left as the other

Dark pummeled him with short bursts of magic that stung viciously. Soon Warrick was being hit from behind with both fists and magic. Warrick let them think they got the better of him and stumbled into an alley.

The Dark were shouting, their eyes going bright red as the craze of battle filled them. Warrick avoided as much of the magic as he could while still getting in enough hits to kill a few Dark.

Several times he had to pull his punches to ensure their attention remained on him. Warrick ducked when he saw a hefty bubble of magic come at him. He glanced behind him to see it barrel into two Dark, knocking them flat so that neither moved again.

Warrick straightened and glanced at the building to see Ulrik scaling the stone with Darcy hanging from his back.

Warrick only got that glance as he was struck again and again by Dark magic. It didn't just burn, it drained him. Warrick stopped pulling his punches and landed whatever he could, whenever he could.

A growl rumbled through his chest when his hand closed around a throat of a Dark Fae. He squeezed and felt the bone snap.

There was a ruckus behind him. Warrick elbowed a Dark Fae in the face, snapping his head as he turned around and saw Thorn standing there with a smile upon his face as he looked at all the Dark.

Warrick spotted the two Dark Thorn was standing on and knew he must have landed on them as he jumped from the roof.

"I couldna let you have all the fun," Thorn said as he faced the Dark.

Warrick renewed his fighting. If Thorn was there, that meant Darcy was beneath the city. Yet the amount of Dark dead at their feet kept piling up, but the number they were fighting kept growing just as fast.

He tripped on a body and fell backward, rolling so that he popped up on his feet. Warrick felt his legs begin to go numb. It wouldn't be much longer before he could no longer stand.

Suddenly a Dark grabbed him. There were so many hands holding him he couldn't dodge any of the magic coming at him. He saw Thorn and a Dark circling each other. Thorn parted his lips and let out a hiss just before the flash of a dagger appeared and was buried in the Dark's throat.

Warrick heard Thorn shout his name. Warrick lifted his head and was able to raise his hand as Thorn's dagger sailed through the air. Warrick snatched it and began to slash at the Dark trying to cart him off.

As they released him, Warrick twisted in midair and landed on one knee. One arm was completely numb. His fingers gripping the dagger were shaking as he tried to hold on.

There wasn't time to heal from the Darks' magic. He had to get to Darcy. Warrick used the side of the building to get to his feet as the Dark ran away.

A moment later the Dark began shouting again. Warrick lifted his head and saw the Druids. They stood like a wall, blocking the Dark, their magic pulsing.

"I'll be damned," Thorn said as he killed another Dark.

Warrick looked over his shoulder to see the Warriors from MacLeod Castle at the opposite end of the alley. They used their powers to combat the Dark until, one by one the Dark teleported away.

Phelan was the first to walk to Warrick. "Darcy is at Dreagan. Fallon teleported her there."

Warrick leaned back against the brick and sighed. "And Ulrik?"

"Walked away."

Warrick knew that wasn't going to be the last they saw of the King of Silvers.

"Let's get back to Dreagan," Thorn said.

Warrick didn't have time to grasp what was happening as Fallon MacLeod suddenly appeared in front of him, his dark green eyes smiling as he laid a hand on Warrick.

The next thing Warrick knew, he was in the kitchen of Dreagan Manor right as his legs gave out.

CHAPTER THIRTY-TWO

Darcy tried to get to Warrick. She was so happy when he appeared in the kitchen she could barely contain herself. He hadn't even seen her before he collapsed.

She gasped and started to go to him. The other Dragon Kings immediately surrounded Warrick and got him upstairs while Thorn was talking to them. Leaving Darcy behind.

"A shower or food?" asked a female voice behind her.

Darcy turned and focused on the three women standing there. They had been trying to talk to her after some man touched her. One moment she was in Edinburgh atop the roof, and the next, she was standing in a large kitchen.

"She looks shell-shocked," said the petite woman with long inky hair and dark eyes.

Darcy blinked. "I am. Am I at Dreagan?"

"Yes, you are," said another woman with wavy blond hair and kind brown eyes.

Darcy didn't quite understand. "How?"

"Fallon teleported you."

Darcy moved her gaze to the third woman who was

stunningly beautiful with her black hair and the silver stripe running along the side of her face.

Dark Fae.

Darcy knew it instantly. She backed up, gathering her magic as she did. She ran into something and looked over her shoulder to see a tall man with wheat-colored hair and shamrock green eyes.

"Is something amiss?" he asked smoothly.

Darcy looked back at the woman. "She's Dark."

"Was," the man said from behind her. "Shara is my mate, Darcy. She was born to a Dark family, but she's now Light."

Darcy recalled Warrick saying something about that, but after all she'd endured at the Darks' hands as well as witnessed, she was slow to let it all go.

"You're safe here," the petite woman spoke again.

The Dragon King walked around her and went to stand by Shara. "I'm Kiril," he said. "I came to let you know that Warrick is fine. He took too much Dark magic."

"I knew it would happen again," Darcy said more to herself than those around her.

Kiril's brow rose in surprise. "Again?"

"It happened yesterday as well. The Dark surrounded him on the street."

"In the middle of Edinburgh?" Shara asked, her shock evident.

Darcy nodded, suddenly very weary.

The tall blonde hurried to Darcy and gently pushed her down into a chair. "I'm Iona. Shorty over there is Lily. It looks like you need food first."

Food and sleep, but Darcy wasn't sure she could do either. Now that she was free of the threat of the Dark, the realization of how close she had come to death descended. She clenched her hands to stop them from shaking, but it didn't help.

Shara took the chair next to her at the round table, her gaze sympathetic. "I know what you witnessed must have been horrific."

"I have no words," Darcy said.

Lily set a cup of tea in front of her. "The best thing you can do is relax and let your mind grasp that you're safe."

Safe. It was a word Darcy had always thought pertained to her. She had magic enough to protect herself against too-frisky dates and anyone attempting to rob her. Yet, she discovered how little her magic helped when facing the Dark.

Iona closed the fridge and looked at her. "I'm not the best cook, but I make great sandwiches."

Darcy smiled, but with the way her stomach felt, she wasn't going to chance eating anything right now. "Thanks, but I think I'm going to have to pass."

"Why don't I show you to a room?" Lily asked. "I'm sure you'd like some time alone and a shower."

Darcy got to her feet with a nod. "I'd like that very much."

She briefly looked at Kiril, Shara, and Iona before she followed Lily out of the kitchen and to the stairs. Darcy looked around, noting all the dragons. Most were made of iron. She loved the dragons that seemed to come right out of the wall, one claw holding a lantern with a light inside.

There were dragon pictures of various sizes. Some of the dragons were prominent. Others you had to search to find.

Then she reached the staircase and marveled at the beauty. There was a dragon newel post that was carved out of a huge piece of wood and looked as realistic as the dragons in her dreams.

"It's a beautiful place, isn't it?" Lily asked.

For the first time Darcy realized her accent was British. "It is. I could spend hours looking around."

Lily smiled over her shoulder. "I've only been a mate

for a short time. I worked for Dreagan, but I didn't see the manor until after Rhys and I had our ceremony. I know I walked around with my mouth hanging open for days."

Darcy couldn't help but smile at Lily's exuberance. "How is it being mated to a Dragon King?"

"Thrilling," she replied as they reached the top of the first flight of stairs. Lily slowed as she turned to the next flight so that Darcy came even with her as her smile faded. "I was in a bad situation before, and I . . . well, I died."

Darcy stopped in her tracks. Surely she'd heard that wrong. "I'm sorry?"

"I died. My brother shot me. It's a really long story that involved the Kings' enemy who used me to get on Dreagan. My brother was part of it."

"I know I've not gotten a lot of sleep these past few days, but if you died, how are you here?"

Lily started up the second flight of stairs. "I didn't know it at the time, but Ulrik brought me back."

Well, if Darcy thought her week had been strange, it now exceeded that.

Lily shrugged. "I don't know why he did it, especially since he was responsible for sending my brother here."

"Wow." What else was there to say?

Lily chuckled. "That pretty much sums it up. I was a little freaked out when I came to and found myself alive once more."

"So you remember what it was like to be dead?"

"It faded pretty quickly," Lily said when she reached the third floor and started down the corridor. "I told Rhys everything, which is why I know what I do. I don't have any memories of it, but based on my description of the man, it was Ulrik."

Darcy thought she knew Ulrik's secrets, but it looked like she knew next to nothing. Why did she think seeing his memories made her an expert? All that did was give her a glimpse into his past. She had seen nothing of his future, and he shared even less.

"I hear you helped Ulrik."

There was no heat in her words, but Darcy heard the censure nonetheless. "I did."

"Why?"

"Because it was a challenge. Because he had been wronged."

"The Kings bound his magic for a reason." Lily's forehead was creased in a frown. "You do know why, don't you?"

Darcy nodded. "Warrick told me the Kings' side of the story."

"And Ulrik told you his?"

"No. I saw his memories."

It was Lily's turn to halt. Her eyes widened in astonishment. "What did you see?"

Darcy didn't want to share Ulrik's memories. They were private. She had no right to them, and even less of a right to tell others of them. "I saw a lot, but I felt even more. He went through hell. There was betrayal, grief, and then anger. They all mixed in such a way that he couldn't tell one from the other."

"You feel for him."

"In a way. I know he has ulterior motives. I helped him because I wanted to see if I could, and then I continued because I couldn't *not* help him. I didn't comprehend my role until he told me the other Druids had died."

Lily continued on to a door on the left and opened it. She leaned against the corridor wall. "Now that you know both sides of the story, will you continue to unbind his magic?"

"I don't know."

"He's evil," Lily insisted.

Darcy glanced at more of the hanging dragon lights

adorning the hallway. "I was raised on the Isle of Skye, and we Druids have edicts we live by. It's so ingrained in us that at twelve, we each spell ourselves to ensure we stick by those rules or lose our magic. We can't use our magic to harm an innocent, and we can never use it to help evil. If Ulrik was truly evil, my magic would have stopped the moment I tried to help him."

"You're the only one who knows both sides of the story, and it does make me think. However, I know that Ulrik cursed Rhys so that he couldn't shift and put him in a tremendous amount of pain. I also know that Ulrik sent my brother after me."

"But Ulrik didn't pull the trigger. Let's not forget that he brought you back from the dead as well. As for Rhys, I don't know anything about that. I know the hate between Ulrik and the Kings runs thick and deep. I wouldn't put it past him."

Lily cocked her head to the side, the length of her long black hair falling over her shoulder. "You don't think cursing Rhys makes him evil?"

"He didn't kill Rhys."

"But he cursed him."

"Is Rhys still cursed?"

Lily paused, taken aback. "No."

"That's good to hear."

Lily pushed away from the wall. "I like you, Darcy, and I know you've been through a lot these past few days. I also know you have your own thoughts about Ulrik, but you might want to think twice before telling others what Ulrik did was nothing. I saw Rhys dying a little every time he couldn't shift and take to the skies. That curse changed him."

"I didn't mean to make light of what happened to Rhys," Darcy hastened to say. "I'm just saying that an evil person would have killed Rhys."

"Mixing dragon magic with Dark magic was enough that it almost happened." Lily held up her hand when Darcy tried to speak again. "I'm not angry. I'm trying to explain. You won't find any sympathy for Ulrik at Dreagan."

Darcy nodded woodenly. "I understand."

"By the way, please don't mention Ulrik in front of Iona. He was responsible for her father's death."

If Darcy didn't feel like the biggest heel before, she certainly did now.

"Make yourself comfortable," Lily said with a tight smile as she motioned into the room. "There's an en suite. One of us will be up later to see if you want any food."

"Thanks."

Darcy watched her walk away before she entered the room and closed the door behind her. She leaned back against it and let out a deep breath.

"Way to go, Darcy. That was a catastrophe. Why didn't I just keep my mouth shut?" she asked herself.

CHAPTER THIRTY-THREE

Con stood at the door of Warrick's room as he lay upon his bed. It was all he could do to hold back his temper as rage burned through him.

The Kings couldn't die by Dark magic, but that didn't mean they felt nothing from it. The fact was, it debilitated them. Depending on how much of the Dark magic they took in, it could be anywhere from a few minutes to hours for the Kings to recover.

Thankfully, it didn't happen often. Most times the Kings fought the Dark in dragon form. If he didn't care that the mortals discovered them, Con could have urged Warrick to shift and put an end to most of the Dark in Edinburgh.

But he hadn't.

"Where's Darcy?" Warrick asked.

Thorn stood with his arms crossed against a wall across from the bed. "She's fine, War. She's with Lily, Iona, and Shara."

"She willna understand Shara," Warrick said and tried to rise.

Kiril put his hand on his shoulder. "I've taken care of it."

Con had to be blind not to see the worry Warrick had for the Druid. Surely Warrick wasn't foolish enough to feel anything for the mortal. She'd aided Ulrik, and in Con's mind, that made her an enemy.

If only he could put the spell back in place that would stop the rest of the Kings from falling in love. It was only a matter of time before another betrayal happened.

That time could be now.

"You're frowning," Kellan said as he moved to stand beside him.

Con smoothed out his features. "I doona like to see any of us brought low by the Dark."

"Horse shit. You've taken notice of how Warrick keeps talking about Darcy."

Con didn't bother to tell Kellan he was wrong. Kellan was the Keeper of the History for the Dragon Kings, and that allowed him to be privy to important incidents and happenings regardless of whether the other Kings wanted him to know or not. Kellan was shown what happened in his mind, and he then recorded it.

His job brought him and Con close simply because Kellan had information about a weapon hidden on Dreagan that could be used against the Kings. The Dark were after it, but Con had yet to share what it was with the other Kings.

Nor would he.

Kellan stared at Warrick who was talking to Guy and Tristan about the Dark attacks. "You can no' keep sending Kings out to watch over females and no' expect something to happen."

"Of course I can."

"Then you'd be an idiot. We're no longer spelled, in case you need reminding."

Con cut his eyes to Kellan and met his celadon gaze. "If I need reminding, all I have to do is look around at all the mates roaming Dreagan."

"You really hate it, don't you?" Kellan asked with a hard look.

Con returned his attention to Warrick. "Nay."

Kellan issued a grunt. "Doona bother lying to me, Constantine. Remember. I know your secrets."

"You know some of them."

"I know the biggest ones."

"Is that a threat?" Con asked and turned his head to Kellan.

Kellan didn't bother to look at him. "Nay. Just a *reminder*. You know, you might no' be such a wanker if you would but—"

"Doona even say it," Con cut him off in a hard voice.

Kellan shrugged. "Denying it willna change things."

Con walked away from Kellan to stand next to the bed. "Who sent for the Warriors and Druids?"

"No' me," Warrick said. "I didna even think of them. I wouldna have agreed to let Ulrik help if I knew they were coming."

Con felt as if someone had just punched him in the gut. "What did you say?"

"Ulrik helped." Warrick struggled to sit up and lean back against the wooden headboard. "He arrived and offered his services. Darcy accepted."

"And you didna stop her?" Con demanded.

Thorn dropped his arms and moved to the other side of the bed. "It was Darcy's life. She was the one to decide."

"Nay," Con said angrily. "We're Dragon Kings. We decide."

Warrick traded a look with Thorn. There was something in Con's voice that told him he was barely containing his anger. "You didna see the Dark that were there, Con. Darcy decided to allow Ulrik to help, and since we wanted her out safely, I didna see another choice."

"Neither did I," Thorn added.

Con's cold black eyes stared at Warrick. "You know what he is."

"Aye," Warrick agreed. "Darcy isna blinded, Con. She might have seen his memories, but she knows there's more to him."

"How did he help?"

Thorn spoke before Warrick could. "Warrick was the distraction. He went into the street to lure the Darks' attention to him. It worked, allowing Ulrik to climb the building behind Darcy's shop, with her hanging on. I kept watch on Ulrik, keeping close in case he tried something. He never got the chance to make it down the other side of the building and beneath the city because the Warriors arrived with the Druids. Once Fallon brought Darcy here, I went to help War."

The room was silent as they all watched Con. Finally, Con said, "You should've killed Ulrik right then."

"Without my sword?" Warrick asked angrily. "Or perhaps I should've shifted, letting the humans see me."

Con's shoulders relaxed as he took a step back. "I'll need to talk with Darcy."

"No' without me," Warrick ordered.

Con glanced at his legs. "You're still recuperating."

"Con!" Warrick bellowed.

But the King of Kings walked from the room without a response.

Thorn put his hand on Warrick's shoulder when he tried to rise. "I'll be there until you can."

"I willna be long."

Thorn flashed a quick grin before he followed Con.

Warrick could already feel the effects of the Dark magic wearing off. He wished it would hurry so he could get to Darcy.

"She'll be fine," Kellan said.

Guy glanced at the door. "I've no' seen Con that angry toward a mortal in a while."

"He wouldna harm her, would he?" Tristan asked.

Ryder stepped into the room with a gloomy look. "Con had me pull everything on Darcy before you were sent to Edinburgh, War. Since then, he's had me dig deep."

"That's no' unusual," Kellan said.

Ryder made a face. "No' really, except that he was trying to connect her to Ulrik. He wanted me to see if she was anywhere near certain places like Iona's land, London during the fiasco with PureGems, or the like."

Warrick didn't like the implications. He liked the idea that they could be true even less. "And?"

"I've no' found anything. I told Con that as well, but he's no' satisfied. He's determined to link her to Ulrik more than she already is," Ryder said.

Guy gave a shake of his head. "If he finds that link, he's likely to throw her in the dungeon."

"Or kill her," Warrick said.

They all shared a look as each recognized the truth in his words.

"Shite," Kellan said as he pivoted and walked from the room with long strides.

Guy, Kiril, and Tristan followed him, leaving Warrick alone with Ryder.

Ryder walked inside the room and softly closed the door. "It should've been more than just you and Thorn in Edinburgh."

"Thorn had to keep hidden as it was. If the Dark knew there were other Kings, they would've attacked more mortals than they did. We saved some, but we couldna help all of them."

"Should Con no' be thinking of retaliation against the Dark instead of concentrating on Ulrik?"

Warrick ran a hand down his face. "Aye. Those buggers knew we wouldna do anything to them. Trust me, they'll be all over now unless we do something about them."

"I willna be the only one game for that."

"We're being divided just as Shara warned us that the Dark would try to do."

Ryder rubbed the back of his neck. "Right now we doona have another choice. There's the Dark, Ulrik, and Darcy."

"We've yet to figure out who sent the Dark for her."

"The Dark, of course."

Warrick wasn't so sure. "They let Ulrik walk right through them and into Darcy's shop. Why would they do that if they were upset he got some of his magic unbound?"

"I doona know." Ryder sank into the chair in the corner and popped his knuckles. "The Dark seem the most plausible, because they're the Dark. Why would they be upset? Ulrik is against us, just as the Dark are."

"Exactly," Warrick said. "If anything, they should be ecstatic that there's a Druid who can help him. They wouldna kill her."

Ryder leaned forward in the chair. "Shit, War. Then that just leaves Ulrik."

Warrick was shaking his head before Ryder finished talking. "Nay. I saw Ulrik with her. Regardless of what we think of him, he needs Darcy. He went so far as to ask Rhi to watch over her."

"If it isna the Dark, and it isna Ulrik, then who?"

"That's what I've been asking myself for days. Could it be the Light?"

Ryder thought for a moment before he said, "What do they care? That would be like the Light minding if we could shift or no'. Besides, would Rhi no' have said something?"

"She did only protect Darcy's flat and no' the shop," Warrick pointed out.

Ryder made a face. "It's Rhi, War. She's always been there to help us."

"And it wasna that long ago that she was in Balladyn's prison with the Chains of Mordare around her wrists being tortured. That's how the Light become Dark. Can you honestly tell me you've no' seen a change in her?"

"Aye, I've seen it. There isna a being alive that wouldna have been affected by what she went through. Rhi has had plenty of opportunities to screw us, and she's no' done it."

That was true. Warrick's head began to ache as he tried to sort through all of this. "Who else is there?"

"The Dark wouldna listen to MI5, but we could ask Henry. He's still keeping tabs on them."

"No need. The Dark doona care about MI5. If the Dark are doing a favor—or taking orders—who could it be other than Ulrik?"

Ryder's hazel eyes narrowed. "Another enemy we doona know about."

"Someone after Ulrik as well as us," Warrick said.

"That means someone who wants to bring down all the Dragon Kings."

Warrick sat up, grateful that the pain was diminishing and the feeling was returning to his limbs. "Another enemy? Do we have any idea who it could be?"

"I can try and find out," Ryder said as he stood. "You want to break the news to Con?"

"He wouldna listen. He believes everything is laid at Ulrik's feet. Until we have proof, that is."

CHAPTER THIRTY-FOUR

Rhi was standing in the desert thinking of her conversation with Balladyn. She shouldn't care about what he said to her. It was all rubbish.

Why then was she there?

She sat and took her boots off to let her toes sink into the hot sand. The sky was cloudless and a startling blue. The sun was unforgiving, and soon she was feeling the heat bake her.

The old Rhi, the one before the torture and Chains of Mordare, would've been with the Druids and Warriors helping Darcy and the Kings. In fact, Rhi had been in Edinburgh watching it all, though she was veiled the entire time.

She'd even contemplated helping. Why hadn't she? What stopped her?

The darkness inside her was growing. She could feel it. Could that be what pulled her toward Balladyn?

There was no point in asking him. Balladyn would tell her whatever he needed to in order to get her to turn Dark. That Rhi would never do.

Yet . . . there was something wrong with her.

Looking back, she couldn't figure out why she had protected Darcy's flat and didn't do the shop as well. She also hadn't responded to Warrick's call.

At least she went and got Phelan and Aisley. Darcy was at Dreagan and safe from the Dark.

Rhi put her head in her hands and closed her eyes. She wanted to throw off the weight that had settled over her. She wanted to be as flippant as she used to be. To drive her Lamborghini around Austin and shop.

She wanted to bask in the warm sunshine on an Italian lake and soak in the beauty. She wanted to enjoy life again.

Truth, Rhi. When was the last time you enjoyed life?

Rhi could pinpoint the exact day, the exact hour and minute. It was right before her lover ended their relationship.

She had been curled in his arms after hours of lovemaking. Her hands had been in his long bl—

"Rhi?"

Her heart stopped at the sound of Balladyn's voice. "Go away."

There was movement in the sand as he sat beside her. "What brings you here, pet? Were you looking for me?"

"Go. Away."

"What's got you in such a mood?"

Rhi lifted her head to find him a mere inch away. His legs were bent with his arms around them and one hand clasped his other wrist. He wasn't looking at her, but had his eyes closed and his face lifted to the sun. It was something he used to do as a Light Fae.

For an instant, Rhi thought they were back in time before he turned Dark. It was the Balladyn who had never let her down beside her. The Balladyn who came up with the dirtiest jokes just to make her laugh.

The Balladyn who had loved the feel of the sun.

"Who am I?" she asked.

His eyes opened as he turned his head to her. "You know who you are, pet. You always have."

"Not anymore. Not after what you did to me. I'm not the same."

He glanced away, a slight frown crinkling his brow. "We all change."

"Nothing has changed for me in . . . eons." She fell back on the sand and threw an arm over her eyes to shade them from the sun.

Suddenly, Balladyn was leaning over her, his hands on either side of her head. "I'd say something has changed. You're talking to me."

"I shouldn't be." She moved her arm to look at him.

"But you like it. Tell me, did you like my kiss as much?"

Rhi didn't have time to respond as he placed his lips on hers. The kiss was slow, searching. When she responded, a moan left him. He deepened the kiss and shifted his weight to one hand.

She knew it was wrong to kiss him, much less talk to him. But Rhi was tired of being alone. She was weary of holding love in her heart that was endlessly being rejected.

Balladyn kissed her with abandon, without restraint. He silently told her his feelings while taking every opportunity to kiss her. He made her feel wanted.

It was a heady sensation, especially mixed with such hot kisses that seemed to never end. It wasn't until his hand cupped her breast that reality struck.

Rhi gripped his wrist to halt him.

Balladyn lifted his head and looked down at her. "Tell me you've not thought of this."

Since she couldn't lie, she didn't respond.

"They why stop me? We were meant to share our bodies."

Kissing was one thing, but Rhi couldn't let another touch her as *he* had done.

Balladyn grew angry, his face hardening. "It always

comes back to him, doesn't it, pet? He's told you he doesn't want you. He ignores you. When will you let it go?"

"I'm trying."

"If I had kissed you before him, would you have let me love you?"

Rhi placed her hand on Balladyn's cheek and looked into his red eyes. "I might have."

"You're strong, Rhi," Balladyn said. "Let go of him and come to me."

"I'm not Dark. I won't ever be."

Balladyn smiled softly. "You'll realize who you really are soon enough. Until then, I'll be waiting."

The sun blinded her as Balladyn teleported away. Rhi rolled onto her side, hating the sting of tears as they fell hot on her cheeks. She should've been done crying for her lover. His soft promises and declarations made her lose centuries as she waited for him. How had he repaid her?

With contempt and disdain.

Another piece of her heart hardened against him.

And the darkness within her grew.

Darcy had a towel wrapped around her as she stood in the bathroom after taking the longest shower of her life. She wasn't about to put her clothes back on again.

She combed out her hair as she looked around at the white bathroom that was accented with black. In the middle of the room, the white tiles on the floor were dressed up with an outline of a rectangle with smaller black tiles.

Curious, Darcy walked into the bedroom and got her first look at it since she'd been too interested in a bath when she first entered.

The bathroom colors were carried over into the bedroom, except in reverse. The metal bed frame was black, as were the two bedside tables, though each table was a different style.

The comforter was a black on black paisley design with a small white stripe along the outside edge. Three pillows—one small white fur one, one small white satin, and a large black and white polka dot one—were on the bed. A black and gray shag rug covered most of the wood floors. Also in the room was a black armoire and a white and black armchair.

Darcy sat in the chair and looked out the window to the pasture where Highland cattle grazed. The sky was clear except for an occasional puffy cloud that drifted lazily by.

All in all, she should be completely relaxed.

Except she was wound tighter than when she was in Edinburgh.

Her head swung around when someone rapped on her door. She glanced down at the towel about her as she got to her feet. Darcy checked to secure the towel and walked to the door.

She opened it to find a tall man with golden blond waves and cold black eyes. Con.

"You know who I am?" he asked.

She nodded. "I do."

"Because you saw Ulrik's memories?"

There was movement behind Con, and Darcy spotted Thorn. She returned her focus to Con. "I'm not exactly dressed for this."

"There's a robe in the bathroom. I suggest you put it on," Con said as he pushed past her and strode into the room.

Darcy waited for Thorn to follow before she made her way to the bathroom and found the robe on the back of the door. She belted it tightly and returned to the bedroom. "How is Warrick?" she asked.

Thorn smiled. "He's getting better."

"Why did you help Ulrik?" Con demanded.

Darcy sighed and sat on the edge of the bed. "I've explained this to Warrick already, and to Lily. It was a challenge."

"A challenge?" Con repeated, his voice as icy as the artic. "You helped a man known for evil and destruction. I'd think as a Druid that you would be more careful about who you helped."

"I take exception to that," she said and returned his glare. "I read people's futures in their palms and through tarot cards. I couldn't see Ulrik's."

Con stood rigidly by the window. "That's your reasoning?"

"Of course not, but it made me curious. Not once have I not seen a person's future. His request was interesting. He told me who and what he was. I knew attempting to help him was harmless. So, I tried it. I was knocked unconscious for a day."

"Was he there when you came to?" Thorn asked as he sat in the chair.

Darcy shook her head. "Ulrik returned a week later. I tried again, and that time I was hit with his memories."

"So I've been told," Con said. "What were the memories?"

"I'd rather not say, but I suspect you won't give up until I tell you. I saw him discover what you did to his woman. I felt the thundering of his multiple emotions. I saw him fighting the humans."

"Is that all?" Con demanded.

She gave him a stern glare. "Actually, it's not. I saw his argument with you when you tried to get him to fight you to become King of Kings."

"Liar."

Darcy fisted her hands in the robe. "You told him that the other dragons needed definitive proof who was King of Kings. Ulrik said he didn't want to fight you, but you kept pushing. He refused."

"Satisfied?" Warrick asked Con from the doorway.

Darcy smiled when she saw him. She started to get up and go to him, but he motioned for her to remain.

"No' nearly," Con told him. "I want to know what else Ulrik told her."

Darcy rolled her eyes and once more took her seat. "He didn't tell me much. He gave me details of the Dragon Kings because I pushed to know."

Con's condemning look was fierce. "You sided with him."

"There are two sides to every story. Warrick told me his. Ulrik shouldn't have attacked the humans, but what did you expect him to do? He was angry at them, and at his friends. He didn't want to hurt any of you, so he did the only thing he could.

"And," she said over Con when he tried to speak. "If he was so wrong, why did so many Kings side with him? Humans were killing dragons, and dragons were killing humans. It had to stop. You did what you had to do. I'm not saying it was right. You could've handled Ulrik better. He was your best friend. He considered you his brother."

Con's nostrils flared as he drew in a deep breath. "He wouldna listen to anyone, especially me."

"He was hurt. You had your pride wounded because Ulrik did his own thing and other Kings followed. You didn't have to bind his magic and banish him. That was you responding to anger with anger."

Warrick braced his hand on the door frame. "You make it sound simple, Darcy, but it wasna. It was total chaos. We sent the dragons away, our family and friends away."

"Because humans were killing them. Did my ancestors kill dragons before or after Ulrik attacked?"

"Before," Thorn answered. "Then again, dragons killed their fair share of humans as well."

Darcy looked at Con then. "How can you place the

blame squarely on Ulrik's shoulders? What about the Kings who sided with Ulrik and you persuaded back to you? Did you punish them?"

"Nay," Con answered tightly.

Darcy shoved her damp curls out of her face. "But they killed mortals?"

"Aye." Con's voice was low, hard.

"Both you and Ulrik are in the wrong. Neither of you would admit it, so the hate grew between the both of you bringing us to where we are now."

Con gave a shake of his head. "Ulrik wants to kill me."

"And you want to kill him."

Thorn said, "He cursed Rhys."

"And killed Iona's father," Con added. "He has aligned himself with the Dark and a faction within MI5 to hunt down any human who has a connection with us. Not to mention he wants to expose us to the mortals. This is the man you're helping, and with every bit of magic he has returned, he gets stronger and does more damage."

Darcy looked at Warrick, but he wasn't going to offer her any help. Not that she'd expected he would. She knew how he felt about Ulrik.

"I've told you my reasoning, and what I know about Ulrik. What else do you want?" she asked Con.

Con's face was emotionless. "I doubt you've told us everything. What I want to know now is how many times have you helped Ulrik against us?"

CHAPTER THIRTY-FIVE

Warrick knew Constantine wasn't going to stop until he was sure Darcy had told them everything. The problem was, Darcy was just as stubborn as Con.

"Excuse me?" Darcy asked Con. "Are you accusing me of being involved in Ulrik's schemes?"

Con stared at her with hard, black eyes. "I am. It's obvious you've helped him."

Darcy made a sound at the back of her throat. "Yeah. I told you. I unbound his magic. That's as far as it went. I didn't know his plans, and not once did I help him in any murder or anything else you think he did," she said with a wave of her hand. "I repeat—in case you're hard of hearing—I didn't help him with anything more than unbinding his magic."

"She's no' lying," Warrick told Con.

Con slid his gaze to Warrick. "How would you know that? Because she told you? And you believe her?"

"I do."

"You accept her word for it that easily?" Con asked, a look of utter contempt on his face.

Darcy stood, anger shooting from her fern green eyes.

"It was three years ago when Ulrik first came to see me. It took me over six months before I was able to unbind some of his magic. Once I did, I didn't see him again until three days ago when he came to warn me that someone might be coming after me."

Con stared at her for long moments. "I have Ryder looking into your whereabouts for the last two and a half years. We'll see if you happened to be in the same places as the incidents we know Ulrik put in motion."

"Did you hear her, Con?" Warrick asked. "It was the same time the Silvers moved and the spell on us broke. We know what caused it now."

Warrick hoped that bit of news would turn Con's mind away from linking Darcy with Ulrik, but judging by the muscle tightening in Con's jaw, it was the wrong thing to say.

"So you're to blame for that as well," Con said icily to Darcy. "Millions of years I ensured that the Kings would never fall under the spell of a human again. By releasing Ulrik's magic, you broke that spell."

"Perhaps your spell wasn't as powerful as you thought," she retorted.

Warrick stepped inside the room and walked to her before Con retaliated. He grabbed Darcy's shoulders and forced her to turn to the side so she would look at him.

She had been accosted by the Dark and seen them do things no mortal ever should. Her shop was destroyed, as was her way of life. She was barely holding it together.

It didn't help that she had no idea that angering Con was the absolute worst thing she could be doing. Not that he blamed her. He would most likely act the same way when confronted in such a fashion.

Few would dare to talk to Con in such a fashion unless they were a Dragon King. Or Rhi. Humans seemed to innately know that he wasn't the type of person to mess with.

"Enough," Warrick said, looking first at her and then at Con. "We're getting nowhere with this."

Thorn stood and shoved a hand through his long dark brown hair. He cut his gaze to Con and said, "Your hatred for Ulrik is leading you down a path that will destroy you."

"It's either him or me," Con stated. "And it willna be me."

Darcy sighed, her shoulders slumping. "I've told you all I know. I didn't help Ulrik with anything. Do your search, Con. I no longer care."

Warrick gently pushed Darcy back down on the bed. "Rest. I'll bring you some food." He then turned to the door and looked pointedly at Con.

Thorn walked past Con into the hallway. It took a moment, but Con finally followed. Warrick glanced at Darcy to find her curling up on the bed as he closed the door behind him.

"Downstairs," Warrick said as he shoved past Con and Thorn.

He heard Thorn chuckle behind him while they descended two levels of switchback stairs. Warrick strode into the kitchen and threw open the pantry door, but he didn't see a single thing that he wanted to fix for Darcy.

With a slam of the doors, he ignored the other two couples in the kitchen and turned to pin Con with a glower. "You took things too far."

"We have to know." Con's famed control was back in place.

How Warrick hated it. But he and Thorn had seen just how rattled Con could get when it came to Ulrik. "You want to blame Darcy for unbinding Ulrik's magic? Be my guest. Darcy has admitted to that part. But I willna let you pin Ulrik's transgressions on her."

"Or to blame her for each of the Kings finding love," Thorn added from beside Con.

Kellan and Denae rose from the table that sat in the middle of the kitchen. A moment later, Rhys and Lily pushed back their chairs and stood. Both Denae and Lily walked from the kitchen without a word, leaving the five Kings.

"I warned you no' to take such an action, Con," Kellan said. "No' until we had proof."

Con folded his arms over his chest, his dress shirt stretching tight over his shoulders. "We doona have time to wait around."

"You took someone we could have as an ally and turned her against us," Rhys said. "Great job."

Thorn walked to the counters and leaned against the kitchen sink. "It was your idea, Con, that we watch over her."

"And learn whatever secrets she has about Ulrik. I'm still waiting on that," Con said.

Warrick rested his hands on the back of a chair at the table. "Usually, you're in control of yourself, or you would realize that condemning her first is the worst thing you could do."

"None of you know Ulrik like I do!" Con bellowed. He dropped his arms, his black eyes narrowed and angry as his chest heaved. "I know what he's capable of."

Rhys snorted loudly. "I do as well. Remember?"

"If you want her to help, give her a reason," Kellan said and looked pointedly at Warrick.

Warrick knew where Kellan was headed and began to shake his head. "I'll no' use her."

"No' even for us?" Rhys asked.

Warrick looked at Thorn who threw up his hands. "Doona look at me. I'll choose the Kings over any other being any time."

"You've already slept with her," Con said. "She trusts you."

Warrick turned away and rubbed his eyes with his thumb and forefinger. He couldn't use Darcy that way. It wasn't right. Not even to save himself and the other Kings.

Was it?

He didn't know what to do. There was no doubt he felt something for Darcy, something strong and raw and visceral. He even wondered—for a second—if she could be his mate.

But he didn't want a mate. So why did it matter what he did?

Because she has been nothing but honest and open from the verra beginning.

"I doona like the idea of it either, War," Rhys said. "Frankly, I couldna have done it with Lily, but I knew she was my mate."

Warrick didn't respond. How could he? He knew Ulrik had to be stopped, but at what cost? The Kings had coexisted with the humans for ages.

It was the mortals who started the first war. Would it be the Kings who began the second with Warrick's betrayal?

Thorn moved to stand in front of him. "Or *is* she your mate?"

Warrick could only stare at Thorn. He couldn't deny that she wasn't any more than he could admit that she was.

"Ah, hell," Rhys said.

Behind him, Warrick could hear Con mumble something to Kellan. The two had quick words, but Warrick didn't pay them any attention. He was too caught up in his thinking of Darcy.

"War," Kellan called.

He turned to face the others. "I doona want a mate."

"That doesna matter, my friend," Rhys said with a sympathetic look. "It happens without any interference from us."

Kellan rubbed his jaw. "Doona use her then. Talk to

Darcy. Get her to understand us and why Ulrik needs to be stopped."

"She willna do it," Warrick said. "She's trying to remain neutral in this fight."

Con's lips compressed. "That isna an option."

"You can no' force her to choose sides," Thorn stated to the King of Kings.

Con raised a blond brow. "If she refuses to help us, then she's taken a side—Ulrik's."

Rhys loudly blew out a breath. "Before Ulrik cursed me, I was one who argued that he might no' be the one pulling the strings. Though I hate to do it, I have to say Con is right in this. Ulrik must be stopped."

"I know." Warrick dropped his chin to his chest. "I'll talk to Darcy. I'll do my best to convince her that she can no' unbind any more of Ulrik's magic."

Rhys clapped him on the back. "It's the right thing to do, War. If you need anything, let us know."

"Why has it been so long since Darcy first unbound Ulrik's magic and him returning to her?" Thorn asked, confusion marring his features.

Warrick's head lifted as he looked at Thorn. "It was his choice. He didna return to her in all that time."

"Do you think she unbound all of it the first time?"

Con shook his head once. "Nay. The Silvers would wake, and Ulrik would come to challenge me. He only has a portion of it back. Of that, I'm sure"

"Enough to use our telepathic link and curse me," Rhys pointed out.

Warrick frowned as he went through what Darcy had told him about Ulrik. "He wants to kill Con. Why wait so long if he could have all of his magic back?"

"Perhaps Darcy couldna do more," Kellan said.

Thorn looked at Warrick. "Or whatever Ulrik is planning isna ready yet."

CHAPTER THIRTY-SIX

Ulrik wanted to pay Mikkel a visit and see how close the female Dark was to him, but there were other, more important matters to attend to. Besides, he couldn't return to Mikkel until he killed Darcy.

It put a definite crimp in his plans. He'd hoped getting her away from Warrick and Thorn for a bit would be all that it would take.

Then the Warriors and Druids arrived. Ulrik chuckled as he recalled how the Druid Laura had looked at him in surprise. He wondered if she remembered how he had paid Charon's pub a visit and spoke with her. Apparently she did.

Once the Warriors and Druids appeared, Ulrik had to amend his plans. He didn't stick around Edinburgh. There was no doubt Warrick and Thorn would get away from the Dark. The Dark had the ability to take a Dragon King, but it was not always an easy thing.

Ulrik stood on a mountain taking in the view of Dreagan in the distance. That was his home he had been forced from. Those were his dragons being held within a mountain.

He was so close to having it all that it was almost too much to take in. For so long, his revenge had been nothing more than wishes and dreams.

For five thousand years he'd forged bonds and alliances that grew through each generation. So what if Mikkel had done the same? The difference between them was that Ulrik knew how to reward mortals.

Mikkel simply killed.

The sound of a motor drew closer. Ulrik looked over his shoulder to see an old baby blue BMW slowly pull to a stop. Agonizing moments later, the door opened and an elderly woman climbed out of the car.

Ulrik walked to the parking area and held out his hand to help her down the few steps to the lookout. "How was your drive, Dorothy?"

"Now I know why I don't leave the city much." She smiled up at him, her face crinkling in deep wrinkles. "I'm always amazed when I see you. It seems like only yesterday when you visited my father and I saw you that first time."

Ulrik nodded. Dorothy MacAvoy had been but a child of five or six the first time he allowed her to see him. The years had aged her, but not once did she forget the bond between her family and Ulrik.

"I did what you wanted with Darcy," Dorothy said. "She's a sweet girl, even if she doesn't tell me the truth in what she sees. It doesn't matter though. I've finished what you asked of me, and I'm ready for my reward."

Ulrik gave her hand a light squeeze. "Thank you. That should be all that's needed to push Darcy where I need her."

"We should've done this sooner. Why did you wait?"

"Some things are out of my control."

She laughed, her craggy face lifting to his again. "I seriously doubt that. Nothing gets by you, Ulrik. You never forget a face, you speak at least twenty different languages, and you always have an answer."

"It's all going to be rectified now."

"Yes, finally. You've waited far too long, my Dragon King. You won't tell me what it is Darcy still needs to do, will you?"

Ulrik shook his head. "No. I've already visited both of your sons and your daughter. They know what's expected of them in the coming years."

"Of course they do," she said and sniffed, affronted. "William and I taught them well. They won't fail you, just as we never did."

"I know they willna." If they did, it was the last thing they would ever do.

Dorothy looked out over the view. "This is a beautiful place. Too bad I can't die here."

"Stay as long as you like."

Ulrik released her hand and walked away. He withdrew a phone from his pants' pocket and sent a quick text with the words: IT'S TIME.

He didn't look back at Dorothy. Their deal had been set in motion ten years earlier. She had held up her end of the bargain. And so would Ulrik.

In an effort to keep a low profile, he'd left his ice blue McLaren Spider in Perth. He walked to the black Mini and climbed behind the wheel before he drove away.

Warrick was on his way up to Darcy's room with a tray when he heard voices coming from the entryway. He paused and listened, picking out Lucan MacLeod's voice as well as Charon Bruce's and Phelan Stewart's.

Damn. He'd wanted some time with Darcy before the Warriors and Druids spoke with her, but it looked like he wasn't going to get his wish.

He took the steps three at a time to her room. Balancing the tray in one hand, he knocked on the door. A moment later and it opened to reveal Darcy's face.

Warrick smiled and held out the tray. "Hungry?"

Her answering smile was weak. "I think I could eat." She opened the door wider so he could walk in.

Warrick carried the tray to the bed and set it down. He took the chair while she gingerly climbed on the bed and inspected the food. He waited until she chose a cracker, a piece of cheese, and some cold chicken.

"I should've known Con would react the way he did," she said after she swallowed her bite.

"Ulrik has done some horrible things."

She nodded and turned the cracker around in her hand as she stared blankly at the tray. "My magic would vanish if I was helping an evil person, Warrick. It's part of what we're taught on Skye as well as the spell we put on ourselves."

"Could you have reversed the spell on yourself?"

Her gaze jerked to him, her expression wounded and angry. "You think I would?"

"It's just a question. Perhaps Ulrik convinced you to do it without your knowing it."

"Not possible. The spell can't be removed or reversed in any way. Do you think I helped Ulrik commit his crimes?"

Warrick shook his head. "The only way you're involved is in unbinding his magic."

"But that is enough to condemn me in most people's eyes. I see the way they look at me here. They're not sure what to do with me."

Warrick wouldn't lie to her. It wasn't going to be easy, but Darcy had to know the truth. "Many of them have had their own run-in with Ulrik. The mates are no' just taking the word of the Kings."

"I see people's futures. I didn't see Ulrik's. I saw a part of his past, but not the recent past. I need to know what all he's done."

He had been hoping that was what she would ask of him. It was going to be hard for her to hear, but it might be what she needed to prevent her from helping Ulrik unbind the rest of his magic.

"You know why he hates us," Warrick began.

"Ulrik hates Con. He's angry at the rest of you," she corrected.

Warrick wasn't sure there was much of a difference. "He has a network of spies that I suspect far exceeds that of MI5 and MI6 combined, or any other government intelligence agency for that matter. We try no' to engage with the mortals, even when they're after us. However, Ulrik uses them often. He has a ring of ex-military mercenaries that he calls upon."

Darcy took another bite of food, nodding as he talked.

"We suspected something was going on when a company named PureGems trespassed on our property."

Darcy shrugged and said around her bite of food, "Perhaps they didn't know it was Dreagan."

"They knew. Elena, who you have no' met yet, was with her boss. Sloan insisted that Elena go caving with her and brought her directly to Dreagan. Sloan died in the middle of their caving. She went down a hole looking for something and the line broke. She fell to her death, leaving Elena in the mountain alone."

"Obviously Elena didn't die," Darcy pointed out.

Warrick shifted to get comfortable in the chair. "Guy and Banan found her. They got her out alive, fortunately. There is a magic barrier around Dreagan to prevent people from stumbling onto our land like that, which is why we were so concerned about their presence. The only place that magic is absent is around the distillery."

Darcy put together another cracker, cheese, and meat. “What happened to Elena?”

“They questioned her involvement.”

“Sounds familiar,” Darcy mumbled.

Warrick hid his grin. “Guy believed in her though. Elena came up with a plan to return to London and PureGems to discover who had sent Sloan. Three Dragon Kings went with her.”

“And?” Darcy urged when he paused.

“Elena learned that PureGems was working to find anything they could on us. Attention pointed to the CEO. We needed to get close to him, so the Kings began following Jane, who was his secretary. Banan was tasked with uncovering what he could on Jane.”

“I’m seeing a pattern here.”

Warrick ignored her comment. “Jane overheard a conversation the CEO had with Ulrik. It put Jane’s life in danger since Dreagan was mentioned. She was kidnapped to lure us out. Since she was Banan’s mate, he and Rhys had to shift into dragons to rescue her. She heard Ulrik, but she never saw him.”

“Heard him?” Darcy asked. “What’s that mean?”

“Ulrik uses a different voice. He drops the brogue and has a cultured British accent. He kept just out of sight so Jane couldna see him.”

Darcy finished off another cracker and began to make another. “Jane became Banan’s mate, just as Elena became Guy’s?”

Warrick held her gaze for a moment before he nodded. “That’s right. After that incident, things got quiet for a wee bit. Or so we thought. We had no idea there was a faction within MI5 that was working with Ulrik and the Dark. They put together a two-person team to infiltrate Dreagan. They chose a cave of a dragon who had been sleeping for over twelve centuries.

"Denae was sent in with a partner, who was supposed to wound her once they were in the cave. Their plan was that they would then see a dragon come after her, apparently to eat her."

Darcy's eyes got big. "Go on."

"Denae didna go down without a fight. She killed her partner, though she was gravely wounded. Kellan woke during Denae's fight, and he carried Denae out of the mountain to be healed."

"Oh, let me guess," Darcy said with sarcasm. "As well as interrogated."

"Questioned," Warrick corrected.

"Hair splitting."

He shrugged. "Regardless, Denae finally agreed to help us. While trying to get her out of the country with another identity, MI5 and the Dark attacked. Eventually, the Dark took both her and Kellan prisoner looking for a weapon. It was Rhi who facilitated in getting the both of them out of the Dark prison."

"And Ulrik was responsible for the MI5 focusing on Dreagan as well as the attack on Denae and Kellan?"

"Aye."

"And the weapon?"

Warrick glanced away as he considered his words. "He told the Dark about the weapon. That's the only way they would know. It was a secret Con held all these years. The rest of the Kings only recently learned of it ourselves."

"That weapon could be a game changer, I'm guessing."

Warrick sighed. "Aye. Ulrik didna give up. We suspect he is either a part of, or runs the Mob. They targeted Jane's half-sister, Sammi. They blew up her pub and shot her."

"How do you know that was Ulrik?"

"The bullet Tristan pulled out of Sammi's shoulder had a dragon etched in it."

Darcy released a breath. "Oh."

"The Dark then stepped in and took Sammi prisoner, hoping it would be enough that Tristan would tell them where the weapon was. During that time, Ulrik tried to convince Tristan to join him. Luckily, Tristan was able to get Sammi out."

"That's quite a list."

"I'm no' done," Warrick said. "Bordering Dreagan is a fifty acre piece of land that has belonged to the Campbells for generations. They made a pact with us to watch over the border between their land and ours."

"Why?" Darcy asked as she dusted off her hands and opened the soda. "Why would you get that close to humans who might spill your secret?"

Warrick hated talking about this part. "There is a spot on their land that is an invisible doorway onto ours. We can no' detect anyone who walks through the doorway. However, it can only be seen by moonlight."

"What genius put the doorway there?"

"We did. It's the spot where we killed Ulrik's woman."

Darcy lowered the can slowly.

Warrick wanted to finish the tale before they were interrupted, which would be any moment. "Iona was raised on that land. Her father was murdered in an effort to get her back to Scotland. It also turns out that the company she worked for was a front put together by Ulrik to track her through her electronic devices."

"Please tell me that's the end of it," Darcy said.

"I wish it were. When Rhys went to Ireland to help Kiril while he was spying on the Dark, Rhys was hit with a combination of dragon and Dark magic. He couldna heal the wound. He had to make a choice to remain in dragon form forever, or human form. He wouldna be able to shift again."

Darcy looked down at her hands. "You told me about Rhys. So did Rhi and Lily."

"I didna tell you about Lily."

"She did," Darcy said as she looked back up at him. "She walked me up here and told me Ulrik's part in what happened to her."

Warrick paused for a moment. "Then there's you."

CHAPTER THIRTY-SEVEN

"You think he's using me?" Darcy asked Warrick.

She was still trying to absorb and sort through everything Warrick had told her about Ulrik. It was too gruesome and awful to be real, and yet there was no denying the Dark were after her.

Warrick's cobalt gaze was steady. "I do."

"He needs me. He told both of us that."

"Aye, and once you have unbound the last of his magic? Do you think he'll need you then? He'll kill you. He willna want a Druid around who can touch dragon magic."

She swallowed, her stomach rolling as she realized the truth in his statement. Why had it taken her so long to figure that out? Because Ulrik had warned her that danger was close? Why hadn't he told her it was Dark Fae? Why did he leave that part out?

"I honestly didn't think Ulrik had anything to do with the Dark after me, but now I don't know," she said.

"You believe me now?"

"I do believe all of that happened, yes. Did anyone see Ulrik?"

Warrick rose to his feet, his frustration clear. "There couldna be anyone else, Darcy."

"Just for a moment, put that thought aside and consider it. We were thinking along those lines while trying to figure out who sent the Dark after me. I have my doubts about a lot of things now. What if there's someone who wants to make everyone think it's Ulrik doing all of this?"

"Because he is."

Darcy drew in a deep breath and grasped the last shred of her patience. "What if it's not all Ulrik? What if he's only part of it?"

"We would know." Warrick stood at the foot of the bed. "There are only so many Dragon Kings. We watched all the dragons leave except for the four Silvers we're holding in the mountain. The only one who can use dragon magic is a dragon. Every King has been accounted for, including Ulrik."

Well, when he put like that, and in such a confident tone, Darcy didn't see the need in continuing her argument. The Kings might be arrogant, but they weren't foolish. They would check every King on Dreagan to see if he was the culprit. That only left Ulrik.

There was a small piece of Darcy that wished the rest of them could've seen the Ulrik she had in his memories. They might not hate him so much.

Then again, it seems he deserved their loathing.

"If Ulrik is such a bad person, why didn't my magic stop?" Darcy asked.

Warrick's lips parted to answer when a knock sounded. He turned and opened the door to reveal Kellan. They both turned to Darcy.

"We've no' had a chance to properly meet," Kellan said as he nodded to Darcy. "I'm Kellan."

Darcy licked her lips and set the can of soda on the tray.

"Warrick was just telling me your and Denae's story. I'm glad both of you came out of that."

Kellan bowed his head. "I appreciate your words. If you're up to it, the Warriors and Druids are downstairs and would like to talk to you."

"Look at me," she said as she glanced down at the fluffy white robe. "I don't have any clothes."

Kellan glanced in the bathroom. "There's some there."

"I was in those for days. I'd rather remain in the robe."

"Nay," Kellan said and pointed. "I see the pile on the floor, but there is another set on the stool."

Darcy walked into the bathroom and stopped as her gaze landed on the clothes. They were stacked neatly, but more importantly, they were her clothes.

She turned and looked at Warrick. "Did you bring these?"

"Nay," he said with a frown. "I think Rhi might have."

Kellan remained near the door. "What should I tell the Warriors and Druids?"

"I'll be right down," Darcy said as she walked to the clothes. She waited until she heard the door close behind Kellan before she asked Warrick, "I know about Druids, but I've heard very little about the Warriors. Should I worry?"

"No' at all. They're good people despite having primeval gods inside them. They've fought for their freedom against *droughs*."

Darcy dropped the robe and lifted the bright pink long-sleeved shirt to find panties and a bra. She hurriedly put them on, and then tugged on the jeans and shirt. When she turned around, Warrick's gaze was heated, the desire blatant.

"It's a good thing they're expecting you downstairs," he said in a thick voice. "Otherwise, I'd throw you on the bed and have my way with you."

Chills raced down her spine at the image his words created. Despite the past few hours, she found herself grinning up at him. "Don't tease."

"That's a promise."

Darcy reached for him at the same time Warrick closed the distance and brought her against him. She melted against him as they kissed. His arms held her tight while he plundered her mouth.

All too soon, he pulled back and looked down at her. "We can no' tarry. They'll come looking for us."

It wasn't until Darcy was in the hallway that she remembered she hadn't looked at her hair. She felt around for the frizz and groaned.

"It looks great," Warrick said with a lopsided grin.

"I bet it does," was her sarcastic reply. There was nothing she could do about it now.

She was nervous about meeting the Druids, but it wasn't until she stepped off the final stair that her heart began to pound in her chest.

Voices were coming from a room off to her right. Warrick led the way, only stopping once they reached the parlor.

"It'll be fine," he leaned down and whispered.

After the welcome Darcy had received from those at Dreagan, she wasn't so sure.

All at once, every eye in the room turned to her. Darcy imagined this was how an insect felt beneath the lens of a microscope.

It sucked.

"Thank you for whisking me out of Edinburgh," Darcy said. "I'm not sure I told any of you that."

A woman with golden blond hair and smoky blue eyes who stood beside Fallon smiled and said, "It's quite all right. That's as close to the Dark as we've gotten."

Darcy nodded at Fallon. They had shared exactly twelve words after he'd told her his name and that he was getting her out of Edinburgh. She had simply replied, "Okay." What else was she to say to him?

"This is my wife, Larena," Fallon said as he glanced down at her. "And the only female Warrior."

Larena beamed up at him.

Darcy looked over to Warrick, but he was staring at another Warrior with very long dark hair and blue-gray eyes.

"Phelan," Warrick said.

The man nodded. "Warrick."

"I expected all of you to be here," Warrick said to the room.

A man who looked similar to Fallon with sea green eyes and long black hair as well as a torc around his neck said, "We thought it might be too much for Darcy after all she's been through."

"Lucan's right," Fallon said. "We can be a bit overwhelming when we're all together. We kept it to just us six. For now. The others are anxious to meet Darcy."

Darcy hadn't had time to count when they all appeared on the rooftop, but it hadn't been a small group. She was glad they weren't all there.

"Perhaps introductions would be good," said a woman with chestnut hair beside Lucan. "I'm Cara, Lucan's wife. You've already meet Fallon and Larena. The other two are Phelan and Aisley."

Darcy said hello to each of them. It wasn't until she looked at Aisley that Darcy shifted under the intense fawn-colored stare.

"Are you really from Skye?" Aisley asked.

Darcy wondered why that mattered. "I am."

"Who's in charge there?"

"Corann. As always."

Aisley and Phelan glanced at each other. Then Aisley asked, "Why did you leave Skye? I would think a Druid would never want to leave."

"You wouldn't think that if you were from there."

"Actually, she is," Phelan said.

Aisley put a hand on his arm. "I wasn't raised there, Darcy. My parents were from Skye."

Another Skye Druid. No wonder Aisley was so interested in her. "Have you returned to Skye?" Darcy asked.

"A short trip," Aisley said evasively. "Will you go back?"

Darcy looked down to see her bare toes. "One day, perhaps."

"What of your family?" Phelan asked.

Apparently they had done some checking on her. So much for privacy. "I talk to them every week."

"What keeps you—" Phelan began.

But Aisley cut him off. "It's none of our business."

"It is if she's helping Ulrik."

Darcy felt everyone's stare. She was tired of everyone condemning her. She nodded stonily, looking at each of them. "Thank you again for helping. There's nothing else to say."

She turned on her heel and started to walk away when Aisley called her name.

Aisley came to stand beside her and touched her arm. "Druids need to stick together. You might need us one day."

Darcy heard her words as if through a tunnel. As soon as Aisley touched her, Darcy saw her future. Aisley and Phelan lived for hundreds more years, with Aisley returning twice in fire.

Phoenix, a voice whispered in her head.

Darcy turned her head and looked at Aisley in shock. The Phoenixes were supposed to be gone. "You're a Phoenix."

Aisley dropped her hand and took a half-step back, her eyes narrowed. "How did you know?"

"I see people's futures. Most times it's through palm readings or tarot cards, but there are rare times I see it when people touch me."

"Yes, I'm a Phoenix. It was handed down to me through my ancestors."

Darcy glanced over her shoulder into the room full of immortals and Druids. They didn't need her, and it was doubtful they ever would. She turned her back to them but stopped short of walking away. Where was she to go? The bedroom for Con to interrogate her more? Back to Edinburgh?

Darcy saw the front door and started toward it, needing some fresh air. She heard footsteps behind her and recognized the long strides as Warrick's.

"You don't have to follow me. I have nowhere to go, remember?"

"I'm no' following you, lass," he replied softly.

She opened the door and walked outside, her feet not happy when she came in contact with the rocks.

"If you wait, I'll get you some shoes," Warrick said.

Darcy shook her head and turned toward the grass. She needed to think, to clear her head.

She needed to be alone.

That thought scattered when Warrick came even with her and slid his hand in hers. "You should give them a chance. Those from MacLeod Castle can be trusted."

"Maybe." She slowed once she reached the grass, but she didn't stop.

They walked in silence. Every time they came to a fence, she climbed it while Warrick vaulted over it with one hand.

Darcy didn't know how far they walked until she glanced behind her and saw the manor was a speck in the distance. She stopped and let her gaze wander the wild beauty around her. "Will they come looking for me?"

"Nay. I told them where we are."

That mental link. She was really going to have to remember that.

"It's going to be all right, Darcy," Warrick said.

She waited until they reached the top of the hill and took in the breathless splendor around her before she asked, "Will it? I'm not so sure. I can't change what I've done, and people want to lump me in the category with evil because of it."

"No' all of us."

Darcy looked up at him. Warrick's hand touched her face before he glided his hand to the back of her neck and bent to give her a soft kiss.

"Come with me," he urged.

As if Darcy could tell him no.

CHAPTER THIRTY-EIGHT

Warrick couldn't wait on Darcy. He picked her up and carried her the rest of the way to the cottage. It was one of three newly built ones after the battles over the past year. He set her down inside and closed the door behind him. As soon as she turned to him, he wrapped his arms around her and crushed her against him as he kissed her.

Their first time together had been frantic and intense. He wanted to go slow, to savor her. Not once did he stop and wonder why, he just accepted it.

Warrick backed her into the living area where a plush fur rug lay between the fireplace and a sofa. He felt her palms against his flesh as she tugged up his shirt and caressed his stomach and chest.

He broke the kiss to remove his shirt, but she stopped him. It took him bending down before she could pull it over his head.

Her fern green eyes were alight with desire that made his balls tighten in need. Warrick put his hands at her waist and slowly, gently raised her shirt enough to get his hands beneath.

He caressed upward, pushing the shirt up as he did,

until he cupped her breasts. Before he took off her shirt, he let his thumbs swipe over her nipples. They were hard instantly.

Warrick grinned in satisfaction.

He took his time tugging the shirt up and over her head before tossing it aside so that she stood in her bra and jeans.

"My turn," she said.

A groan locked in his throat when she cupped his aching cock through his jeans. After a soft squeeze, she unbuttoned his jeans. Then, with agonizing slowness, she pulled the zipper down.

Their gazes locked as she knelt before him and yanked his pants down past his hips to his knees and wrapped her hand around his cock.

Warrick fisted his hands in her hair and closed his eyes as the full measure of pleasure surrounded him. A moment later, her mouth enveloped his rod. He moaned, his hips moving of their own accord. Her hot mouth was bliss, her hands stroking his length as she took him deeper was pure ecstasy.

Darcy loved the feel of his arousal. It was velvet wrapped around steel. She'd barely gotten started when he withdrew from her mouth and picked her up so that she wrapped her legs around his waist.

"You'll be the death of me," he said with a grin.

She wound her arms around his neck. "Enjoyed that, did you?"

"Verra much."

"Then why did you stop?"

"Because I want you stripped."

Darcy looked into his cobalt gaze as he dropped to his knees, and then slowly lowered her onto the fur rug. He kicked his pants off and unbuttoned hers before he looked at the fireplace.

"Let me," Darcy said and snapped her fingers.

A large flame burst around the logs set there, shedding a red-orange glow around the room. Warrick's smile grew. He jerked her zipper down, and then tugged the jeans over her hips and down her legs.

Darcy didn't realize until the air touched her that he'd removed her panties with her jeans. He laughed as he leaned over her and rolled them so that she was on top of him. She straddled him and felt her bra give as he unhooked it.

She pulled it off as she sat up and tossed it away. Then she touched his face. He'd come into her life so suddenly, saving her from beings she hadn't known existed. He'd risked his life for her. Something no one else had ever done.

The only time she felt as if she had someone who understood her was when he was near. She trusted him. Completely, wholly. Implicitly.

"What?" he asked softly.

She leaned over him so that their lips were almost touching. "I owe you so much."

"Nay," he whispered as he slid his hands in her hair.

He brought her head down for a kiss. It was slow, erotic, and seductive. It teased her senses, tantalized her soul.

Darcy let go of all the weight of the happenings over the last few days. She ran her hands over his rock hard chest, his thick shoulders.

Time was lost as their hands caressed and stroked, learning and studying the other. The fire within them burned hotter, brighter.

Stronger.

Moans and soft sighs filled the cottage. Their breaths mixed, their limbs tangled as they rolled around the rug while desire swelled.

Need, thick and strong, tightened within her when the head of his arousal pressed against her. Then he thrust and slid inside her.

Darcy marveled at the sinew beneath her palm. She loved the weight of him as he settled over her. He was passion and pleasure in one tasty package.

Warrick ground his teeth as her tight sheath gripped him. He pumped his hips, their bodies sliding over each other.

He couldn't get enough of her. He couldn't kiss her enough, touch her enough. And he feared what that meant.

Looking down at her, Warrick knew. She was his mate. It didn't matter whether he wanted one or not. She was his. All he had to do was take her.

Her auburn curls were spread around her, her swollen lips parted as soft cries fell from them. She was the most beautiful thing he had ever seen. Fern green eyes opened and met his gaze. Her legs tightened an instant before she climaxed. At the feel of her clamping down on him, Warrick felt his own orgasm take him.

They rocked against the other, each lost in the pleasure—and each other.

Warrick held her close as he rolled to his side. The aftermath of their lovemaking sheltered them from the harsh realities of the outside world.

"Well?" Con asked the Warriors and Druids as he walked into the sitting room. "What do you think of Darcy?"

"We just met her," Lucan said.

Fallon nodded. "It's hard to say."

"No' for me," Phelan replied.

Aisley looked at him askance. "Are you serious? After what we went through? I was *drough,* Phelan."

"And you knew what you were doing," he said.

Larena blew out a breath. "I believe Darcy does as well. She's wary, as she should be."

"Especially after enduring the Dark," Cara pointed out.

Con had expected the Druids would side with Darcy. "She didna endure anything other than being stuck in her shop while War and Thorn fought off the Dark."

"I wouldn't say she came out of that unaffected," Larena said, a hard edge to her voice. "Darcy saw things she didn't know were even around."

Lucan scratched his chin as he thought. "Aye, but she knew she was helping a Dragon King. Before Ulrik she didna know the Kings were here either."

"So we've been told," Phelan said.

Aisley rolled her eyes. "I love you, Phelan, but you can be so thick sometimes."

"You know as well as I do that Corann knows more than he tells anyone," Phelan argued.

Just what Con had wanted someone to mention. "So you think Corann knows of us?"

Phelan shrugged. "I'm saying it's a possibility. If he does, he wouldna share that with the others."

"So he wouldna have told Darcy," Fallon said.

"This can be solved easily," Cara said. "We need Reaghan."

Con crossed his arms over his chest. The Druid who could tell if someone was lying with a touch. Just what they needed. Con knew that Warrick wasn't about to let him near Darcy again, but Con had to know the truth.

All of them did—no matter how hard it was.

"What if she's innocent?" Lucan asked.

Con shrugged. "She's no'. She unbound Ulrik's magic."

"Some of it," Aisley corrected.

"Some, all. It matters no'," Con stated.

Fallon glanced at Larena before he looked at Con. "It does. If the worst thing Darcy did was help Ulrik, then you need to find who sent the Dark after her."

"Do I?" Con asked.

Aisley gave him a dubious look. "You know the Skye Druids put a spell on themselves so they can never harm another with magic or help evil."

"But there's no doubt Ulrik is evil," Phelan argued.

Cara lifted one shoulder. "Apparently there is some doubt, because as soon as she tried to help him, her magic would've vanished." Cara turned her head to Con. "Did you consider that?"

"Of course." As if he hadn't considered every possibility.

Larena raised a blond brow. "If Darcy had never unbound Ulrik's magic, then your Kings wouldn't have found love."

"I know." The spell would still be in place, and Con wouldn't have to worry about a human betraying them again. "We wouldna be fighting MI5 or the Dark."

"We wouldna be happy," said a voice behind him.

Con turned to the side to see Hal, Kiril, Guy, Tristan, Banan, Kellan, Laith, and Rhys. The eight of them radiated fury. But Con didn't care. They didn't know what it meant to be responsible for an entire race. They didn't feel the weight of decisions or the blanket of worry that he could never shed.

They thought him callous and cold. Let them. It was better that they thought the worst of him, because he had long ago realized he would do whatever it took to ensure that the Dragon Kings lived in as much peace as they could.

He wouldn't be a part of that serenity, but it was a price he would pay for his men.

"It's the truth," Con told them. "If this is what it's like with only some of Ulrik's magic returned, can you imagine what it'll be when he has it all? We'll be fighting the Silvers to keep them locked away while also battling Ulrik, the humans, and the Dark. All of that can be easily stopped."

"You wouldn't," Aisley said in a strangled voice.

Con took a deep breath. "Sacrificing one to save our race? Aye, I certainly would."

CHAPTER THIRTY-NINE

Warrick felt the push in his head from Con, but he decided not to answer. He wanted time alone with Darcy that didn't involve thinking about the Dark Fae, Ulrik, or her involvement.

He wound an auburn curl around his finger as they lay on their sides facing the fire. Warrick rose up on his elbow and looked down at Darcy.

She turned her head to him and smiled. "I forgot what this feels like."

"What?" he asked, intrigued.

"To do nothing. To be alone." She faced the fire again. "We don't have long, do we?"

"We have as long as you want. We're still on Dreagan, so you doona need to worry about the Dark."

"I was talking about Con and the others."

He paused as he heard Con's voice in his head call his name again. "I'll keep them away for as long as I can."

"Why don't you see me as they do?" she asked softly. "Why don't you condemn me? I see how they look at me, how they speak to me. You don't. Why?"

Warrick swallowed. A few minutes earlier, he'd been ready to declare to the world she was his mate. He wouldn't deny it now, not even to himself. But that didn't mean he was ready to tell Darcy or anyone else either.

"Because I know you," he said.

She snorted and shot him a quick glance. "Not really. We've been forced together. I doubt you would've been so ready to hear my story otherwise."

"I'm no' so sure about that," he said, recalling how he felt the first time he laid eyes on her. "I would want to know all about you regardless."

"Don't be nice. I can't handle that right now."

He frowned and rolled her onto her back so he could look down at her. "You think I'm being nice?"

"We just had sex, Warrick. We're naked in a cottage together. Of course I think you're being nice."

"Then you doona know *me* verra well." He was hurt by her words. Warrick got to his feet and began to gather their clothes. "I brought you out here to get you away from the manor."

"Or to get me to trust you more so I might tell you anything I could be keeping secret."

It was so close to what Con had suggested that Warrick paused and looked at her. "Did it never occur to you that I'm trying to help?"

She sat up and brought her knees to her chest. "Yes. I also remember that Con wanted you to bring me to Dreagan so I could tell him everything I knew about Ulrik."

"Which you have."

Darcy looked at the fire and nodded. "Yes."

Warrick knew she was referring to the fact he hadn't told her he was initially sent to find out about Ulrik. Of course she would wonder if he was using their connection now.

"I'm no' here on Con's order. I'm not with you to get close to see if you know more about Ulrik. I'm here because I want to be."

"Do you believe me?"

He stared at her for a moment, hoping she would look at him. Finally, he answered. "Aye. I do."

"You're the only one."

"I'm on your side, Darcy."

When she refused to look at him, Warrick got dressed. He didn't know what else to say to convince her. Everything that came out of his mouth only seemed to agitate her more.

It's one of those times he hated that he didn't converse well with others. Not to mention he didn't understand females at all. He'd thought Darcy was happy with him in the cottage, but she looked dejected and miserable.

Perhaps she required a little time to herself. Warrick knew he needed advice on how to handle the situation. He only hoped one of the other Kings would actually help him with her.

He understood their animosity toward her helping Ulrik. The fact Darcy kept taking up for Ulrik didn't help. Warrick didn't like that she kept doing that either. But, in a way, he understood.

She wasn't taking up for Ulrik. She was taking up for herself. Darcy was proving to herself and everyone else that she hadn't done wrong since she still had her magic.

If she still had her magic, Ulrik couldn't be evil.

The problem with that was that everyone knew he was evil.

Warrick ran a hand down his face. "I'm going to collect some firewood. Do you need anything?"

"No, thank you."

Warrick dressed, his gaze never leaving Darcy. If only

she would look at him, he could gauge her feelings. Yet she kept her face toward the fire.

Once he finished putting on his shoes, he paused beside her and tugged on a ringlet. "I'll no' be gone long."

Darcy waited until the door closed behind Warrick before she buried her face in her hands. The tears had been slowly falling, but now the floodgates were open.

Her shoulders shook as she let all of her emotions out. She had really thought Warrick cared about her. So much so, that she let herself think there might be something more between them.

What a fool she had been.

It had been in front of her from the very beginning. She might not have wanted to see it, and even refused to see it at the manor. But she couldn't deny it anymore.

Mainly because after making love to him again, Darcy knew she had feelings for Warrick—deep feelings. The kind that made her nauseous and excited at once. The kind that made her want to tell him how she felt.

What a disaster that would be.

Darcy lifted her head and wiped the tears away. She stood, shivering without Warrick's heat and looked down at the fur rug. The tears started all over again.

Why did she have to ask him why he was with her? Why couldn't she have been content with the way things were? Why couldn't she have left well enough alone and enjoyed their time together until she could leave?

She hiccupped. Because she wouldn't be leaving. As soon as she did, the Dark would descend upon her.

Darcy reached for her clothes through her tears. Her foot missed the opening to her jeans three times. She fell back on the sofa as the tears came harder.

Long minutes passed as she cried. When the grip on her heart lessened enough that the tears slowed, she sniffed and slowly dressed.

Images of Warrick making love to her flashed in her head. He was a good man. And he might actually believe her. If he did, the other Kings and their mates would start treating Warrick as they did her. That wasn't something Darcy could handle.

However, if Warrick didn't believe her, then he was once more doing what Con wanted. And he'd just lied to her. She wanted to be angry, and a part of her was. Another part understood.

Ulrik was after the Kings, and he would stop at nothing to get what he wanted. It wasn't just about revenge. Ulrik wanted to be King of Kings.

Everyone at Dreagan was fighting for their way of life.

Although she might appreciate their motives, that didn't help Darcy in her own feelings. She knew she couldn't remain near Warrick and not let him kiss and hold her again. It felt too damn . . . right.

Darcy angrily wiped at her eyes in an attempt to remove any trace of her tears. But when she thought of her feelings for Warrick, they started all over again.

She didn't know how long she stood and stared at the rug before she heard a mobile chime a text. At the second chime, Darcy shook herself.

Her hands went to her back pockets before she realized she didn't have her phone. It had been left behind at the shop. Curious, she began to look for the phone on tables and on the mantel, but found nothing.

The sound had been close, so she knew it was in the room with her. She removed the cushions on the sofa, looked in a vase, and even lifted the rug.

When it chimed for a third time, Darcy followed the sound down to her hands and knees and looked beneath the sofa. That's when she found the mobile. She grabbed it and saw the screen flashing a text. It was gone too fast for her to read. Darcy unlocked the screen and stared in stunned silence at the text.

I'VE FOUND A WAY TO KEEP YOU AWAY FROM THE DARK. U.

As if there were any confusion to what the U stood for. Ulrik. How did he get the number to the phone? More importantly, how did the phone get here?

She hurriedly typed a response.

WHY?

Darcy knew she shouldn't be talking to him, but if he could get her away from the Dark, then she could leave Dreagan behind—and Warrick.

That way she might save her heart.

I'M TRYING TO HELP. UNLESS YOU WANT TO STAY.

As if. He must know how she was being treated. Everyone guessed it except for her. Warrick hadn't treated her badly, and neither had Thorn for the most part. How stupid of her to think others would be just as understanding.

I KNOW WHAT YOU'VE DONE.

Darcy wasn't sure why she wrote that text. Perhaps because she wanted Ulrik to stop lying to her, even if it was by omission. Part of the blame lay with her since she hadn't dug deeper into his past. She'd been so amazed by his story and the glimpses she had seen, that she hadn't stopped to think about what he might do with his magic.

She knew he wanted revenge. She knew he wanted to kill Con, and for the few things she saw in his memories, she was sympathetic with his need.

But the rest? All those killings? That she hadn't ever considered on any level. She'd assumed Ulrik was just after Con, and that's where she went wrong.

I WOULD'VE TOLD YOU HAD YOU BUT ASKED.

She snorted as she read Ulrik's reply aloud. "Right," she said to herself.

THEN ANSWER ME THIS. DID YOU SEND THE DARK AFTER ME?

She tapped her fingernails on the phone, waiting for his reply.

NAY.

Darcy expected just such an answer. She wasn't sure if she believed him or not. He needed her, but how far would he go to ensure that he got what he wanted?

CON WON'T STOP UNTIL HE HAS EVERYONE CONVINCED YOU'RE HELPING ME. DO YOU REALLY WANT TO BE THERE FOR THAT?

"Hell no," she whispered as she stared at the screen.

If anyone knew what Con would do, it was Ulrik. Darcy had seen for herself how furious Con was, and how quick to judgment he was. However minute the proof was they found, it would be enough to convict her in his eyes.

HE'LL KILL YOU, DARCY. YOU'RE THE ONLY ONE ABLE TO UNBIND MY MAGIC. IF YOU'RE GONE, THEN SO IS ANY THREAT I HAVE.

Darcy swallowed hard. Ulrik's words were easy to believe, because she saw Con's hatred toward her. Whether they promised to protect humans or not, the Kings would protect themselves first and foremost.

Where did that leave her? Would Warrick stand against Con and the other Kings? That was assuming he believed her. Most likely it would be her standing by herself. Even on the off chance that Warrick did side with her, it would mean his possible death as well.

Neither scenario was one she wanted to be involved with. It had been too easy to think Dreagan would be the place she could be safe and free. She should've seen it coming, but she had been too filled with fear of the Dark Fae that she hadn't thought it through.

The only place for her now was Skye.

DARCY?

She looked at the rug and the roaring fire. If only time could've stopped for her and Warrick. If only she were still in his arms.

Her gaze lowered to the phone as she began to type.

HOW DO I GET OFF DREAGAN WITHOUT BEING SEEN?

CHAPTER FORTY

Warrick was about ready to explode. Con wouldn't leave him alone, and now Thorn's voice sounded in his head as well. All Warrick wanted was some time with Darcy. He wanted to calm her down and let her feel safe again.

Only then would he even consider allowing Con to see her. The others, well they could just wait. Darcy had been through too much to be faced with such anger from the others.

Everyone just needed to take a step back and consider the other side. He couldn't say that to Darcy without her thinking he was doing Con's bidding. It never occurred to her that Warrick was trying to help.

He was walking in the Dragonwood trying to sort out the conversation he and Darcy had had when an arm reached out and grasped him.

Warrick jerked out of the hold and spun, ready to shift when he spotted the culprit. He frowned, confused. "Thorn? What the hell?"

"I said your name three times, and I've been trying to contact you through the mental link," he replied tersely.

Warrick relaxed his stance. "I didna want to talk to anyone."

"You're going to change your mind after I tell you what Con has planned."

"More interrogating?" he asked wearily, using Darcy's word.

Thorn's lips flattened as he glanced away. "He wants to kill her."

"What?" Warrick exploded. A mixture of rage and fear enveloped him.

Thorn hastily looked around and held up his hands. "Quiet, War," he said in a strained voice.

Warrick drew in a deep breath as he stared at Thorn. He struggled to get his emotions under control. "Is this a joke?"

"I wish." Thorn ran a hand through his long dark hair. "Con isna going to wait to see if he can connect Darcy to anything else Ulrik has done. He wants her dead before she can finish unbinding Ulrik's magic."

"And the others are accepting this?"

Thorn gave a half-shrug. "Aisley is the only one vocally speaking out against it. Kellan is trying to talk Con out of it. The mates doona want to see her killed, but neither do they want Ulrik to have his magic restored. Too many have suffered from Ulrik's quest for revenge to stand up and speak for Darcy."

"Then I will."

"I doona recommend that."

Warrick looked aghast at him. "I'm no' going to stand by and let Con kill her."

"Neither am I. We need to get her away from Dreagan."

"Nay," Warrick said as he looked to the mountains. "I'll take her to my cave."

Thorn gave him a wry look. "How long do you plan on

keeping her there? She's human, War. She needs sunshine and fresh air, food, and to roam. None of them do well confined for any length of time."

"Rhi could get her out."

"Good luck with that. I've been calling for her for half an hour. She's no' responding."

Warrick looked helplessly around. This couldn't be happening. He'd known Con would want to talk to Darcy, but never in his wildest imaginings did he think the King of Kings would want to kill her. Warrick would never have brought her to Dreagan if he'd had the slightest sense that Con would put such a plan into motion.

"We're her only hope," Thorn said.

Warrick put his hands on his hips as he briefly closed his eyes. "No' her only one."

"You've got to be kidding," Thorn said in outrage. "Ulrik? Really?"

"He needs her."

"For now."

Warrick dropped his hands and paced. "We'll have to tell her to drag it out until we can find another place for her."

"And you think she'll believe us?"

That brought Warrick to a halt. "She already questions why I doona treat her as the others."

"Did you tell her it was because she's your mate?"

Warrick dropped his head and shook it from side to side. "I didna want a mate."

"So you would let her go?"

"I thought I could." Warrick lifted his head. "But I can no'."

Thorn blew out a breath. "Looks like we've got some convincing to do in regards to Darcy."

"I need to talk to Ulrik first. He might no' help."

"I've got a feeling he will," Thorn said with a twist of his lips.

Movement down the hill caught their attention. Warrick looked through the trees to see someone walking their way.

"I'll be damned," Warrick said.

Warrick wasn't sure how he felt seeing Ulrik walking among the Dragonwood. He put that aside for the moment, because Darcy's life was once more at stake.

When Ulrik finally reached them, he stopped and leaned back against a thick oak as he regarded them. "I'm a Dragon King. Did you think I couldna come onto Dreagan?"

"You were banished," Thorn pointed out.

"After my magic was bound." Ulrik shrugged. "Things have changed."

That fact was becoming more and more apparent with each passing day. Warrick never thought he would go against Con. He also never thought he would take a mate either.

Ulrik turned his attention to Warrick. "When is Con coming to kill Darcy?"

"How did you know?" Thorn asked.

Ulrik made a face. "Con is predictable. He feels threated, so he wants to kill the one human who threatens his way of life."

"You will destroy all of this as soon as you have your magic returned," Warrick pointed out.

Ulrik held Warrick's gaze for a moment. "I'll destroy Con, aye. As for Dreagan? I helped find this land. I helped build the caves well before I was betrayed. Why would I destroy it?"

Thorn gave a loud snort. "Because you blame all of us as well."

"So I do."

Warrick scrubbed a hand down his face. If he let Ulrik take Darcy, he was sentencing them all to potential death. Ulrik might be focused on Con right now, but if he defeated Con, then Ulrik would turn to the rest of them.

If Warrick kept Darcy on Dreagan, then he was condemning her to death.

"What will it be, War?" Ulrik asked. "Will you send Darcy with me, or will you let Con kill her?"

Warrick got in Ulrik's face, his teeth bared. "Con willna lay a hand on her!"

Ulrik smiled coldly. "I knew she was your mate. I wondered if you realized it yet back in Edinburgh."

"How did you know?" Thorn asked him.

"Darcy," Ulrik stated, as if it was obvious. "It was the way she looked at him, spoke about him. Cared about him."

Warrick turned away and walked in a wide circle to calm himself. His reaction to Ulrik's statement confirmed what he was about to do. It was the only way to keep Darcy alive, but why was his stomach in knots over it?

"How much time do we have?" Warrick asked Thorn.

Thorn threw out his hands. "No' long."

"I'll get Darcy." Warrick turned to retrace his steps back to the cottage.

Ulrik's voice stopped him. "You might want to bring Thorn with you. I'm sure Darcy is confused and a bit leery. She's endured quite a lot these last few days."

Warrick looked over his shoulder at Ulrik. "We'll meet you here."

"I'll need to leave with Darcy straight away. Meet me at the border."

That was miles away, but Warrick would rather be the one getting Darcy through the Dragonwood than Ulrik.

He nodded to Ulrik and looked at Thorn who moved

to his side. They walked away, leaving Ulrik behind them.

"I'm having a hard time deciding if we made the right decision," Thorn said.

"Ulrik knew Con would kill her. Ulrik knew and we didna." Warrick shook his head in frustration. "How did I no' see what Con's move would be?"

Thorn threw him a hard look. "I didna either."

"Do you believe Darcy?"

"I believe all she's done is unbind Ulrik's magic. I doona think she had a hand in anything else he's done," Thorn added.

Warrick breathed easier. For a moment, he thought Thorn might have been sent by Con. "Are we the only ones?"

"I doona think anyone wants to kill Darcy, but the thought of ending all of this shite we've been going through is too good to pass up."

"Killing Darcy willna stop Ulrik. He still has magic."

Thorn nodded. "Aye. Without Darcy, he willna have the full force of his magic, but he has enough to still cause problems."

"Just no' enough to challenge Con or come after the rest of us."

"It's taken millions of years, but Ulrik found a way to get his magic back. How long do you think it would be before he found another Druid to help him if Darcy died?"

Warrick glanced at Thorn as the cottage came into view. "Hopefully just as long."

Thorn chuckled. "Do you think we could get that lucky? Because I doona. We ran out of luck the day we bound Ulrik's magic. It's just been a matter of time before it all came back on us."

The conversation halted as they approached the cottage

door. Warrick was the first to enter. He found Darcy sitting on the sofa dressed and staring into the fire.

"That's a lot of wood you found," she said without looking at him.

Warrick didn't try to lie about not having any wood. He stepped aside to let Thorn enter. Warrick closed the door and said, "We've got a problem, Darcy."

"Oh? What's that?"

Warrick exchanged a look with Thorn. He didn't like Darcy's glib attitude. Warrick walked to the sofa and sat on the edge, facing her. "I know you doona believe me, but I'm on your side. I doona think you did anything more than unbind Ulrik's magic."

She didn't so much as look at him.

Warrick took a deep breath and tried again. "Darcy, I brought you to Dreagan because I knew the Dark wouldna be able to get to you. Con wanted to talk to you, but I didna realize he would harbor such . . ." He paused, searching for the right word.

"Hate?" Darcy supplied.

Thorn moved to stand in front of the fire to lean a hand on the mantel. "Con has never been particularly happy that any of the Kings found mates. I've only ever seen him this angry at one other mortal."

Darcy slid her gaze to Thorn. "Ulrik's woman. Con is going to kill me, isn't he?"

"He's going to try," Warrick said. As soon as her fern green eyes looked at him, he let out a little sigh. "I'm no' going to let him hurt you."

"What do you suggest?" Darcy asked. "Have the Dark stopped looking for me? Can I leave?"

Warrick took her hand in his. "Ulrik is here. He is going to get you away from Dreagan."

"Where can he take me that will keep me from the Kings and the Dark?"

Thorn dropped his arm from the mantel and crossed them over his chest. "I'm guessing his shop in Perth for the time being."

"Just until I can talk some sense into Con, and then I'll return for you," Warrick said. "I'm no' going to force you to go. This is your life. You need to dec—"

"I'll do it," she said and got to her feet. "Take me to Ulrik."

CHAPTER FORTY-ONE

It was everything Darcy could do not to break down in tears again as soon as Warrick returned to the cottage. His arrival wasn't a surprise. However, she had been more than taken aback by his and Thorn's talk of Con coming to kill her.

Before she could get a handle on that, Warrick told her he wanted her to leave with Ulrik.

Darcy had already decided to go to Ulrik after their text messages. Now she didn't have to sneak out and worry about Warrick finding her. But that didn't make leaving him any easier.

She was under no illusions. Once she left Dreagan, she would never return. No matter what. She was putting Dreagan, Warrick, and her growing affections behind her.

Nor was she idiotic enough to help Ulrik further. Oh, she would attempt to help him, but she wouldn't actually do it. Eventually, she would be able to return to Skye once Ulrik realized she couldn't unbind the last of his magic.

Darcy reveled in Warrick's hand on hers. For a few short moments. Then she stood and told them to take her to Ulrik. She was surprised her voice came out as strong as it did. Inside, she was shaking and nervous. And scared.

Warrick's cobalt gaze narrowed a fraction before he got to his feet to stand beside her. "I'm on your side, Darcy," he said in a soft voice.

She blinked but didn't keep eye contact with him. It was too difficult. Besides, she was tired of crying. The sooner she got away from Warrick, the sooner her heart could begin to heal.

"We need to get going," Thorn said.

Warrick glanced at her feet. "She's barefoot."

Darcy walked past the both of them to the door. She opened the door, but Thorn pulled her back so he could exit first. He shot her an annoyed look.

After Thorn had a look around, he motioned them to follow. Warrick stayed beside Darcy the entire time. He shortened his strides while his hand rested on the small of her back. It was both comforting and irritating. She wanted to turn and bury her head in his chest and have his strong arms wrap around her again.

"What happened?" Warrick whispered. "One moment you were smiling, and the next you wouldna look at me."

She quickened her steps, hating to be exposed. Darcy was happy they were headed toward the woods. They would provide some cover, at least.

"Facts," she said.

"Facts? I doona understand."

Darcy glanced at him, and then regretted it when she saw the confusion reflected in his eyes. His blond hair was mussed from constantly running his hands through it. "You're immortal. I'm mortal. You fight against Ulrik. I unbound his magic. Your place is on Dreagan. Mine isn't."

"You didna mind these 'facts' when we were making love," he said tightly.

Darcy's heart broke a little more. Why did she have to like him so much? Why couldn't he have kissed badly or had bad breath or something? Why did he have to be so damn perfect for her?

She didn't get a chance to respond because Warrick grabbed her hand and started running to the woods. He pulled her along, while she struggled to stay on her feet and not face-plant.

Once they reached the woods, Warrick stopped and pulled her against him. He pressed her between his chest and a pine tree.

Darcy peered around him and saw Thorn to their left. He gave Warrick a nod, and they began to make their way quietly through the woods.

There was no more time to talk, no more time to share any last thoughts—or regrets. Darcy held onto Warrick's hand tightly, wishing there was some way they could be together. There was just too much standing between them.

They moved quickly and quietly, stopping occasionally to listen. Darcy's feet ached from the cold earth and the many pine needles, pinecones, and other sticky things that poked her feet ruthlessly.

Several times she had to bite her tongue not to cry out. It seemed an eternity later that Thorn and Warrick stopped and Ulrik walked from around a tree.

"I was beginning to think you changed your mind," Ulrik said to Warrick.

Warrick's hand tightened on hers. "It wasna my decision to make."

"You're really going to let her go?"

Was it just Darcy, or was there a double meaning to Ulrik's words?

There was a long pause before Warrick said, "For now."

"He'll never forgive you for this," Ulrik told both Warrick and Thorn. "I hope you understand what it means to have Con turn against you."

Warrick looked down at Darcy. "He'll never know."

She hoped for Warrick's sake that Con never did. But even if Con discovered the truth, she was sure Warrick could take care of himself. He was too strong, too good.

"Be safe," Warrick said.

Darcy nodded, feeling those damn tears again. "And you."

"I want you to know th—"

"Warrick," Thorn interrupted as he looked back the way they had come.

Warrick followed his gaze. "Shite." He turned to Darcy and released her. "You need to go. Now!"

"Come on," Ulrik said urgently and grabbed her arm.

Ulrik pulled her after him until Warrick was out of sight. Darcy had thought her heart was heavy before. Now, it felt as if it were weighing her down.

"You shouldna have left him," Ulrik said.

Darcy jerked her gaze to him. "What?"

"You're Warrick's mate. Con wouldna have killed you once Warrick admitted it. He's made that mistake before."

"Then why am I here?"

"Because Warrick doesna want to admit you're his. He's never wanted a mate."

Darcy tried to stop, but Ulrik was too strong and kept pulling her after him. "Warrick wouldn't have let Con touch me."

"Nay, he wouldna have."

"Then why did you talk me into coming with you?" she demanded.

Ulrik finally stopped and faced her. "Because I need you."

She shivered and tried to pull her hand from his, but

his grip was too tight. "You're a fool if you think I'm going to unbind any more of your magic here. We're too close to Dreagan."

"Did you stop to wonder why I didna come see you for several years after you first unbound my magic?"

Darcy frowned. Ulrik's voice had changed. It was soft, too soft. "Of course I did. I assumed you needed time."

"Assumed," he repeated with a wry smile. "You mortals always make the mistake of assuming things. Why would I need time? I finally had a Druid who was able to touch dragon magic and begin to undo what Con and the others had done. I should've returned the next week and had you keep going."

"But you didn't." Shit. What had she missed? Was it right in front of her? Because it was obvious Ulrik had been doing something. "Did you find another Druid?"

He chuckled and shook his head. "There's no' another like you, Darcy. That fact made me reconsider things. It would only be a matter of time before Con discovered you and what you had done. I'm no' without my share of enemies. I knew they too would find you."

"I don't understand."

"I had to have another way of gaining my magic."

Darcy rubbed her temples. She was cold, tired, and getting pissed. "I had to touch your magic."

"And you did. Through another Druid. You know her as Dorothy MacAvoy."

Her knees threatened to buckle as the world began to spin. Every week Mrs. MacAvoy would come in. Every week Darcy read her palm. There were Druids who could take in another's magic without them realizing it. Was that what Dorothy had done? It was the only explanation.

"Ah. I see you've figured it out," Ulrik said.

Darcy tried to pull her hand from his again, but he tightened his grip. She gritted her teeth and yanked her hand free. "Do you have all your magic?"

"I think I'll keep that to myself."

"You don't need me anymore."

Ulrik held her gaze without responding. But that was answer enough.

"What now?" Darcy asked, dread making her stomach drop to her feet. "Why did you talk me into coming with you?"

"Because I refuse to allow Con to have you."

Darcy gasped when she saw him pull back his hand and spotted the curved knife.

CHAPTER FORTY-TWO

"That went too easily," Warrick said.

Thorn grunted, his gaze on the sky. "Way too easily."

"I wish I could've spoken to Darcy and figured out what was wrong."

"Did you no' see her eyes?"

Warrick frowned as they crested a hill. "What about them?"

Thorn cut him a dark look. "They were red-rimmed, War. She had been crying."

Crying?

Warrick halted. "Why would she be crying? Because I went for a walk?"

Thorn let out a loud sigh as he turned to face Warrick. "For all the things she said to you before we reached the Dragonwood. She didna want to leave, but she felt that she had no choice."

"She has a choice. If I tell Con she's my mate, he willna touch her."

Thorn's dark brows rose. "You might want to rethink that. Con considers her a threat, more so than Ulrik's woman ever was. He'll kill Darcy the first chance he gets. It's why I didna suggest you keep her here. She's better off far from Dreagan."

"Perhaps, but I'm no' better off." Warrick turned back around.

"Ulrik needs her. Right?" Thorn asked worriedly.

Warrick looked at Thorn. Without another word they started running back toward Darcy. Warrick would stand against Con if he had to for Darcy.

He spotted her and Ulrik talking. At least they were still near. All Warrick had to do was make it back to Darcy and talk to her. Then he saw her yank her hand away from Ulrik and step back. It wasn't until Warrick saw the blade in Ulrik's hand that he bellowed in fury and shifted. He threw his protective magic around Darcy.

But it was too late. Ulrik plunged the knife into Darcy's stomach.

Warrick's roar shook the earth as his massive wings knocked down trees before he could tuck them against him. He was too close to the border to take to the skies. Warrick barreled through the trees with Thorn on his right side in dragon form as well.

Ulrik looked at them with a smile before a Dark Fae appeared beside him and teleported him away.

Warrick reached Darcy and shifted back into human form so he could lift her in his arms. Her eyes were closed and blood gushed from the wound. There was the barest of breaths coming from her, but it was growing shallower by the moment.

"Nay," Warrick said as he touched her face. "Darcy, open your eyes. Look at me, lass."

Her head lolled to the side.

"You can no' leave me," he whispered, emotion tightening his throat.

He could feel the life draining from her. In all his endless years as a Dragon King, there was only one other time he had felt so utterly helpless.

"He's fucking gone!" Thorn bellowed. "I'm going to kill him!"

Warrick heard Thorn, but he couldn't respond. He was too desolate, too wrecked to do more than hold Darcy. He hadn't told her she was his mate, hadn't told her how much he cared for her—how much he loved her.

Why had he been so against taking a mate? She could've been under his protection this entire time. Had he taken her as his mate, Ulrik couldn't have hurt her. She wouldn't be bleeding out in his arms.

"Move!" said a female voice who shoved at Warrick's shoulder.

He looked up and saw the faces, but it took a moment for them to register. He blinked at the Druids.

"You need to step aside," Aisley said from beside him. "We can help Darcy."

He looked down at Darcy and tightened his grip. "You'll have to do it with me holding her. I'm no' releasing her."

Warrick vaguely realized the Druids circled around him and joined hands. They began to chant, their magic filling the air. Warrick felt their magic touch him before shifting to Darcy.

He opened the tear in her shirt to look at the wound and saw it begin to heal. Hope flourished inside him. This could work. The Druids could save her.

He could have a second chance.

No sooner had that thought gone through his mind than the wound opened back up and blood flowed quicker. Warrick covered the wound with his hand and tried to stop the flow of blood.

He dropped his forehead against Darcy's, because he knew he was losing her. He had been so against wanting a mate that fate was taking her from him before he ever had her.

A large hand fell softly on his shoulder.

Warrick looked up to see Con. "Get away from her. Ulrik did what you were going to."

Con didn't say a word. He merely squatted beside them and put a hand on Darcy as his eyes closed. His face contorted for a moment. Then he opened his eyes and stood. "Dragon magic was used," he said.

Warrick looked from Con down to Darcy. He lifted his hand to see that the wound was closed with just a small pale scar to show what had happened.

Darcy took a deep breath, but she didn't open her eyes. Warrick's throat clogged with emotion. He lifted her in his arms and stood. That's when he saw not just the Warriors and Druids, but the Dragon Kings as well.

Kellan gave him a nod, as did Guy and Tristan. Warrick held Darcy closer and started toward the cottage. He knew there were those who followed him, but he didn't care. He could handle whatever came now that Darcy still lived.

He shouldered his way into the cottage and lay her on the sofa before he covered her with a blanket. Then he turned and faced the others.

Warrick's gaze landed on Con first before moving to Thorn, Kellan, and Rhys. "Why did you save her?" Warrick demanded of Con.

"Because I saw Ulrik plunge the blade into her." Con's black eyes glanced at Darcy, his lips flattening for a moment. "She was right. I let my hatred cloud my judgment."

"I doona like that she unbound Ulrik's magic, but that's all she did. She didna curse me or shoot Lily. That was all Ulrik's doing," Rhys said.

Kellan nodded in agreement. "Denae reminded me that

she was accused as well and had no involvement. She keeps telling that a person is innocent until proven guilty."

"Thank you," Warrick said to them. "Though it might go a long way if you tell Darcy all of this yourselves."

Rhys smiled. "We'll do better than that. Bring her back to the manor when she's ready."

The three filed out of the cottage, leaving Thorn. Thorn looked at Darcy. "You're verra lucky, War. You got a second chance to set things right. Darcy is your mate. If you let her go this time, you may no' get another chance."

"I know. I doona plan to rest until she's mine."

Thorn looked at him and winked. "I knew you'd come around."

As soon as Thorn left, Warrick looked about the cottage. "I've got one shot to convince her to be mine. It's got to be perfect."

Darcy woke to the sound of thunder and rain hitting glass. She opened her eyes to see the fire roaring. She sat up, the blanket falling from her as she looked around the cottage.

Wait. What was she doing in the cottage? The last thing she remembered was talking to Ulrik and then the knife. Darcy looked down to see the dried blood and the tear in her shirt. She lifted her shirt, but there was no wound.

A piece of paper floated to the ground from the arm of the sofa. Darcy bent and opened it, reading aloud. " 'Your bath is waiting.' "

Darcy rose and walked around the sofa to the hallway. She found the bathroom and the huge oval copper pedestal tub sitting under a window.

Steam rose from the water. Darcy glanced around, but still didn't see anyone. She walked to the tub while removing her clothes. As she neared, she saw the rose petals floating in the water.

On the other side of the tub was a tray set on a stool.

There was a glass of champagne and a bucket of strawberries.

Darcy stepped into the tub. She sighed when she sat down and leaned back, the water reaching all the way up to her neck. It felt heavenly, the heat seeping into her muscles to relax her.

She sat there for several minutes savoring the warmth before she plucked a plump strawberry from the bucket. As she chewed the tasty berry, she wrapped her fingers around the champagne glass and brought it to her lips.

Darcy had never tasted champagne before. The bubbles popped along her tongue before she swallowed. She loved the taste of the golden liquid, but she made sure to take small sips.

After she drank half of her glass and ate several more strawberries, Darcy simply soaked in the tub and closed her eyes. The thunder was rumbling and the rain continued to pour, but she was warm and toasty.

Only when her fingers began to wrinkle did she sit up. She saw something out of the corner of her eye and jerked her head to the window, but all she could see was rain.

She rose from the water and reached for a towel. Darcy stepped out of the tub and dried off, keeping her eyes on the window. No matter how hard she looked, she didn't see anything.

"Oh well," she said to herself. "I must be seeing things."

An image of Ulrik flashed in her mind with him holding the knife. Darcy immediately closed her eyes and tried to think of anything else.

She found herself imagining a dragon, a jade dragon.

Darcy inhaled deeply and slowly released the breath. As she did, she opened her eyes. She looked at herself in the mirror.

"What happened?" she asked herself.

She recalled her conversation with Ulrik. She saw the

dagger. She also remembered all too well the feeling of the blade cutting into her body.

It had been . . . horrific.

The agony had taken her breath, the pain exploding throughout her body in suffocating waves.

And all the while, all she could think about was Warrick.

Darcy turned away from the mirror and saw the cream robe hanging on a hook. She took the garment and slid it on, rubbing her hands along the plush dark fur that lined the inside of the robe before she belted it.

She spent a few minutes trying to work out some of the tangles in her hair. Then she walked out, fully expecting to see Ulrik.

But once more, she was alone.

Darcy looked to the left where the living room and kitchen were. Then she turned to the right. There were three more rooms.

She checked out the one nearest her and found a bedroom colored in a dark silver and pale gray. She moved to the room across the hall and discovered a massive bedroom with a king bed.

A solid white comforter without any adornments covered the mattresses. There was a single accent pillow in a deep burgundy upon the bed. As she let her gaze wander the room, taking in the light tan walls and wide white trim, she spotted more burgundy throughout the room.

Darcy then turned to the door between the two rooms. She gasped when she opened it and found a dressing room. An armoire stood off to the side nearly as tall as the ten-foot ceilings.

There was a makeup vanity and stool, as well as a chaise longue in a soft cream. A large rug of burgundy covered the wood floors.

Darcy walked into the room and touched each object

as she inspected it. It was a woman's dream. The perfect place to put shoes, clothes, scarves, and jewelry. Add in the makeup vanity, and she was in heaven.

She turned to the chaise again. That's when she saw the clothes. Darcy recognized the black sweater as hers. She picked up the sweater and saw the jeans as well as another bra and a pair of panties. Sitting beside the chaise was a pair of her boots.

Squeezing her toes into the plush rug, Darcy eyed the clothes. Was Rhi responsible for this as well? Or had Warrick gotten it for her?

Not that it mattered. It would be nice to be in clothes not soaked with blood.

Darcy removed the robe and looked down at her stomach. She touched the spot she knew the knife had entered. It was a little numb. She walked to stand in front of the makeup vanity and looked at her stomach in the mirror.

A two-inch, narrow, pale line cut across her abdomen. How had she healed? She couldn't remember anything. Unless she was dead.

Darcy spotted a couple of candles and snapped her fingers to light them. But nothing happened. She frowned and tried again. No flames appeared.

She shivered and quickly dressed. After the last boot was zipped, Darcy stood in front of the candles and snapped her fingers again and again.

No matter how many times she did it, she couldn't get them to light. She searched inside herself for her magic. To her horror, it took several tense moments before she felt it.

It was dim, as if it were fading away.

Darcy's legs gave out and she crumpled to the floor. She couldn't be losing her magic now. Not when she needed it so badly.

She held on to the last ribbons of magic and closed her

eyes as she sought out the ancients. Minutes ticked by with nothing.

"Please," she whispered. "Talk to me."

The faintest beat sounded. She held her breath, waiting to see if the ancients would deem her worthy to talk to her now. She felt something wet drop onto her hand, but she ignored the tears and kept silently calling to the ancients through what was left of her magic.

There was a rush of air that blew her hair back and made her brace against the force of it. As soon as the wind brushed past her, the drums began to beat and the chanting filled her head.

"Thank you," Darcy said.

"Why should we talk to you?" the thousand voices asked in unison.

Darcy licked her lips. "I don't know what happened. Why is my magic leaving me?"

"It's been gone for many years."

What? "That's impossible. I used my magic yesterday."

"That wasn't your magic," the ancients said.

Darcy squeezed her eyes closed. This couldn't be happening. "When did I lose my magic?" But she already knew.

"The moment you unbound Ulrik's magic. He has done evil. As a Skye Druid, you know the consequences of such an act."

"I didn't know he was evil."

The ancients let out a sound that reminded Darcy of a snort. *"You were too interested in the money he offered and discovering if you could help him."*

"Druids take money for their magic all the time. I've been doing it for years by reading palms and tarot. Never when I touched him or the dragon magic did I feel evil. I would've stopped."

The ancients sighed loudly. *"What's done is done, Darcy. It cannot be undone."*

"Whose magic has been supplementing mine? That's the only explanation of why I still had magic."

"An old Druid. She died a few hours ago. With her life force gone, her spell no longer worked. The little magic you feel now is all that's left within you."

It wasn't even enough to light a candle. Darcy opened her eyes as the drums and chanting faded away. The ancients hadn't had to talk to her. She was thankful they had, but that didn't make things any easier.

Darcy jumped up and ran through the cottage to the front door. She threw it open and ran out. She didn't know where she was going, and it didn't matter.

She was a Druid without magic.

The rain mixed with her tears. She stumbled over rocks but kept running. It didn't matter that it was raining and cold. She had to do . . . something, anything to stop the pain that was threatening to burst from her chest.

Something swooped over Darcy low enough to ruffle her hair. She looked up and saw the jade dragon a moment before he dipped down into nothing. She slid to a halt a few feet from going over the side of a cliff.

Darcy fell to her knees as she blinked the rain and tears from her vision. She watched the dragon dip a wing and circle back around to her. It was her first good look at Warrick, and she was awed. He was massive, his scales gleaming even in the rain.

A crest of membranes ran from the base of his skull to his shoulders, while two large frilled membranes shot from either side of his head, framing his face. It was the sheer size of the dragon, as well as the long spike at the end of the tail that kept her riveted.

As he drew closer, she looked into his large eyes the

color of the sun. He was the dragon of her dreams, the one she kept seeing over and over again.

Darcy dropped her face into her hands and sobbed. The ground trembled as Warrick landed. Suddenly the rain stopped. Darcy looked up and saw Warrick holding his wing out to keep the rain off her.

She stood and walked to him. With a hiccup, she leaned against his front leg and wrapped an arm around him. His scales were slick from the rain, but warm. To her surprise, he shifted and opened his other hand. Darcy eyed the talons that were a shade darker than his jade scales. She looked up at him, and he nodded.

It wasn't like she had anything else to lose.

CHAPTER FORTY-THREE

Con sat in the cavern with the Silvers and sharpened the blade of his sword. When Ulrik came, he would have his Silvers. Con would only have himself.

It wasn't the first time Con wished he had kept one of his Golds, but he couldn't choose one over any of the others. So he'd let them all go.

Besides, if he kept one, every King would've wanted to keep one. That would've defeated the purpose of sending the dragons away.

Things were coming to a head quickly. It wasn't just that Ulrik could come onto Dreagan without any of them being alerted, but there was the fact Warrick and Thorn had conspired with him.

Con knew why Warrick had done it, but he wasn't sure about Thorn. Not that Warrick's excuse was acceptable, but a King would do anything for his mate. Fortunately Warrick was going to allow him to talk to Darcy for a bit. Ulrik had used Darcy, tricking all of them. He also had all of his magic returned to him, and Darcy no longer had any.

What she did still have was knowledge about Ulrik as

well as his memories that she'd seen. Con was leery of digging into those memories, because there could be a chance Darcy had seen the one thing Con didn't want anyone to know.

Now that she was Warrick's, she was part of Dreagan. He still didn't trust her. She could betray Warrick just as Ulrik had been betrayed, but Con would wait and see.

For now his attention was focused solely on Ulrik. But he would be keeping an eye on Darcy.

Con set aside the whetstone and polished his blade. His gaze jerked to the Silvers when one of their tails banged against the cage.

The battle he always knew would come between him and Ulrik was soon to arise.

Warrick anxiously waited for Darcy to climb onto his opened hand. The vicious grip around his heart loosened when she finally did. He gently closed his hand so that he held her securely without squeezing her. Darcy rested her arms along one thick digit and looked at him.

"My magic is gone."

He blew out a breath and glanced away. The Warriors had told him as much. He wondered when she would find out. At least now he didn't have to break that bad news.

"So you know," she said. "What am I to do without magic?"

He suddenly leapt into the air, his wings stretching to catch the air. She let out a gasp, her hands clutching him.

Warrick wanted to show her what it was like to see the world from a different vantage point. He remained low, keeping out of the clouds. They were safe on Dreagan, but it was more about giving Darcy a few moments where she could forget what had happened to her and enjoy things.

He remained in the sky for over thirty minutes, flying over a large chunk of Dreagan, but staying far away from the manor. The rain lessened significantly by the time they returned to the cottage.

Warrick landed and set her down before he shifted. Darcy was staring at him, her lashes spiky from her tears.

"What happened? I don't remember anything after Ulrik stabbed me."

Warrick fisted his hands as he fought not to pull her against him and just hold her. Never had he been so terrified as when he'd felt the life draining from her. To be such a powerful being and not be able to save the person he loved was alarming.

"You were dying," he said. "I can use my power to protect you, but I could do nothing to heal you. The Druids tried, but Ulrik used dragon magic. It was Con who saved you."

Her eyes widened in surprise. "Con? The same Con who was going to kill me?"

"The verra one."

"And my magic?"

"The Warriors can sense a Druid's magic. They told me yours has faded. I'm sorry, Darcy."

She looked down at the ground. "It seems mine has been gone for almost three years now."

"What?" She couldn't be right. Warrick frowned and took a step closer.

"The moment I unbound Ulrik's magic, mine left me."

"How did you no' know?"

She shrugged and looked back at him. "I wasn't exactly conscious afterward. Then I was recovering from that, so I didn't pay attention. Apparently, there is an old woman who used her magic to supplement mine so I would assume I still had magic."

Her face crumpled as more tears came. Warrick closed the distance between them and wrapped his arms around her. He held her as she cried, letting her get it all out.

Warrick guided her back into the house once the worst of the crying was over. He took her into the bathroom and undressed her. Then he turned on the shower and pulled her into the hot water with him.

"It was a client I trusted who didn't just supplement my magic. She took what was left of mine from me and was able to use it to help Ulrik."

Warrick squeezed his eyes closed for a moment. "I doona want to talk of him right now. Did you mean what you said when I was taking you to Ulrik? Do you really think there can be nothing between us?"

He held her with her back against the water. She looked up at him. "After what I've done, I'll never be able to look anyone at Dreagan in the eye again."

"I didna ask about everyone. I'm asking about me."

She laid her hand over his heart. "I should never have questioned you. You're the only one who has been honest with me. You deserve someone worthy of you. I'm not her. No matter how much I wish I were."

"You are worthy," he whispered and bent to place a light kiss on her lips. He leaned back enough to look into her fern green eyes. "I couldna imagine going through a day without you."

She smiled sadly. "All I could think about after I was stabbed was you. I've been dreaming of a jade dragon for months."

"Why does that make you sad?"

"Because I love you, and I've screwed things up."

Warrick wanted to shout with joy. He held her tightly as she ducked her head in his neck. "Let's revisit that first sentence. You love me?"

She nodded.

Warrick smiled and looked up at the ceiling. His greatest fear was that she didn't love him. Now that he knew she did, the hardest part was over.

"That's good news, since I love you."

She jerked out of his arms to stand against the far wall of the shower. Her brow was puckered as she stared at him. "What?"

"I love you," he said slowly, wondering if he had said it wrong.

Darcy shook her head. "No. That can't be. You're a Dragon King. You're not supposed to love me. I'm the one that started all of this crap by unbinding Ulrik's magic. I'm to blame."

"We're all to blame." Warrick reached for her, non-plussed when she batted his hand away.

She shook her head. "You might forgive me, but the others won't. And I can't forgive myself. I released evil, Warrick. I can't even light a candle," she said and snapped her fingers.

Warrick glanced at the candles on the windowsill and saw all of them flicker for a moment, but none of them remained lit.

"Everyone makes mistakes," he told her. "You can help us stop Ulrik. With your knowledge of him and his memories, we can beat him."

She dropped her head to his chest.

Warrick kept her under the hot water because he didn't want her getting ill. "You asked me earlier why I was with you. I couldna tell you then that you were my mate. I've been denying it. I never wanted a mate. Until you."

"So you have no choice," came her muffled reply.

Warrick chuckled and lifted her chin so that she was looking at him. "I have a choice, Darcy. I didna have to tell you that I loved you. I didna have to tell you that I know you're my mate, but I did. I told you because I want you in my life."

"You've no idea how hard this will be, Warrick. What the others will do to us and how they will treat you."

"You'll be a part of Dreagan," he told her. "Besides, I already had a little talk with the Kings."

She blinked. "You did?"

"Of course. I willna stand for my woman to be treated badly."

Darcy licked her lips, her chest rising as she took in a deep breath.

"Make up your mind, because I doona know how much longer I can stand here without taking you," he said as he looked down at her breasts. Water was running to the tip of her nipples before falling down. It was driving him mad with lust.

Her smile was slow, but grew quickly. "Is that right?"

"Aye," he said and brought her close enough to feel his hard cock.

"Impressive." Her smiled died. "What if you regret it? We haven't spent that much time together."

"No one says we have to do the ceremony immediately. What about next week?" he teased.

That had her laughing. "Smart ass."

"Laith and Iona have no' done the ceremony either. I'd do it right this minute if I could so that I didna have to worry about Ulrik attacking you again, but I'd rather wait so you know for sure. There's no divorcing a Dragon King, Darcy. Once we're mated, we're mated for eternity."

"I know," she said with a nod. "I don't see any children around. Is it forbidden?"

Warrick turned her so that her back was against the wall. "It's no' forbidden. Unfortunately, a mortal can no' carry a child from us to term. Most miscarry early in the pregnancy. A few have delivered babies, but they were all stillborn."

"Oh."

"Did you want children?"

Darcy shrugged. "I hadn't thought about it. I always figured it would come after I got married, but since I never expected to find someone I would want to spend my life with, I never saw myself with children." She swallowed and rose up on her toes to wrap her arms around his neck. "The answer is yes, Warrick."

He didn't let out a whoop, because he saw that she wasn't finished talking.

"However, if you don't mind, I'd rather take it slow. I want to give each of us time to figure out if this will work. I want you to make sure you can love a woman who might have begun the downfall of your race. And I need to come to grips with the fact that I'm in love with a Dragon King."

"I'll give you as much time as you want. Just tell me you love me again," Warrick said as he nuzzled her neck.

Her hands smoothed over his back. "I love you, Warrick. I love you, I love you, I love you."

"You're mine," he whispered right before he took her mouth in a savage kiss.

EPILOGUE

Two weeks later . . .

"Admit it," Warrick pressed.

Darcy rolled her eyes as they crossed the bridge to get to the Isle of Skye.

"Come on. You said if everyone treated you as if nothing happened that you would admit you were wrong," Warrick said as he glanced at her while he drove.

She laughed and threw up her hands. "All right. I admit it. You were right."

"Exactly," he said with a satisfied smile. "Then again, it might have helped that we spent an entire week at the cottage."

"You're probably right," she said as she looked at him.

The SUV got quiet as they drove across the Skye Bridge. It had been seven years since she'd left, and it felt odd to be back after so long.

"Nervous?" Warrick asked.

She nodded, looking at the water from the window. "I've not seen my family since my mother died. I should've known better than to keep reading her future. No good can ever come of that."

"Is that why you willna read mine?"

She glanced at him with a smile. "Oh, I've tried. I can't see anything. I'm not sure if it's because I no longer have my magic, or if it's because you're immortal. I couldn't see Ulrik's either, remember."

"I doona need my future read. I know it involves you, and that's enough for me."

Darcy took his hand in hers and brought it to her lips for a kiss. "I need to warn you that my family can be . . . well, they can be a bit much. They're loud and everyone talks at once."

"I'm going to love them."

"No, you won't," she said with a grin. "They can only be endured in small doses."

With their talk, Darcy didn't realize how close they were to her family's home. Her stomach tied in knots. It wasn't about her not having magic anymore. Her family didn't need to know about that.

It wasn't even about Warrick and keeping him and Dreagan a secret. That was the easy part.

It was seeing her family after so long. So much had changed her that she wondered if she would see them differently. Or would she be different?

All too soon Warrick pulled into the drive and parked the Range Rover. He turned off the vehicle and turned his head to her. "Ready?"

"I don't think I can do this," she said, suddenly sick to her stomach.

The front door opened and her father walked out, followed by her two aunts, one of her uncles, her grandmother, and her sister. It was her sister who came running to the SUV and opened the door to envelop Darcy in a tight hug.

Darcy was promptly hauled out of the Range Rover and passed from one person to another. She was finally able to search for Warrick, and she found him standing off to the side with her father, talking.

Warrick winked at her and mouthed, "I love you."

Despite everything that had happened to her, and that she had caused, Darcy was alive and in love with a dragon. Could life get any better?

But she knew the answer to that. It was yes. Just as soon as they were mated, and she was officially his.

Dublin, Ireland

Rhi was on her fifth whisky. It was Jameson. Good stuff, but she still preferred Dreagan.

Damn it.

She tossed back the last of the whisky and caught someone staring at her through the mirror behind the bar. This was the third Fae club she had visited since picking herself up off the sand in the desert. All the clubs were neutral ground, so the Dark and Light mingled together.

The Light staring at her reminded her that she was looking for a fight. She wanted to pick a fight with Balladyn, but she couldn't find him. This guy, however, would do.

Rhi turned on the bar stool and raised a brow as she looked at him. He stood in the corner wearing all black from his shirt down to his boots.

The top part of his midnight hair was pulled away from his face with a strand or two falling free to lay against his chiseled cheek.

It was hard to determine just how long his hair was by the way he stood. Not that his thick shoulders and don't-fuck-with-me attitude scared her away.

She hopped down off the stool, her four-inch heels not wobbling once. Rhi flicked her hair over her shoulders and was about to walk to him when she picked up hurried whispers running throughout the club.

"The Reapers," someone said in a panicky voice.

Rhi snorted. As if. The Reapers were a myth, legends and tales told to frighten children—and even a few adults.

She ignored the talk and headed to the man. Not once did his gaze waver from hers. No one went near him, not even the waitresses. Rhi grabbed a whisky off a passing tray and tried to hand it to him when she reached him.

"You might actually get someone to take your order if you were friendlier."

His eyes dropped to the whisky she held out before skating back to her. His silver eyes watched her, studied her.

When he didn't take the whisky, Rhi shrugged and tossed back the alcohol. She waited until another waitress walked past and put the now empty glass on the tray.

Rhi turned back to him. "The silent type, huh? I've never understood males like that. Is it because you have nothing to say? Or is it because you think females like it?"

There was a ruckus at the front door of the pub. Rhi turned to see what was going on. As usual it was a Dark causing the problems.

"This would be a nice establishment if the Dark weren't allowed in."

She laughed at her own joke and turned back to Mr. Silent.

Only he was gone.

Rhi looked around, but there wasn't another sign of him. She shrugged and went back to the bar to order another whisky. "His loss," she murmured before ordering another drink.

Thorn walked into the cavern and paused. The last time all the Kings had been awake and gathered together inside the mountain was when they had bound Ulrik's magic.

Surely Con wouldn't try that again.

Thorn looked at the King of Kings at the front of the cavern standing on a boulder as Thorn walked to the opposite side. There were many faces he hadn't seen in thousands of years. It felt right to have all the Kings awake once more.

He leaned against a carving of a group of dragons. A few minutes later, Ryder came to stand beside him. Thorn glanced at Ryder, but Ryder's gaze was on Con.

"This isna good," Ryder whispered.

Thorn leaned against the stone and crossed his arms over his chest. "Do you know what this is about?"

Ryder gave a nod to the entrance of the cavern. Thorn followed his gaze and saw Henry North, MI5 agent and friend to the Kings, walk in.

"I'll be damned," Thorn muttered.

Con raised a hand to quiet the cavern. "A mortal has never been allowed in this cavern. No' even a mate. But times have changed. We've enemies at every corner. Ulrik has his magic returned. It willna be long before he awakens his Silvers. But that's no' why I've called you here."

Thorn's frown deepened.

"The Dark attacked two of our own in Edinburgh," Con said. "We didna respond for fear of the humans seeing us. Because of that, the Dark have been spotted all over Scotland. I can no' allow that to continue."

Thorn smiled. "About damn time."

Con's gaze jerked to him. "Groups of two Kings will be sent out all over the UK to bring the Dark to heel. Our rules remain in place. Only shift at night when there's no' a chance the mortals will see you, and kill as many Dark as you can. The majority of us will remain on Dreagan to ensure the Silvers remain asleep." Con paused and motioned for Henry to join him. "Henry has been tracking the Dark all over the world. He has a map of where they're concentrated the most."

"The fuckers are everywhere," Henry said flatly as he held up a large map and began to talk.

Thorn's attention was pulled from Henry as Con walked to him. Thorn had been expecting some sort of . . . discussion . . . after he helped Warrick get Darcy to Ulrik.

He just hadn't expected it in the middle of a meeting.

Thorn straightened, dropping his hands. He faced Con, assuming the worst.

Con stopped in front of him. "I'm sending you back to Edinburgh."

"Good." Thorn had hoped he would get sent out. After what Warrick endured at the hands of the Dark, the two of them were ready to get back out there and kill Dark Fae.

"With Darius."

The smile forming halted on Thorn's lips. He wouldn't argue with who he fought beside. It was enough that he would get to fight. There was movement out of the corner of his eyes as Darius came to stand beside him. "I doona care who I fight beside."

Thorn started to walk away when Con said his name. He stopped and turned back to Con and glimpsed Ryder watching them.

"I've no' forgotten your betrayal," Con said.

Thorn closed the distance so he stood just a few inches from Con. "I didna betray you. I helped a friend."

"You helped Ulrik."

"I never sided with Ulrik. No' back then, and no' now. You're worried about us fracturing? Take a look in the mirror, Con. You're the culprit."

Thorn began to respond when Con shifted his gaze to Darius. "We're missing a few Kings."

"I was wondering how long it would take you to notice.

Arian will be here soon. He wanted another day to himself. I arrived with Roman and Nikolai just now."

Thorn was looking over the group as Darius spoke. There was something in his tone that had Thorn jerking his head to Darius.

"What is it?" Con asked, a frown forming.

Darius blew out a breath. "I went to one mountain, but it was empty."

"Empty?" Thorn repeated in confusion.

Con lowered his voice as he asked, "Who?"

"V," Darius said.

Ryder visibly jerked.

"He could be anywhere, Con," Darius said.

A muscle in Con's jaw twitched. "Aye. Anywhere but Dreagan."

"We need to find him," Thorn said.

Ryder pushed away from the wall. "I can start looking. I've got a dozen new monitors arriving tomorrow."

"Nay." Con's one word stopped them all. "We've got bigger things to worry about. V will find his way back home."

No one mentioned that V could've gone to Ulrik.

Read on for an excerpt from the next book by
Donna Grant

PASSION IGNITES

Her defiant words appealed to him on a primal level, but her precarious position made his blood turn to ice. Thorn had been so enraged, so incensed that he had one thought—save Lexi.

It wasn't until it was over that Thorn realized what he had done. She had seen him shift. Lexi now knew the secret that everyone at Dreagan worked so tirelessly to protect.

"You're the other beings killing the Dark," she said.

He closed his eyes. "Aye."

"You're a dragon."

His chin dropped to his chest. There were many reasons he hadn't intended to tell her what he was, but the biggest was the way she was handling things now. She was in shock at all she had seen. When that shock gave way, she would be too frightened of him to even be in the same city.

"You're a damn dragon!" she yelled.

Thorn was going to have to have Guy come and wipe Lexi's memories of anything to do with him. It might even be better if she didn't remember the Dark either.

"Look at me," she demanded.

He whirled around and held out his arms. "What do you want me to say? Yes. I'm a dragon!"

"How?" She gave a small shake of her head, her voice breaking on the word.

"We've been here since the beginning of time."

"Impossible. We'd have found something."

Thorn lifted one shoulder. "We have some human allies who have helped to keep us hidden."

"This makes no sense." She looked around at the warehouse as if seeing it for the first time.

"None of this would be an issue if you'd remained in the flat as I told you."

Her gaze narrowed on him. "Told me? I'm not some dog to be ordered around."

"Nay, you're a human who has stepped in a war she has no business knowing about!"

"Maybe if more of us *humans* did know we wouldn't be dying by the dozens every day because of the Dark!"

Thorn took a step toward her. "You really think knowing of the Dark would stop the deaths?"

"It certainly couldn't hurt," she replied, moving toward him.

"That simple thinking is why the Fae came for you to

begin with. You think in the entire universe that you're the only beings? Do you really think there aren't other planets with life on them?"

"I don't care about them, I-"

"Well you should care," he interrupted. He took another step. "Use your brain, Lexi. You're smart. Look around at your world. Do you really think cancer can't be cured when your doctors have cured almost everything else? The Dark keep preventing it. They want you weak and stupid."

"I'm not stupid"

"I told you how dangerous it was out on the streets. I told you to remain inside the flat."

She rolled her eyes. "I had every intention of doing just that except I saw you jump off a six-story roof. Humans can't do that."

"That still doesna mean you should've followed us!"

They were so close he could see the black circle around her irises. Her gray eyes were stormy with anger, fear, and anxiety.

"I used my head," she retorted.

Thorn looked down at her and nearly groaned when he felt her breasts rub against his chest. To his horror, the fury in her gray eyes turned to desire.

No matter how hard he tried he couldn't stop himself from yanking Lexi against him as he took her lips in a savage kiss.

He spun her around and pressed her up against a wall.

Her hands delved into his hair as she answered his kiss with one just as fierce and violent as his.

Thorn came to his senses and lifted his head. He looked down at her swollen lips and his hard cock begged him to continue. Whatever thought he had vanished with his craving of her.

He touched her cheek before he slid his hand around to the back of her neck and held her head as he slowly kissed her, tasting the passion and need.